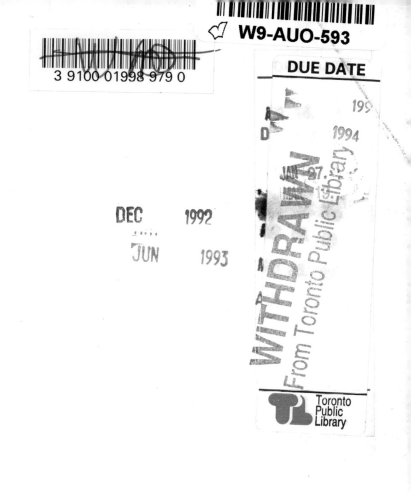

SHANNON'S WAY

SHANNON'S WAY

by

A. J. CRONIN

LONDON
VICTOR GOLLANCZ LTD
1978

Copyright 1948, by A. J. Cronin

ISBN 0 575 00923 3

First published 1948
Tenth impression March 1967
Eleventh impression March 1971
Twelfth impression May 1975
Thirteenth impression March 1978

068449

Printed in Great Britain at
The Camelot Press Ltd, Southampton

BOOK ONE

CHAPTER I

O N   A   D A M P   E V E N I N G in December, the fifth of that
month, in the year 1919—a date which marked the
beginning of a great change in my life—six o'clock had
struck from the University tower and the soft mist from
the Eldon River was creeping round the Experimental
Pathology buildings at the foot of Fenner Hill, invading
our long work-room that smelled faintly of formalin, and
was lit only by low, green-shaded lamps.

Professor Usher was still in his study—from behind the
closed door on my right, with eardrums unnaturally
attuned, I could hear his precise tones as he spoke, at
length, upon the telephone. Surreptitiously, I glanced at
the two other assistants who, with myself, made up the
Professor's team.

Directly opposite, Spence stood at his bench, racking
culture tubes, awaiting the arrival of his wife. She called
for him regularly, every Friday night, and they went out
together to dinner and the theatre. A slanting beam drew
a cruel caricature of his broken profile upon the wall.

In the far corner of the laboratory Lomax had knocked
off work and was idly tapping a cigarette upon his thumbnail—signal for a departure which he generally contrived
to make easy and negligent. Presently, in a bored manner,
surrounded by a languid cloud of smoke, he stood up,
adjusting the wave in his hair at the mirror he kept over
his sink.

"Let's go somewhere to-night, Shannon. Have dinner
with me and we'll take in a cinema."

The invitation was flattering, but, of course, this evening
I declined it.

7

"How about you, Spence?" Lomax turned towards the other bench.

"I'm afraid Muriel and I are going out."

"This is a beastly unsociable town," Lomax complained.

Neil Spence hesitated, almost apologetic, covering his chin with his left hand, an instinctive gesture, which seemed to give him confidence and which always touched me, increasing the sympathy and deep affection which I felt for him.

"Why don't you come along with us?"

The suggestion halted Lomax.

"I shouldn't want to butt in and spoil your evening."

"You wouldn't."

Just then there came the sound of a motor horn, and almost at once Smith, the attendant, entered and announced that Mrs. Spence had arrived and was outside.

"Don't let's keep Muriel." Spence, having put on his overcoat, waited companionably for Lomax at the door. "I think you'll enjoy the show . . . it's *The Maid of the Mountains*. Good night, Robert."

"Good night."

When they had gone I breathed a little faster and my eyes, wandering round this world I loved, this inner, secret, mysterious world of the laboratory, came to rest, with apprehensive expectation, upon the Professor's door.

At the same instant it opened and Hugo Usher came out. His exits and entrances, indeed all his movements, had a slightly theatrical quality, which so completely fitted his severe figure, iron-grey hair, and cropped imperial that he gave me always the uncomfortable impression of being less a distinguished scientist than an actor playing too perfectly that part. He drew up by the Hoffman centrifuge, near my bench. Despite his well-controlled expression, it was not difficult for me to read,

8

in the faint constriction of his frontal muscles, a disapproval of my peculiarities, from the shabby naval uniform I persisted in wearing, to my failure, during the past six weeks, to evince enthusiasm for the research he had compelled me to take up.

There was a pause. Then, with that infusion of geniality which he assumed to temper his severity, he said, briefly:

"No, Shannon . . . I'm afraid not."

My heart ceased its bounding and sank slowly, while my face coloured with disappointment and mortification.

"But, surely, sir, if you've read my memorandum . . ."

"I have read it," he interrupted me and, by way of evidence, laid upon my bench the typewritten sheet which, earlier that day, I had presented to him and which now, to my burning eyes, presented the soiled and deplorable appearance of a rejected manuscript. "I regret that I cannot accept your suggestion. The work upon which you are engaged is of very considerable importance. Impossible . . . to allow you to discontinue it."

I lowered my eyes, debarred by my hurt pride from pressing my request, knowing also that his decisions were always irrevocable. Although my head was bent, I could feel his gaze resting upon the batch of slides stacked on the acid-charred wood of my bench.

"You've finished our latest counts?"

"Not yet," I told him without looking up.

"You know I particularly want our paper ready for the Spring Congress. As I shall be away for several weeks, it is imperative you press forward with all possible speed."

When I did not answer his half-frown deepened. He cleared his throat. I thought I was about to receive a dissertation on the nobility of pathological investigation, particularly as it related to his favourite subject, the theory of opsonins. However, after playing for a moment with his

9

wide-brimmed soft black hat he flung it on the back of his head.

"Good evening, Shannon."

With that formal withdrawing bow he had picked up abroad, he went out.

I sat for a long moment, completely still.

"I'm ready to close up, sir."

Lean and cadaverous as ever, out of the corner of his eye, Smith, the attendant, was watching me, the same Herbert Smith who, when I first entered the Zoology laboratory six years before, had damped my youthful enthusiasm with his pessimism. Now he was head attendant in the Pathological Department, but the attainment of this better position had not changed him, and he displayed towards me a morose suspicion which my few successes, including an honours M.D. and the winning of the Lister Gold Medal, had increased rather than dispelled.

Without a word I shrouded my microscope, put away the slides, took my cap and went out. My thoughts were bitter as I walked down the dark, dripping avenue of Fenner Hill, crossed the crowded thoroughfare of Pardyke Road—where, beneath misty arc lights, the trams clanged and bounded over greasy cobblestones—then entered the drab district of Kirkhead. Here, terraces of old-fashioned houses, clinging desperately to respectability against an invasion of public-houses, ice-cream saloons and tenements for the workers at the nearby docks, raised their tall grimy fronts, with broken stucco cornices, slipped porticos and fallen gutters, weeping, it seemed, for their former glory, beneath the eternally smoky sky.

At Number 52, which bore on the fanlight the polite name ROTHESAY, and below, in discreet letters of peeling gilt, GUESTS, I mounted the steps and went in.

CHAPTER II

My ROOM, AT THE TOP of the boarding-house, was small, almost an attic, furnished sparsely with an iron cot, a white wooden washstand and a black-framed woolwork text. But it had the advantage of communicating with a little green-painted glass conservatory still equipped with stands and benches, a relic of the palmy days of the mansion. Although cold in winter and sweltering in summer, this served me adequately as a study.

For this accommodation, with two meals a day, I paid the Misses Dearie, co-owners of the establishment, the moderate sum of thirty-four shillings a week—which, I must at once acknowledge, was quite as much as I could afford. The money I had inherited from my grandfather, "to put me through college," had no more than fulfilled its purpose, while the honorarium for my assistantship, and for the extra work of demonstrating in Bacteriology to the third-year students, amounted to one hundred guineas a year, a delusive suggestion of gold pieces which concealed the fact that in Scotland they are cautious about spoiling their budding genius. Thus, on Saturday, when I had paid my board and lodgings, I had barely five shillings in my pocket to provide myself with midday luncheons at the Union, with clothing, shoes, books tobacco—in brief, I was outrageously poor, compelled to wear my obsolete uniform, which so offended Professor Usher's sense of propriety, not from choice, but because it was the only suit that I possessed.

However, these pinched circumstances scarcely troubled me. My upbringing in Levenford had inured me to such vicissitudes of the Spartan life as lumpy porridge, watery milk of singular and unforgettable blueness, made-down clothing, and thick-soled boots studded with "tackets" to make them last. Besides, I regarded my present state as purely transitory, precursor of a splendid future, and my mind was too desperately engaged by the enterprise which would carry me to a great and immediate success to worry about trifles.

When I reached my lofty garret, from which I had a view of a blank brick wall topped by the smoke-stack of the city incinerator, I stood for a moment in determined thought, studying the paper which Usher had restored to me.

"You'll be late for tea."

With a start, I turned to the intruder who stood diffidently upon my threshold. It was, of course, Miss Jean Law, my next-door neighbour in the corridor. This young woman, one of the five medical students who lodged at Rothesay, was taking my Bacteriology class, and all through the present session had made me the object of her neighbourly attentions.

"The gong went five minutes ago," she murmured, in her Northern accent; and, observing my irritation, she had the grace to blush—a warm, modest flush which suffused her fair skin yet did not cause her to lower her brown eyes. "I knocked, but you didn't hear me."

I crumpled up the paper.

"I've asked you, Miss Law, not to disturb me when I'm busy."

"Yes . . . but your *tea*," she protested, more than ever rolling her *r*'s in her confusion.

I could not help it—at the sight of her, in her blue serge skirt, her plain white blouse, black stockings, and sturdy shoes, entreating me with such earnest solicitude, as though the loss of my tea were a mortal calamity, I was obliged to smile.

"All right," I consented, imitating her tone. "I'll come this very minute."

We went down together to the dining-room, an appalling chamber, furnished in worn red plush, the very linoleum impregnated with the smell of boiled cabbage. Upon the mantelpiece, which had a tasselled velvet fringe, stood the pride of the Misses Dearie, token of their departed sire's prestige and of their own "ladylike" upbringing: a hideous green marble clock, stopped, but supported by two gilt-helmeted figures carrying axes and inscribed *Presented to Captain Hamish Dearie on his retirement from command of the Winton Fire Brigade.*

The meal, pale and meagre shadow of the traditional substantial Scots "high" tea, had already begun, and Miss Beth Dearie was presiding at the mahogany table covered with a mended but clean white cloth, bearing a few plates of bread, scones and seedcake, an ashet of kippers, one for each person, and a Britannia metal teapot, encased in a blue knitted "cosy."

As she poured our tea, Miss Beth, a tall, correct, angular spinster of forty-five, with faded good looks, whose hair-net and a high bone necked lace dress seemed to emphasize her air of reduced gentility, gave us—although she had due respect for my medical degree, and Miss Law was certainly her favourite—her pale, "suffering" smile, which vanished only when I dropped a penny in the little wooden box placed beside the empty biscuit barrel in the centre of the table, and marked "For the Blind." Punctuality, like politeness, was one of the elder Miss Dearie's many principles, and all who came after she had "asked the blessing" were supposed to make atonement, although one must be forgiven for doubting, in unguarded moments, if this tribute ever reached its proper destination.

I began in silence to eat my kipper, which was salt, greasy, and more than usually undergrown. These two worthy gentlewomen had a hard struggle to make ends meet, and Miss Beth—who "managed" the establishment out in front, while Miss Ailie cooked and cleaned in the background—saw to it that the sin of gluttony was never committed in her presence. In spite of this, the scrupulous reputation of her house was recognized by those connected with the University, and she seldom had a vacancy. To-night, I saw that out of her complement of six, Galbraith and Harrington, both fourth-year undergraduates, were absent, having gone home for the week-end, but opposite me sat the two other medical students, Harold Muss and Babu Lal Chatterjee.

Muss was an undersized youth of eighteen, perpetually spotted with acne pimples, and endowed with a most striking set of protuberant buck teeth. He was only in his first year, and ɪor the most part maintained deferential silence, but occasionally, when he thought someone had made a joke, he would burst suddenly into a wild and hoarse guffaw.

Lal Chatterjee, a Hindu from Calcutta, was older than Muss, actually about thirty-three, extremely plump and podgy, with a smooth saffron complexion set off by a trim little black beard and a beaming, ineffably stupid face. For at least fifteen years he had been waddling in and out of the Winton classrooms, wearing baggy trousers which hung down at the seat like an empty potato sack, and carrying a large green umbrella, trying without success to obtain his medical degree. Good-natured and garrulous, with an incessant flow of amiable small talk, he was nicknamed "the Babu" and had become, at the University, a comic institution. Immediately we entered, in a high "singsong" voice which seemed always, like the cry of the muezzin proclaiming the hours of prayer, to be pitched in the minor key, he began:

"Ah, good evening, Dr. Robert Shannon and Miss Jean

14

Law. I am afraid we have almost eaten all the food. For your lateness you may perhaps perish of malnutrition. Oh, yes, perhaps, ha, ha. Mr. Harold Muss, please to pass me the mustard, thank you. I appeal to my fellow doctor. I ask you, Dr. Robert Shannon, does not mustard stimulate the salivary glands, of which there are two, the sublingual and another whose name I have safely in my notebook? Sir, excuse me, how does that other gland call itself?"

"The pancreas," I suggested.

"Ah, yes, sir, the pancreas," agreed the Babu, beaming. "That is exactly my own view."

Muss, who was drinking tea, suddenly choked violently.

"The pancreas!" he gasped. "I don't know much, but that's in the stummick!"

Lal Chatterjee gazed reproachfully upon his convulsed fellow student.

"Oh, poor Mr. Harold Muss! Do not exhibit your ignorance. Please to remember that I am many more years an undergraduate than you. I had the honour to fail B.A., Calcutta University, probably before you were born."

Miss Law was attempting to catch my eye and to draw me into her conversation with Miss Beth. They were discussing, with the grave yet eager interest of those banded by evangelical sympathies, the coming performance of *The Messiah* at St. Andrew's Hall—always a notable winter event in Winton—but since I had, for reasons of my own, a particular reticence towards religious matters, I fixed my gaze upon my plate.

"I do so like choral music, don't you, Mr. Shannon?"

"No," I said. "I'm afraid I don't."

At this point, Miss Ailie Dearie entered from the kitchen, silently, in her broken-down felt slippers, bearing the "crystal," the glass dish of stewed but stony prunes which, on "kipper nights," with the inevitability of death, terminated our grim repast.

Unlike her sister, Miss Ailie was a soft and tender creature, rather untidy in her appearance, with a thickset, slow-moving figure and hands knotted and disfigured by housework. It was rumoured—probably a piece of student nonsense, encouraged by the fact that her one relaxation, in the evenings, was the reading of romantic novels from the public library—that as a young girl she had suffered a tragic love affair. Her kind face, flushed from the stove, patient under her sister's acid tongue, was sad and wistful, with a thin strand of hair falling so constantly over her forehead that she had the curious habit of pursing her lips and, with a gentle upward breath, puffing it away. Perhaps her own difficulties made her sympathetic towards my problems. Now, with kindly interest, she bent over and murmured in my ear:

"How did things go to-day, Robert?"

To reassure her, I forced a smile, at which she nodded with a pleased expression, puffed away her hair and went out.

Miss Ailie's heart was softer than her prunes! For the next five minutes, no sounds were audible but those of troubled mastication, the clash of Muss's errant canines upon the flinty fruit.

When nothing edible remained on the table, the meal ended with Beth Dearie rising like the chatelaine of a castle who has dispensed a banquet. We then dispersed to our rooms, Harold Muss absently extracting fish-bones with his forefinger, Lal Chatterjee belching musically, with a kind of Oriental majesty, *en route*.

"Mr. Shannon." Hastening after me, Miss Law breathed my name—I had at last broken her of the habit of addressing me as "Doctor," a title which, with its implications of professional mediocrity, I at this stage

16

thoroughly resented. "I'm not sure of the paper I've written on *Trypanosoma gambiense* . . . you know the question you set us to-day. It's so specially interesting to me . . . Would you . . . could you be so terribly good as to look it over?"

Although harassed and preoccupied, I had not the strength of will to refuse—somehow that unguarded freshness in her face turned back my rudest answers.

"Bring it along," I growled.

Five minutes later, sustained by the broken springs of the one chair in the conservatory, I read her paper, while she sat very erect on the edge of a stool covered with cracked waxcloth, her hands clasping her serge skirt across her ankles, watching me with an earnest and anxious air.

"Will it do?" she asked, when I had finished.

The essay was remarkably well done, with several quite original observations, and a series of sketches of the flagellated parasite's development, extremely accurate. As I considered her, I had to admit that she was not like most of the young women who came in droves to the University, presuming to "go in" for medicine. Some of these came for a lark, others were pushed forward by aspiring middle-class parents, a few were merely seeking to get married to an eligible young man who would one day, in some suburban community, become a stodgily respectable practitioner, more or less incompetent but financially secure. None had any real talent or capacity for the profession.

"You see," she murmured, as though to encourage my opinion, "there's work waiting for me. I am so anxious to get my degree."

"This is well above pass standard," I said. "In fact, it's extremely good."

A warmth crept into her soft cheeks.

"Oh, thank you, Dr. . . . Mr. Shannon. That means everything, coming from you. I can't tell you how much we students respect your opinion . . . and your . . . Yes, please let me say it, your brilliance. . . . And of course I know what a hard time you had in the war."

I took off my slipper and examined the crack beginning in the toe. I have tried to explain why I could not wound this strange neighbour of mine; nevertheless I had to have some outlet for my vexed sensibilities. My nature was reserved and secretive, I was not constitutionally a liar, yet under that starry, trustful gaze, some devil, which perhaps I had inherited from my incorrigible grandfather, had begun, in these past weeks, screened by my thoughtful, even melancholy visage, to play outrageous pranks.

During our frequent conversations I had confided in her that I came of a wealthy and aristocratic Levenford family, but that, being left an orphan and preferring medical research to the career mapped out for me, I had been cut off and forbidden my ancestral home.

Her innocent credulity goaded me to further efforts.

For the four years of the war I had led an uneventful, dreary existence as the surgeon of a light cruiser detailed for duty with submarines in the North Sea. Our weekly missions through the enemy mine-fields were probably dangerous enough, but they were unutterably dull. In harbour we drank gin, played van-john, and fished for eels. Once our senior officer was surprised in undress uniform in his cabin with a pretty woman to whom, he subsequently told us, he was teaching the abstruse arts of navigation. Beyond this, nothing broke the monotony until we got into the Battle of Jutland, then everything happened so quickly that there remained only a confused impression of noise and light flashes, of myself sweating between decks in the sick-bay, doing everything badly, with shaking fingers, my inside so turned to water that

18

for a whole week afterwards I suffered abominably from colic.

Naturally, this would not do for Miss Jean Law, so while she hung upon my words I invented a new and more picturesque adventure. We had been torpedoed, marooned for days in mid-Pacific on a raft, there were dramatic scenes of thirst and hunger, we fought off sharks, and so on, through the most horrific hazards, until I woke up, pale but triumphant, a hero in fact, in a South American hospital.

During my present silence she had apparently been nerving herself, and now her eyelashes began to flicker, always a sign of her inner stress.

"I've been thinking . . . I mean . . . it seems scarcely fair, Mr. Shannon, that I should have learned so much about you . . . while you know nothing about me." She faltered slightly, then continued valiantly, her colour high. "I was wondering if, some Saturday, you would care to come out to my home at Blairhill."

"Well," I said, rather taken aback. "I'm going to be pretty busy all winter."

"I realize that. But you have been so kind to me I'd like you to meet my people. Of course," she added hurriedly, "we're very simple folk, not like you. My father"—and again she flushed, yet, with the air of one who after long self-communion has taken a difficult resolution, went on bravely—"is not a very important person. He is . . . a baker."

There was a longish pause. Not knowing what to say, or do, I sat rather too still. I was beginning to feel uncomfortable, when suddenly she smiled, showing that some spark of humour enlivened her seraphic fervour.

"Yes, he bakes bread. Works in the bakehouse with my young brother and another man. And sends the batches round the countryside by a horse-drawn van. Quite a small business, but old-established, as you might gather. So although you are so well-connected, please don't look down on us."

"Good Lord, what do you take me for?" Stung, I threw her a quick glance, but she was quite innocent of any double meaning.

"Then you'll come." With a pleased expression she rose, took up her paper from the arm of my chair and stood looking at it. "I'm most grateful for your help with these trypanosomes. Tropical medicine interests me so much." My inquiring glance provoked a final confidence. "You see ... we belong to the Brethren in Blairhill ... and ... immediately I get my degree ... I am going out as a doctor to our settlement ... at Kumasi, in West Africa."

My jaw must have dropped at least an inch. Was there no end to her preposterous capacity to startle me? My first impulse was to laugh, but the look in her eyes, which shone as though she glimpsed the Holy Grail, restrained me. And as I considered her, I had to admit that at least she had the virtue of sincerity.

"How long have you had this wild idea?"

"Ever since I started Medicine. That's why I went in for it."

So she hadn't come to the University for a lark, or to get married, like the others. Even so, I still was unconvinced.

"It all sounds very noble," I said slowly. "Romantic and self-sacrificing ... on paper. But if you did go ... I wonder if you really know what you'll be up against."

"I ought to." She smiled calmly. "My sister has been out there as a nurse for the last five years."

That silenced me. She paused at the door and with a smile slipped from the room. After an interval during which I sat motionless, staring somewhat foolishly at nothing, and listening unconsciously, rather uncomfortably, to her quiet movements next door, I shrugged my shoulders and, with compressed lips, turned to the consideration of my own situation.

Must I submit to Professor Usher's direction or should I in my own way, seen as unclear and hazardous, take issue with authority and fate?

CHAPTER III

THE NEXT DAY, Saturday, was my weekly holiday, and at six o'clock in the morning, I set out from the sleeping house to walk to the village of Dreem, some twenty-six miles away. The Winton streets were still dark, damp with dew, and except for the footfalls of an early workman, silent and deserted. When the sun broke through I had passed the city outskirts, leaving behind, with relief, the last of the bungalows scattered among market gardens, and was in open country, with the broad estuary of the Clyde reaching away to the sea before me, a luminous, familiar vision which always lifted up my heart.

Towards noon I ate an apple which Miss Ailie, daring her sister's displeasure, had slipped in my pocket the night before. Then, crossing the river at Erskine Ferry, five miles above the town of Levenford, I entered the stretch of splendid farm land which fringed the waters of the Firth, a terrain richly pastoral, with sheep and cattle grazing on the rolling meadows, enclosed by grey stone walls.

As I approached my destination, the purpose of this journey, naïve though it might be, dominated my mind. All that year, since the University Senate, following my demobilization in 1918, had awarded me the Eldon Fellowship, I had been employed by Professor Usher upon a routine investigation of certain opsonins, a subject interesting to him, but regarded by me as of slight importance—indeed, the entire opsonic theory was already being discredited by advanced scientific workers.

Perhaps I was prejudiced by my deep regard for the previous head of the Department, Professor Challis, who, at the University, had taught and inspired me: a fine old man, now retired, at the age of seventy, to the obscurity of private life. Yet I neither liked nor trusted his successor. Frigid, at times ingratiating, spurred by a rich and socially ambitious wife, Hugo Usher seemed lacking in inspiration or creative force, unprepared to make the sacrifice of blood and tears demanded by research, an opportunist who had achieved his position through a facility for tabulating statistics, but more especially through push, well-timed publicity, and a remarkable capacity for picking other people's brains. By attaching promising young men to his department, he had acquired a reputation for original investigation—my previous monograph, for example, on Pituitary Function, a small drudgery perhaps, yet painfully achieved, had been published as the joint work of Professor Hugo Usher and Dr. Robert Shannon.

While under this bondage, I had been seeking, with pathetic eagerness, a really significant subject for research, a broad, original thesis, a thesis so unmistakably momentous that it would influence, or even alter, the course of general medicine.

A tall order, naturally. But I was young, only twenty-four, passionately bound up in my work, burning with the painful ambition of a silent and retiring nature, longing, in my poverty and obscurity, to astound the world.

For months I had sought in vain until suddenly, out of the blue, an opportunity presented itself. During that autumn a number of rural areas all over the country had been stricken by a curious epidemic which, perhaps for lack of a better term, had been loosely classified as influenza. The death rate of the infection was high and its incidence wide—in the popular Press there had been sporadic headlines of a sensational nature and indeed, in the medical journals I had traced several reports from America, Holland, Belgium, and other foreign sources recording outbreaks of a comparable condition. The symptoms of acute chill, fever, intense headache, and body pains were of considerable severity, often leading to a fatal pneumonia or, in cases which recovered, to prolonged after-effects of debility. And as I studied them I began to feel that here was a new and different disease, a suspicion which increased as time went on, and sent a current of excitement through my veins.

My interest in this matter was further heightened by the fact that one of the main local centres of the epidemic was the neighbourhood of Dreem. And now, at three o'clock in the afternoon, as I trudged into that little village of low, grey houses, straggling along the bank of a placid stream, always a quiet place, but at present, because of the recent sickness, even more silent and deserted, my eagerness, conquering fatigue, made me go faster. Without pausing for my usual bread and cheese at the one small village tavern, I went immediately to Alex Duthie.

He was in his cottage, seated, pipe in mouth, in his cosy kitchen, while Simon, his little boy, played on the rug at his feet and Alice, his wife, a sedate, matronly woman, rolled out pastry at the table.

Alex was a short, steady-looking man of thirty-five, dressed in clean moleskin trousers, thick socks, and a striped flannel shirt. He greeted me with an impenetrable motion of his head, a flicker rather, of his features, so faint as to be almost invisible, yet which somehow had more welcome than the longest speech. At the same time he took in, not without irony, my tired and dusty appearance.

"Did you miss the bus?"

"No, Alex. I wanted the walk." Unable to restrain myself, I went on: "I hope I'm not late. Did you . . . make the arrangements?"

He appeared not to have heard; then, guardedly, he smiled, and removed the pipe from his lips.

"Ye're a fine chap to choose Saturday afternoon. Most

folks like a rest then . . . especially after what we've been through." He paused long enough to make me anxious. "But I managed the most of them for ye. We'll drop down to the Institute now."

As I gave an exclamation of gratitude, he got up, went over to the fender and began to lace on his boots.

"Do you fancy a cup of tea, Doctor?" Mrs. Duthie asked. "A body needs something hot, a time like this."

"No, thank you, Alice. I'd rather get to work."

"You're having supper and spending the night with us," Alex announced, in the tone of one who will take no refusal. "Sim here wants to show you the new fishing rod I cut down for him."

He took his peaked cap and we went out. Sim, five years old, a self-contained and silent soul like his father, followed us to the door.

"I'm a confounded nuisance to you, Alex," I said as we walked down the road. "I wouldn't have asked you to do this if I didn't think it was important."

"Ay," he agreed wryly. "Ye're a bit of a bother, Rob. But as we happen to be fond of ye, we maun put up wi' it."

My association with Alex Duthie, and indeed, with Dreem, went back six years, to before the war, when as a lonely student at the University I had forsaken my books to indulge my passion for fishing in those tidal waters where, each spring, the silvery sea trout make a wonderful run. On the river-bank, one evening, Alex had helped me to land a tremendous fish; and in that hectic encounter, in the exquisite triumph which succeeded it, the seeds of enduring friendship had been sown. Although a working man, being employed as head herdsman by the Dreem Farms Company, Duthie was locally a highly respected figure and for several years past had been elected to the office of "provost" of the little community. His manner could be difficult at times and his tongue, when he used it, was often rough, but never once had I known him do a mean or shabby thing. Since the village was too remote to possess a resident doctor, it was to him that I made my present unorthodox request, a request which could have come only from an ingenuous and enthusiastic young man, which in fact had in it a touch of the absurd.

The Institute was a small brick building, recently erected by the Farms Combine, and containing various club-rooms and a library. Alex led the way into one of the rooms off the main corridor where about thirty persons were gathered, reading and talking, but with an air of expectancy. A silence fell as we went in.

"Well!" Alex exclaimed. "Here's Dr. Shannon. Most of ye know him as a pretty fair fisherman. But forbye, he's a sort of professor at the University, and he wants to find out about this damn 'flu that's laid us out here. He's come to ask a favour of you."

This struck the right note and several of the people smiled, though many of them still looked pale and ill. When I thanked them for coming, I explained what was wanted and promised not to keep them long. Then I removed my haversack, took out a series of numbered capillary tubes and systematically set to work.

They were, of course, all village folk, most of them men who worked in the fields, and they had all had the recent infection. Some I knew personally, big Sam Louden, who often tied flies for me, keen-eyed Harry Vence, and others whom I had met, at twilight, knee-deep in the water, casting their long greenheart rods. It was a simple operation to obtain from each a small blood specimen and their friendly, good-natured patience made things easier. Even so, I took longer than I had expected, for, as I went on, a fine tremor crept into my fingers as I realized what this might mean to me.

At last it was over, my final subject had rolled down his

sleeve, shaken hands with me and gone out. Then, as I looked up from my note-book, I saw Alex, seated on a nearby bench, watching me in alert summation of my character—a queer, penetrating look, mingled, too, with intelligent interest which, as our eyes met, he took pains to conceal.

There was a pause. I had already told him what was in my mind. I said steadily:

"I have to do it this way, Alex. I can't help myself . . . I simply must find out."

A silence followed; then, slowly, Duthie came over and gripped me by the hand.

"Ye're a clever chap, Rob, and I'm sure I wish you luck. If I can help again, in any way, just let me know." A dry smile wrinkled the corners of his eyes. "Meantime, come on back to supper. Alice has a grand steak-and-kidney puddin' for us."

I smiled back at him.

"You go ahead, Alex. I'll join you when I finish off my notes."

"All right, lad. Don't be long."

When he had gone I worked for half an hour, checking and tabulating the specimens, then with my rucksack across my shoulder I left the Institute and walked up the narrow wynd towards Duthie's cottage. A clear darkness was falling and a thin moon with its attendant star had risen in the frosty sky. The lightly textured air was cold and still, and suddenly my mind lifted in a surge of exhilaration at the prospect which lay before me, this voyage of discovery, beset with difficulty and danger, into uncharted seas.

Outside Alex's door I paused. The lights of the village twinkled around me and beyond flowed the waters of the estuary, shadowy and mysteriously spangled. While I stood there, quite motionless, watching the moon drift

27

higher in the heavens, listening, as the last whisperings of the earth died in the boreal stillness, I felt the mantle of an eternal solitude enwrap my spirit. I knew then what I was, and must always be—alone, one against the world.

I shivered, recollected that I was hungry; and aware that I should find food, fire, and friendship there, and the quiet laughter of little Sim, I went in to Alex's house.

CHAPTER IV

On the following Friday, there took place the event I had anticipated, and upon which my plan of action was based.

All that week, at the University, as I automatically performed the task to which I was handcuffed, I observed that Professor Usher was unusually pleasant to us, moving about incisive as ever, yet wearing a smile so artificially agreeable it caused the hairs on the back of my neck to bristle.

On Friday afternoon this bland assumption of the co-operative spirit reached its height as he made a little tour of the laboratory and finally, having cleared his throat, faced us with a confidential smile.

"Gentlemen, as you are no doubt aware, I have been honoured with an invitation to act as chairman of the advisory committee for the coming Pathological Congress, a distinction which obliges me to make a tour of the various universities with my distinguished colleague, Professor Harrington, in order that we may draw up a suitable and comprehensive agenda."

After an impressive pause he went on.

"Mrs. Usher and I leave for London to-night at six. We shall be away for eight weeks. I know, of course, that in my absence the work of the Department will proceed smoothly and expeditiously, in accordance with the best traditions of research. Are there any questions?"

No one answered. He nodded, as though establishing the fact that an understanding had been reached between us; then, looking at his watch, he bowed to each of us in turn and left the Department. Smith went with him to see to the luggage.

I could scarcely contain my emotions as the door swung shut, for although I had expected a brief respite from the attentions of my taskmaster, the news that he had gone, actually, for eight weeks was so wonderful it bowled me over. What could I not accomplish in that time!

Lomax had already risen and, lighting a cigarette, was glancing across at me with his fatigued smile.

"Didn't you sense we were being put in the frame of mind to work continuously while he was away? I'm so fond of him, I can't bear to see him go."

Pale, with discontented eyes and blond wavy hair, and wearing usually a faintly cynical expression, Adrian Lomax was about four years older than I, one of those fortunate persons who attract instinctively by their charm and good looks. He was an only son, with a rich mother, a widow who lived in London, and he had been educated at Winchester and Oxford, impressed at these colleges with a stamp of manners and good breeding. After his graduation he had meant to continue his studies abroad, but the war had intervened, and now, because of some remote connection between Professor Usher and his family, he had come to Winton to "put in" twelve months' post-graduate research. In his tastes, he affected the exotic, despised most things, aloofly, and cast down all that could not be explained in terms of natural science. His languid scepticism suggested deep reserves of knowledge; and with his half-shrug, his supercilious smile, his metaphysical expositions, he attempted frequently to put nails in the coffin of my belief. Self-centred and affected, his too conscious absence of condescension towards Spence and myself concealed a spoiled vanity. Yet he had a most engaging way with him. Preparing for a distinguished career, but disdaining the vulgarity of too obvious effort, he worked spasmodically; and, while bewailing his exile, carelessly contrived, in his comfortable rooms furnished expensively by himself, to exceed his generous allowance and have the best of everything.

Meanwhile, he had been rummaging in his locker, from which he now produced, with an amused air, a bottle of Benedictine.

"This happens to be on hand. Let's mark the occasion. Immediately." He drew the cork and poured generous measures of the golden liquid into three clean beakers.

Neil Spence, the third member of Usher's team, apart from those regular weekly outings with his wife, was not inclined to gaiety—like the hermit crab, he ventured out of his shell only on the rarest occasions—but now he came over sociably and joined Lomax.

So too did I. The thought of my tremendous decision to use the University laboratory for my own experiments gave to me a sense of freedom and excitement, which rose almost to exaltation, and sent a desire to celebrate surging recklessly within me.

"Absent friends." Lomax drank. "Coupled with the name of Herr Professor Hugo. I hope you like this stuff. Nothing too good for my distinguished colleagues."

"It's extremely nice," Spence said in his quiet, matter of-fact voice.

"Made by the monks." Lomax turned his ironic gaze towards me. "That should please you, Shannon. You are a Catholic, aren't you?"

"Yes . . . of course." I gave my answer a disarming assurance.

Lomax refilled the beakers with a faintly quizzical smile.

"But, Robert, I thought you were a scientist. You can't reconcile Genesis and the mutation of species."

"I don't try to." I took a sip of the warm and mellow liqueur. "The one is a sordid fact . . . the other a romantic mystery."

"Hmm," said Lomax. "What about the Pope?"

"He's all right with me."

"You're fond of him?"

"Absolutely." I stopped smiling—Lomax's wit on this topic usually ended by annoying me. "I admit I'm not a shining example . . . quite the reverse, in fact. All the same, there's something that I can't ever get away from . . . against reason if you like. . . . I hope you don't wish me to say that I regret it."

"Far from it, my dear fellow," Lomax said easily.

Neil Spence was glancing at his watch.

"Nearly six o'clock. Muriel ought to be here any minute."

He took his handkerchief and began, surreptitiously, to remove the moisture that escaped from the corners of his lips.

One night, in a trench near the Marne, in the muddy darkness, as he rose unguardedly to ease his cramped position, Spence's lower jaw had been shattered by a burst of German shrapnel; and although the plastic surgeons had patched him wonderfully with one of his own ribs, the result was a sad distortion of the human face: the chin supplanted by an angry scar, with drawn lips emerging from the cicatrix, a cruel contrast to his fine, broad brow, beneath which his dark, rather haunted eyes retreated instinctively. What made the disfigurement worse was the fact that Spence had been a handsome youth, much sought after at the local dances, picnics and tennis tournaments in the staid but comfortable society of Winton.

"Your wife is charming," Lomax remarked politely. "I enjoyed the theatre last week immensely. Shall I pour another libation to Herr Hugo?"

"No, don't," Spence said, sensibly. "We've had enough."

"But he asked us to drink in the best traditions of the Department," I said.

32

We all laughed, even Spence. It was a thing he rarely did; it contorted his face so badly. At that moment we were interrupted by a sound behind us.

Mrs. Spence had come in to the laboratory, unannounced, with the daring air of one who has broken rules and knows it. She smiled at us vivaciously from behind the dotted veil which fringed her hat and gave piquancy to the slightly hollow contours of her face.

"Smith wasn't to be found, and I waited . . . and waited . . . like a lost soul."

Muriel Spence was about twenty-seven, of medium height, rather thin, yet graceful, with delicate wrists and ankles, light brown hair and a narrow, somewhat colourless face in which, however, at times her grey eyes were wide and girlish. Without exaggeration, she could be regarded as the alleviation of Spence's misfortune. Before the war he had been engaged to her, and when he returned, quite broken up, she had stood by him, resisting the pressure of her family and his own efforts to give her back her freedom. Their wedding, largely attended, had created widespread interest. Now, although she had lost much of her youthful prettiness and was somewhat artificial in her manner, she still was attractive, and in her dark costume and necklet of brown fur she brightened our dull work-room. Because of Spence, who was my closest friend, I had tried to like Muriel; yet my nature, awkward and difficult no doubt, found always in her a quality which threw me back, as though unwanted, upon myself.

She raised her veil and kissed her husband lightly on the cheek, remarking, with a tinge of reproof:

"We shall be late for our dinner engagement, dear. Why aren't you ready?"

"Of course, Mrs. Spence," said Lomax, elevating one eyebrow in his best manner, "now you're in, you may never get out of this chamber of horrors."

She tilted her head to one side, touching me with her bright, provoking glance.

"I feel quite safe with Mr. Shannon here."

At this, for some reason, Lomax and Mrs. Spence smiled. Spence, whose dark eyes rested with almost dog-like devotion upon his wife's face, had put on his overcoat, and now she tucked her gloved hand under his arm.

"Neil and I are going your way, Mr. Lomax." She spoke invitingly. "Can we drop you?"

There was a slight pause.

"Thank you," he said, at length. "You're very kind."

I left with them, and at Muriel's runabout, parked outside the entrance to the building, we parted. While they set off in the car towards the city, I walked down Fenner Hill, bent on retrieving the Dreem specimens from my lodgings and returning with them, immediately, to the laboratory.

In Eldon Park, to my right, the ornamental lake was "bearing," crowded with skaters. I could hear in the still air the keen, gay ring of the steel blades upon the ice. Elevated by the Benedictine, and the delicious thought of Usher's departure, I felt like singing. There was a pleasant giddiness in my head, the world seemed an altogether delightful place.

As I approached the familiar boarding-house, the door of Rothesay opened and there appeared Harold Muss, accompanied by Miss Law, both bearing skates which swung from straps upon their wrists. At this, the liqueur, belying its monastic origin, proved more potent than I had imagined. I couldn't explain why, but the sudden apparition in such company of Miss Law, wearing a neat white sweater and a woollen cap, with a red tassel, upon her hair, bent, not on succour and salvation, but upon healthful exercise, sent me into a silent fit of laughter.

"What's the matter, Mr. Shannon?" At the sight of me she drew up. "Are you ill?"

"Not at all," I answered, leaving hold of the railings. "I am in perfect mental and physical condition . . . ready for an effort which may shake the world. Do I make myself clear?"

Muss suppressed a snigger; he guessed the nature of my symptoms, but Miss Law's modest countenance expressed only sympathy and a deeper concern.

"Won't you come with us to the lake? The breeze might do you good."

"No," I said, "I won't come to the lake." I added, logically: "I have no skates."

"I could lend you skates," Muss suggested slyly, "but the ice is slippery."

"Shut up, Muss," I said sternly. "Don't I work my fingers to the bone for you . . . and for all humanity?"

"You've been keeping at it much too hard, Mr. Shannon." In her perplexity, Miss Jean had taken my words quite literally. "You know you promised to come out to Blairhill. I go home to-night. Do take the day off and visit us to-morrow."

Gazing into her soft brown eyes, my powers of invention seemed suddenly to fail me. Finding no excuse, after a moment, lamely, I muttered:

"All right. I'll come."

CHAPTER V

THE ONE-THIRTY TRAIN for Blairhill was painfully slow, its ancient compartments so foul that with every jolt of the engine a puff of dust exhaled from the mouldy seat covers. As it dragged across the smoky, industrial Lowlands, past belching factory chimneys, with never a blade of grass in sight, stopping at every little station, I blamed myself for fulfilling a promise I had never meant to make and took little comfort in arguing that a day off would send me back refreshed to my research.

At last, about an hour after leaving Winton Low Level, having escaped the worst of the "black country," we bumped into Blairhill. So that the unhappy traveller should not miss his fate, the name was worked in white pebbles, between two fierce-looking Scots firs, upon the station embankment. And there, waiting on the platform, rising a little on her toes, scanning eagerly with bright eyes the curved flank of the stationary train, was Miss Jean Law.

As I opened the door and came towards her, I perceived that, in honour of my visit, or merely, perhaps, because of her week-end vacation, she was wearing, beneath a loose coat, her knitted white sweater and, upon her brown curls, which seemed more noticeable than usual, that little tasselled woollen cap known in Scotland as a "cool." Discerning me amongst the milling passengers, her face lit up in welcome. We shook hands.

"Oh, Mr. Shannon," she exclaimed, happily. "It's so nice you could come. I was almost afraid . . ."

She broke off, but I finished the sentence for her.

"That I would let you down."

"Well . . ." She coloured, as she did so easily. "I know

36

you're a busy man. But you're here, anyway, and it's a lovely afternoon, and I've so much to show you, and although I shouldn't say it, I think you'll enjoy it."

As she spoke, we were walking together up the narrow main street. The town was less spoiled than I had expected; it lay within the wide domain of the ducal family of Blairhill and had the air of an old-fashioned country borough, with hand-hewn setts upon the pavements, unexpected winding alleys, and an old market-place. Full of pride in her native place, my companion explained that "the present Duke," in conjunction with the Blairhill Historical Society, had done much to preserve the local antiquities, and she assured me, seriously, enthusiastically, that, when the formalities of introduction were completed, she would take me upon a comprehensive tour of inspection.

At the head of the incline she paused suddenly, opposite a little low-browed building, and, with a nervously conscious air betrayed by her fluttering lashes, she remarked:

"This is our bakehouse, Mr. Shannon. You must come in and meet my father."

I followed her, beneath a low archway into a little cobbled yard, past a varnished van, its shafts directed towards the sky, then down, through a narrow doorway, between piled sacks of flour, into a dim, sweet-smelling, earth-floored basement lit by the dull red radiation of two charcoal ovens. Gradually, as my eyes became accustomed to the dark interior, I made out two shirt-sleeved figures, each armed with a long wooden paddle, working energetically at the open ovens, their white aprons made ruddy by the glow as they drew the batches of bread on to long wooden trays.

For several minutes we watched in silence this operation, which appeared to demand energy, adroitness, and speed. Then, as the new batch slid into the ovens and the iron doors clanged shut, the foremost of the two turned immediately and came towards us, wiping his hand upon his apron and holding it out, the nails still slightly encrusted with dried dough.

Daniel Law was about fifty-five, of medium height, pallid from his occupation, yet vigorous-looking, with thick shoulders and a sturdy frame. Despite his steel spectacles and the close black beard which somewhat masked his features, he had a frank, earnest expression and an open brow, at present beaded with sweat. Obviously he did not smile easily; yet as his warm fingers grasped mine his lips parted slightly, in greeting, exposing strong teeth, somewhat spoiled, however, by the flour, which was everywhere.

"I am glad to make your acquaintance, sir. My daughter has told me of your great kindness to her at the coll-edge. Any friend of my daughter is welcome here."

His deep voice had a patriarchal quality, enhanced by his pronunciation of the word "college," and his bespectacled eyes, as he made reference to Miss Jean Law, glinted fondly. He went on to apologize.

"I'm sorry we're so rushed the now. My son and I manage by ourselves, Saturday afternoons." He called over his shoulder. "Luke! Step up here a minute."

The young lad of seventeen, who advanced, smiling and pulling on his jacket, bore a close resemblance to his sister, having similar colouring of complexion and eyes. He had a warm, cheerful, human air which made me take to him at once. He could not stay, having to harness the horse and drive the van upon its country round. Indeed, I perceived that Law himself, despite his courtesy, was pressed; so, with a side glance at my companion, I indicated that we must not trespass upon his time.

Law nodded.

"Our customers maun have bread, sir. And to-morrow's

the Sabbath day. But we'll see you later at the house. Around five o'clock. Meantime, my daughter will take ye in hand."

Outside, and continuing our way to the outer fringes of the town, past newer houses standing in little garden plots, my companion kept stealing glances at me, half anxious, half eager, as though trying to gauge my opinion of her relatives. Presently, at a turn of the quiet avenue, overhung by the bare but drooping branches of some chestnut trees, we approached a small stone villa, neat and unpretentious, with a trim privet hedge in front and immaculate lace curtains shrouding the windows. Here, unable to contain herself, with her hand upon the iron gate bearing, on a brass plate, the name SILOAM, Miss Law exclaimed:

"They both liked you—my father and Luke. I could see that. Now you'll meet my mother."

While she spoke, the front door opened and a slight woman, silver-haired and comely, with a delicate, transparent skin, her figure shielded by a black alpaca wrapper, appeared to greet us. After a quick glance at her daughter, making no effort to conceal the feather duster in her hand, she turned upon me for a long moment the scrutiny of her confidently tranquil eyes. Then, as though reassured, she fell into the vein of small talk.

"You caught me before I got changed, Mr. Shannon. I was just finishing my parlour when I happened to see you walking up the avenue. Come in and sit down."

"No, Mother," Miss Jean protested quickly. "We're going out to make the best of the afternoon."

Mrs. Law bent upon my companion her calm, experienced gaze, which, though fond and tolerant of such youthful impatience, preserved a certain element of maternal condescension.

"You've plenty time, child."

"Not for what I've planned."

"Are you taking Malcolm with you?"

"Of course not, Mother." Her daughter answered a trifle fretfully. "You know he's away this afternoon."

Who was Malcolm? I wondered absently, perhaps some juvenile relation, possibly a dog.

"Well, well . . . Off you go then," agreed Mrs. Law with her air of quiet reasoning. "But be sure you're back for supper. We'll all be here and I'll be ready to dish at six o'clock sharp. Goodbye for just now, Mr. Shannon."

While she smiled and retired, competently, to her parlour, Miss Jean Law, with the slightly relieved air of one who has successfully gone through the preliminaries, took me exclusively in hand.

"Now," she exclaimed, with energy, "I can show you round."

Leading the way, she took me out into the back garden of about half an acre, and toured me painstakingly along its gravel paths, between the tidy beds, the rhubarb patch, the washing green. When I approved its order, she flashed me a grateful smile.

"Of course, it's very tiny . . . suburban you might even say. I'm sure, Mr. Shannon, it's nothing like your home."

Affecting not to hear the mildly searching lift in her tone, I pointed, hastily, to the toolshed, where a red motor-cycle was propped upon its stand.

"Luke's." She answered my unspoken inquiry indulgently. "He's mad on motor engines and knows a lot about them, too—although Father doesn't approve. But poor fellow, he has to go so slow in the van, he likes to make up for it on his Indian."

My opinion of Luke, already high, rose considerably. For a long time, as one yearns for the moon, I had coveted such a machine, which was capable of bearing its rider exquisitely through the air at a speed of at least seventy miles an hour. I should have liked to halt to inspect its

40

perfections, but Miss Jean was hastening me back, past the house, and into the public roadway. Tucking her "cool" more firmly upon her curls, she glanced methodically at her watch and remarked crisply:

"We have a good three hours. We'll try to get in everything."

"Shouldn't we rest for a bit, first?" I suggested, casting a glance towards two chairs which stood in a sheltered corner of the veranda. I had been up half the night trying to plan out a culture technique for my specimens.

She laughed quite gaily and remarked, archly, as though I had said something funny:

"Really, Mr. Shannon, you are a *cure*. Why, we've only just begun."

Never was there a more scrupulous sightseer, a more devoted cicerone—that I am prepared to swear—than this pretty daughter of the baker of Blairhill.

Earnestly, indefatigably, she paraded me round the royal and ancient borough. She showed me the Town Hall, the public library, the Masonic Temple, the ducal mausoleum, the old weavers' houses on Cottar's Row, the remains of the Roman wall (three decayed boulders), and, with a reverent air, in Lamb Lane, the Meeting Hall of the Brethren. She even exhibited to me the exact spot at the Cross where Claverhouse, dispersing a Conventicle, had been providentially thrown from his charger.

Then, while I rejoiced that our pilgrimage was over, she gave me, scarcely pausing for breath and with a bright nod, the mysterious glance of one who has saved the best treat for the end.

"We can't miss the White Cattle," she declared, adding, primly, as though quoting from a guide-book: "They are quite unique."

To view these fabulous animals, which, she advised me, were part of the famous herd of Château-le-roi, imported from France by "the late Duke's father," we were obliged to retrace our steps for about two miles and to enter, through pillared gates, an extensive demesne known as "the High Parks," which "the late Duke" had graciously detached from his own policies and donated to the town.

It was undoubtedly a lovely stretch of woods and meadows, still maintaining—since not a soul was in sight—its previous air of privacy.

But Miss Law could not find the cattle. Although she sought them vigorously, ardently, as though her honour were at stake, drawing me with her, up hill and down dale, over wooden stiles and under bushy glades, her seeking eyes meanwhile exhibiting an increased concern, her expression lengthening with dismay, she was forced, eventually, to pull up upon the summit of the last grassy hill and, facing me, with shame, to admit defeat.

"I'm afraid . . . Mr. Shannon . . ." Then, with a final explosion of pique: "Really, it's beyond understanding."

"They're probably hiding from us, up the trees."

She shook her head, refusing to see humour in the subject.

"Such lovely animals. Milky-white and with beautiful curving horns. They must be 'in' for the winter. I'll show you them another time."

"Do," I said. "Meanwhile, let's sit down."

The afternoon was extremely calm, warm for the season, with the sun, partly veiled, diffusing an amber light, which seemed to steep the landscape in the stillness of an undiscovered world. The contours of the muted woods fell away beneath our feet, hiding a little stream which, hushed by the prevailing mood, crept from pool to pool, holding its breath, imposing an equal silence upon us.

Beside me, chewing a blade of the brown tussocky grass and gazing straight ahead, Miss Jean Law sat erect, still nursing her discomfiture and, as I rested on my elbow, I began, unconsciously, to study her, trying, in a random

42

fashion, to dissect her personality. I could not, of course, revise my opinion of her *naïveté*, yet I was compelled to admit that of the few young women I had met, she was the most supremely natural. She had, especially in this setting, a striking, youthful freshness. Her brown eyes, hair, and skin matched the woodlands, as did her firm little throat and chin. Her teeth, as she munched the wiry grass, were white and wholesome. Observing from underneath, one could almost see the flow of warm blood through the soft curve of her upper lip. But, more than anything, she looked, and smelled, so extraordinarily clean. I decided, idly, that, since this virtue came next to godliness, she must wash thoroughly, all over, night and morning, with Windsor soap. Everything visible about her and, I felt sure, the invisible also, was neat and spotless.

Suddenly, while I critically took stock of her, she turned her head and met, unexpectedly, my examining gaze. For a moment she sustained it with her usual fearless honesty, then her modest eyes fell and a slow, sweet flush spread all over her cheeks. There was a strained pause, a silence that was part, somehow, of the greater surrounding stillness of Nature and which, as though inviting a word, an action upon my part that did not come, was filled with an almost painful expectation. Then, almost angrily, as though refusing to surrender to confusion, she glanced at her round silver watch, jumped quickly to her feet.

"It's time we got back." She added in a low voice, which she tried to make practical, "You must be starving for your tea."

When we reached Siloam the entire family awaited us in the immaculate back parlour, Mrs. Law wearing her "company" dove-grey silk, Mr. Law and Luke spruced-up in linen collars and decent broadcloth suits. There was also present, rather to my surprise, another guest, introduced to me as Mr. Hodden, who answered, with an agreeable

43

smile, to the name Malcolm, who at once attached himself to Jean, and who was, indeed, on terms of devoted intimacy with all the members of the Law family.

He was a correct, dependable-looking young man of about twenty-five, with a well-set-up figure, an open, faintly serious expression, firm lips, and a square, compact head, dressed with methodical neatness in a brown tweed suit and a high stiff collar. Prone always to envy in others those qualities opposite to my own, I felt myself dim slightly in his presence, for he had about him a calm solidity, the air of one who exercises every day at the Y.M.C.A., a look of manly frankness as though, conscious of his own uprightness, he was resolved to find in his fellow man an equal attribute. His top right vest-pocket carried a tuning fork and a row of sharpened pencils, which served doubtless to facilitate his occupation, which I soon learned was that of a teacher in the Blairhill elementary school.

When he had offered me a friendly hand, Mrs. Law set the seal upon our meeting.

"You two young men ought to have much in common. Malcolm is quite one of ourselves, Mr. Shannon. He takes our Sunday School every week. A real worker, I can tell you."

Since supper was ready, we took our places at the table, Daniel gravely repeated a lengthy grace in which, with a veiled glance towards her photograph, in nurse's uniform upon the mantelpiece, he made a rather touching reference to his absent daughter Agnes "now working in foreign fields." Then Mrs. Law began generously to portion out the large cut of boiled salmon that stood before her.

Sharp set, I fell to with the appetite to be expected from one of Miss Dearie's boarders. There was in addition to the generous fish a plenitude of everything, potatoes boiled in their jackets, winter greens, cold ham and tongue, pickles, pots of home-made preserve; indeed, the simple goodness of the meal would have delighted a palate far more expert than mine. In honour of my visit, the baker had made a special sponge cake, iced with marzipan and adorned with frosted cherries. But what pleased me most was the bread. Light and well risen, with a crisp, crackling crust, it exhaled a delicious fragrance and melted upon one's tongue. When I ventured to compliment him upon his product, Law looked gravely pleased. He picked up a slice from the plate, tested its consistency, sniffed it delicately, then broke it, with a sacramental air, between his fingers. Glancing across the table, professionally, at his son, he remarked:

"A shade underfired to-day, Luke . . . but not at all bad." Then, turning to me, he went on, with great simplicity. "We take our trade seriously, sir. The staff of life, that's what our bread is to many of the poor country folks. They don't get much else—colliers, ploughmen, farm labourers, with large families, working maybe for thirty-five shillings a week. That's why we make it wi' nowt but the best flour, and the sweetest barm, all mixed by hand."

"The finest bread in the country," Malcolm interposed, with a nod towards me. He was sitting next to Jean and passing plates in an undercurrent of quiet merriment.

Daniel smiled.

"Ay, they walk five miles, some of these bodies, to meet our van to buy it." He paused, drawing himself erect, with dignity. "You are probably aware, Mr. Shannon, of the scriptural significance of the article we produce. You will mind how the Saviour multiplied the loaves to feed the multitude, how He broke bread wi' His disciples at the Last Supper."

I gave a confused murmur of assent and, as Luke relieved my embarrassment by passing me the strawberry jam, with the faintest droop of his left eyelid, I attempted, in an undertone, to engage him in conversation on the merits of his motor-cycle. Daniel, however, was not to be denied. Head of this household, preacher at the Meetings, he was accustomed to hold forth, and now, beaming his grave and well-disposed regard across the table, he seemed determined to sound me out.

"Of course, Doctor, you follow a noble profession yourself. To heal the sick, restore the maimed, cause the lame to walk, what could be more meritorious? It was a proud and happy moment for me, sir, when my daughter decided to dedicate herself to that great and splendid work."

I kept silent, since I could not well advise him that it was my intention never to practise, but to devote myself exclusively to the pursuit of pure science.

Undeterred by my reticence, and with that strange interplay of dignity and humility which characterized him, Daniel returned to the subject, touched upon the brotherhood of man, upon the Christian virtue of helping one another; then, having worked himself into position, he faced me directly.

"May I ask, sir, what is your persuasion?"

I took a prolonged draught of tea. Except for Hodden, whose gaze betrayed a mild alertness, they were all viewing me with kindly attention, waiting in warm interest for my reply as though, in fact, it were the crux, the necessary keystone which would complete the firm edifice of their united approval. Miss Jean in particular, a trifle flushed from the strong, hot beverage, was viewing me with parted lips and starry eyes.

What on earth was I to say? I knew enough of these small town inter-denomination feuds to realize what a commotion I would cause if I spoke the naked truth—that I was a Catholic, who had strayed occasionally into the less dark corridors of scepticism, but who still, at heart, clung to his first belief. The thought caused me to fall back for support upon the structure I had already created for Miss Law. After all, what did it matter? I should never see this worthy family again, I preferred not to disrupt the harmony of the occasion, and if I were skilful I need not lie.

"Well, sir," I said, with a fluency which shocked me, as though this congregation of goodness evoked the worst subtleties of my character, "I must confess that my biological work has somewhat restricted my opportunities for churchgoing. But I was brought up, in Levenford, in an exceedingly strict Nonconformist atmosphere. In fact"—still drawing upon the facts of my chequered upbringing, I improved modestly upon one of my grandmother's less credible boasts—"a great-uncle on my mother's side was one of the Covenanters who gave testimony, with his blood, on Marston Moor."

There was a pause. Then as my answer slowly sank in, I perceived that its effect was not only satisfactory, but highly impressive.

"Do you tell me!" Daniel inclined his head with excusable interest. "Marston Moor! Ay, that was a martyr-dom of the saints. You should be proud of such a forebear, Mr. Shannon. And," he added with gentle cunning, "I hope in future you'll mind his good example."

This obstacle surmounted, the evening continued on a note of amiable concord. When Malcolm, with profuse expressions of regret, was obliged to take his departure to conduct some night classes at the Blairhill Institute—extra work, Mrs. Law confided to me, which he was undertaking to support his widowed mother—we adjourned to the par-lour, where Miss Jean was induced to perform upon the piano, a piece by Grieg. Then there was talk of the distant Agnes. Her latest letter, extremely cheerful, was proudly read aloud. Snapshots were passed, tenderly, one by one, all yellowish and slightly fogged—native children in groups, spindly and large-eyed, wearing white pinafores, strangely pathetic, sustained by a staunch and smiling nurse's figure; clusters of wooden huts, a glimpse of a barren compound, and always the lush background of forest beyond, strange fernlike trees, the whole shot with shafts of sunlight and sullen, blinding shadow.

When eight o'clock struck, I rose to leave amidst protests and cordial handclasps.

"We were honoured, sir," said Daniel—and, with an unexpected warmth in his eye: "Maybe next time ye visit us, ye'll bide overnight."

"Yes, come again soon." Mrs. Law pressed a package into my hand, murmuring confidentially, "That's a nice bit Scots shortbread to help out things at Miss Dearie's."

Darkness had fallen as Luke and his sister escorted me to the station. On the way down Luke generously offered to lend me the motor bike whenever I could use it. As the train gathered steam, Miss Jean Law walked along beside my window.

"I hope you enjoyed your visit, Mr. Shannon. I know we all did, very much."

Alone, in the compartment, I subsided in a corner, exhausted by this excess of sociability, trying to assess my own reactions to it. To be truthful, contact with this simple, zealous family had filled me with a distaste for myself stronger even than usual—I felt cheap and shabby, yes, for some reason I felt a regular sneak.

And suddenly I had a vision of Jean Law's face as, innocently, she blushed with downcast eyes, beside me, in the High Parks. I had slight experience of women, and in this respect was entirely without conceit. But now a thought went through me like an arrow. I started, sat up, shocked, in the empty carriage.

"Oh, no!" I exclaimed aloud. "She couldn't . . . she can't . . . It would be too absurd."

CHAPTER VI

February came in with sharper frost, with cold, clear, sparkling days which stirred the blood. For over a month now I had flung myself, with complete abandon, into my own work. It felt good to be alive.

Naturally, Lomax and Spence noticed my activity, but Smith, although I occasionally caught him staring at me and biting the ends of his ragged moustache, could not guess what I was up to. Now that Professor Usher was away, he spent most of the day in the bar of the University Arms.

It was not an easy process I had set myself. Do not imagine that original research is accomplished in a fine poetic rapture; before the dawn appears one must drudge along the labyrinthine ways, or roll the stone like Sisyphus, endlessly uphill.

Yet, after experimenting with many media, and finding them useless for my purpose, I had at last succeeded in growing, in peptone broth, from the Dreem specimens, a culture which I believed to contain the causal organism of the epidemic disease. As I gazed at the delicate yellow strands forming in saffron threads within the topaz clear liquid, enlarging and coalescing, like a glowing crocus, yet more beautiful to me than the rarest flower, my heart kept pounding with a deep excitement. This was a growth I did not recognize, which gave promise of something strange and new, which reinforced the trembling structure of my hopes.

As the time at my disposal lessened, I increased my efforts, by a method of selective culture, to produce a strong, pure strain of this precious organism. I had a key for the side door of the Pathology building that gave me access to the laboratory when everyone had gone. After tea at Miss Dearie's, I returned to the Department, remaining there, submerged like a diver, connected to the world by only the thinnest cord of consciousness, in the cool, green-shaded solitude, until midnight boomed across the silent University. These were the most productive hours of all.

I was confident that I could finish this essential phase by the following Saturday, February 1st, and remove all traces of my experiments that same night. It fitted beautifully, like a well-designed mosaic—Professor Usher had written that he would return on Monday, the 3rd, and I should be at my bench, busy with his tests, when he came back.

On the Wednesday evening of that last week, shortly after nine o'clock, I felt that, at last, the culture was ripe for examination, and with a platinum loop I smeared and stained a microscope slide. It was a crucial moment. Holding my breath, I placed the slide under the oil immersion lens; then, as the dark forms leaped up against the shining background, I gave a sharp involuntary gasp.

The field was loaded with a small, comma-shaped bacillus which I had never seen before.

For a long time I sat immobile, gazing at my discovery, suffused by an exaltation which turned me giddy. At last, collecting myself, I opened my note-book and began, with scientific accuracy, to write a specific description of the organism, which from its shape, I named, provisionally, Bacillus C. For perhaps fifteen minutes I continued, but suddenly my concentration was broken by a flood of light through the workroom fanlight. A few seconds later I heard steps in the passage, the door opened, and, while I turned cold with consternation, Professor Usher walked into the laboratory. He wore a grey suit with a dark cloth cape thrown across his shoulders, and his pale, stiff face was stained with the grime of travel. At first I could not believe that he was real. Then I saw he had just come off the train.

"Good evening, Shannon." He advanced slowly, in a measured fashion. "Still here?"

I blinked at him across the culture flasks. He was looking at them.

"You show remarkable industry. What's this?"

Utterly unnerved at being caught, I was silent. Why, oh, why had he come back before his time?

Suddenly, behind Professor Usher, I saw that bird of ill omen, standing, without his white coat, in an ill-fitting street suit, his long neck drooping, his orbits hollow—Smith. I realized, then, that I would have to tell him.

As I began haltingly, yet with jealous reserve, to speak, Usher's manner grew more distant and severe. When I finished his face was wintry.

"Do you mean that you have deliberately shelved my work in favour of your own?"

"I'll resume the counts next week."

"Since I've been away how many have you done?"

I hesitated.

"None."

His narrow, ingrained features turned grey with anger.

"I especially told you I wished our paper finished by the end of this month . . . for Professor Harrington . . . whose hospitality I have been enjoying . . . my old friend and colleague. Yet the minute my back was turned . . ." He stuttered slightly. "Why? Why?"

I kept looking at the lining of his cape. It was made of dark green silk. I muttered:

"I have to find out about this . . ."

"Indeed." Even his nostrils turned white. "Well, sir, let us not beat about the bush. You will abandon it at once."

I felt myself wince, but steadied my unruly nerves.

"Surely my fellowship gives me some say in the matter?"

"As Professor of Experimental Pathology, I have the last word."

I was not easily aroused, in fact my nature was retiring and inoffensive, I believed profoundly in universal tolerance, in that blessed motto, "Live and let live," yet now a reddish haze swam up before me.

"I can't give up this investigation. I consider it of far greater importance than the opsonin tests."

In the background Smith swallowed suddenly, his bony Adam's apple shuttling up and down his throat, as though relishing a savoury morsel. Usher drew himself to his full height, his lips wire-thin.

"You are a singularly graceless fellow, Shannon. I observe it in your manners, which are deplorable, in your dress, totally unsuited to your professional standing, and in your outrageous disrespect towards myself. I am accustomed to co-operating with gentlemen. If I have been lenient towards you it was because of my belief that with proper guidance you might go far. But if you choose to behave like a boor, we know how to deal with you. Unless by Monday you hand me a written apology for this almost unpardonable lapse I must ask you to leave my Department."

A dead stillness followed.

After a fitting interval, Usher took out his handkerchief and wiped his lips. He saw that he had silenced me and, as usual, his sense of self-interest came to the surface.

"Seriously, Shannon, for your own good, I advise you to take yourself in hand. In spite of everything, I am reluctant to break up our collaboration. Now, if you will excuse me, I have not been home yet."

With a matador-like sweep of his cape, he spun round and went out. At his departure, Smith stood a moment, then began to whistle softly under his ragged moustache, and, not looking at me, to make pretence of cleaning out Spence's sink.

He was waiting for me to speak, of course, and I was a fool to fall into the trap.

"Well," I said, bitterly. "I suppose you think you've queered my pitch."

"You heard the Chief, sir. I must carry out his orders. I have my responsibilities."

I knew this to be sheer hypocrisy. The truth was that, for the most incredible of reasons, Smith nursed against me, in his heart, an almost morbid jealousy. A poor youngster like myself, he had once aspired towards the highest scientific goal. Now, beaten, frustrated, and consumed with envy, he could not endure that I might succeed where he had failed.

"It's no fault of mine, sir." He swabbed at the sink with a defiant smirk. "I only done my duty."

"I congratulate you."

I put away my cultures, set the regulator of the incubator to the requisite temperature, while he stared at me, sideways, in an odd manner. Then I took my cap and went out.

Sick with resentment, I walked down Fenner Hill, in the darkness.

At the intersection of Pardyke Road and Kirkhead Terrace, to clear my head, I stepped into the cabman's shelter upon the corner, and ordered a mug of coffee. Seated on a high stool, with my elbows on the counter, I sipped the dark, gritty fluid, blind to the surrounding swirl of the night life of this poor quarter—the familiar crowds gathered round the pubs and fried-fish shops, the hucksters shouting at their barrows under naphtha flares, the slowly promenading women, the newsboys darting, between the traffic, shouting the latest sensation.

A moment later, as I sat brooding, I felt the tap of an umbrella upon my shoulder and, turning, I saw the Babu at my elbow, beaming, full of friendship and affection for his fellow men.

"Good evening, sir."

I scowled at him, but he slid forward a stool and pantingly elevated his flabby bulk to the level of the counter.

"Most fortunate meeting. I have been to Alhambra Varieties, second house naturally, so extremely jolly." He rapped for attention with his umbrella. "Coffee, please, with plenty sugar. And one large portion fruit cake. Give nice piece, please."

I turned my back. But Chatterjee, between noisy draughts, and with many giggles, persisted in describing his evening's entertainment, in which the famous Scots comedian, Sir Harry Lauder, had played a prominent part.

"Tee, hee, hee. At the frolics of that hilarious nobleman, I laugh so heartily I nearly fall from my front position in the balcony. I tell you, sir, I am so fearfully enamoured of the Scottish music, I am sincerely wishful of learning to play bagpipes. Can you suggest instructor, sir?"

"For God's sake leave me alone."

"But how nice, sir, for my Calcutta friends if, when returning with my degree, I also dispense Scottish airs while attired in kilt." Waving a pudgy forefinger, he lilted in a high falsetto. "*Ay, ay, ay . . . la, la, la . . . lassee by the side . . . on banks of bonnee Clyde . . . When sun go down to rest . . . that is hour that I love best . . . roaming in the . . . roaming in the gloaming*. Excuse me, Dr. Robert Shannon, what is precise meaning of Scottish 'gloaming'? A wood, forest, nullah or concealed place, probably, suitable for love? Hee, hee, hee. Am I right, sir?"

I felt in my pocket for a coin, placed it on the counter to pay for my coffee and got abruptly to my feet.

"Wait, wait, wait, Dr. Robert Shannon." He tried to detain me, with the crook of his umbrella. "Guess, sir. In the audience to-night, who do I see from my high front place in the balcony? It is two of your friends, in front stalls, Dr. Adrian Lomax and the lady of Dr. Spence, both together, enjoying performance. Don't go, sir. I wish to accompany you."

But I was already outside the shelter. A new fear had entered my mind, driving me to retrace my steps hastily towards the Department.

" 'I must carry out his orders.' "

As I raced back, I kept thinking with increased foreboding of that last gleam in the attendant's eye.

The place was in total darkness when I got there. Hurriedly, I opened the side door, went into the laboratory. Even as I entered I missed the faint reassuring hum of the heater. With a sinking heart I switched on the light above my bench and opened the incubator. Then I saw with certainty. Smith had thrown out my cultures, the flasks stood empty on the bench, and four weeks of my hardest work had gone to waste.

CHAPTER VII

Upon the following morning I did not go to the University, but made my way, after breakfast, to Parkside Crescent, where, in a quiet and unobtrusive terrace overlooking Kelvingrove Gardens, Professor Challis lived in retirement. I felt sure I should get advice and help from this good old man who had so often encouraged me in the past. When I rang the bell it was Beatrice, his married daughter, who opened the door—a pleasant young woman, wearing an art print overall, with her children, two bright-eyed little girls, peeping at me from behind her skirts.

"I'm sorry to trouble you so early, Beatrice. Could I see the Professor?"

"But, Robert," she exclaimed in her warm voice, smiling in spite of herself at my anxious face, "didn't you know. . . ? He's away."

My disappointment must have shown only too plainly, for, with a change of manner, she went on quickly to explain that her father, who suffered severely from arthritis, had been taken by some friends upon a trip to Egypt for his health. He would be away all winter.

"Won't you come in a moment?" she added kindly. "The children and I are having biscuits and hot cocoa."

"No, thank you, Beatrice." I tried to smile as I turned away.

Most of the day, which was grey and overcast, I walked aimlessly about the city, along Sinclair and Manfield Streets, staring unseeingly into the windows of the large shops; then, in the afternoon, I wandered to the docks where, wrapped in a chilly mist, the black and white river steamers lay paddle to paddle, laid up for the winter. I came back to the boarding-house and, more from habit than anything else, drifted into tea.

Out of the corner of my eye I noticed that Miss Jean Law, who had been away—where, I did not know—for the past three days, was again in her usual place. I thought she looked queer, quite ill, in fact—she was pale and her nose and eyes were swollen, slightly inflamed, as though she had been suffering from a severe head cold—but I was too moodily preoccupied to give her more than a single glance. She left the table early.

However, when I went upstairs, ten minutes later, I found her standing, erect, in the corridor, with her back to my door. She addressed me in a stiff, unnatural tone.

"Mr. Shannon, I should like a word with you."

"Not just now," I answered. "I'm tired. I'm busy. And my room's in a mess."

"Then come into mine." Her lips became resolute.

She opened her own door and, before I could protest, I was in her small room which was, in contrast to my littered and untidy den, a model of cool propriety. As, for the first time, I viewed the narrow, neatly "made" white bed, the hand-hooked rug, the shining, silver-framed photograph of her parents placed on the little table precisely set out with her comb and brush, I vaguely recollected her having told me that, to help Miss Ailie, she "did" her room herself.

"Sit down, Mr. Shannon." As I was about to rest on the window ledge, she interposed with a sudden quiver of irony: "No, not there . . . take the chair, please . . . it's much more suitable for a gentleman like you."

I glanced at her sharply. She was breathing quickly and was paler than ever—a pallor that darkened her swollen brown eyes and made deeper the shadows which lay beneath them. I also saw, with surprise, that she was trembling. But, keeping her gaze unwaveringly upon me, she began, steadily, and with a curl of her lip:

"Mr. Shannon, I owe a great deal to you. It's really remarkable, in fact, that one in your exalted position should have condescended to be good to a poor creature like myself, a petty tradesman's daughter."

In spite of myself, I was now listening to her with moody attentiveness.

"You may have observed that I've been absent for a few days. Perhaps you'd care to guess where I've been?"

"No," I said. "I wouldn't."

"Then I'll tell you, Mr. Shannon." Her dark eyes sparkled. "I've been visiting in your part of the country. Every year my father goes to speak at the Tent Meeting and, though it may amuse you, I go with him. This year the Tent was pitched at Levenford."

I began vaguely to see the shape of things to come, and an added bitterness corroded me.

"I hope it didn't blow down on you."

"No, it didn't," she answered hotly, "though I'm sure you wish it had."

"Far from it, I rather like a circus. What did you do? Jump through paper hoops?"

"No, Mr. Shannon." Her voice quivered. "We had a splendid, fruitful mission. There are some good people in Levenford, you see. I met one of them, after our first meeting. A fine old lady . . . Mrs. Leckie."

In spite of having steeled myself, I flinched. Although I had not seen her for more than twelve months, I had every reason to remember this indomitable woman, the support yet flail of my childhood, this paragon who wore six petticoats and elastic-sided boots, whose bed I had occupied at the tender age of seven, the patron of open-air Conventicles, of Gregory powder and peppermint

58

imperials; now—I computed rapidly—eighty-four years old. She was my great-grandmother.

Standing there, her eyes flashing fire, Miss Law saw that she had touched me on the raw. She began to tremble all over.

"Naturally, in your native place, we spoke to her of you. My father inquired, in fact, if some of your wealthy relatives might not be induced to support our cause. She stared at us, then she laughed. Yes, Mr. Shannon, she laughed *out loud*."

I felt myself redden at the vision of that wrinkled, ochreous grin, but my tormentor, relentlessly, cuttingly, went on.

"Yes, she told us all about you. At first we couldn't believe it. 'There's some mistake,' my father said. 'This young man is most highly connected.' Then she took us across the Common."

"Shut up," I exclaimed, in a rage. "I'm not interested in what she did."

"She took us and showed us your country estate." Pale and quivering, almost gasping for breath, Miss Jean Law choked out the words. "A dreary, poky little semi-detached, with weeds all round and washing on the line. One by one, she exposed all your beastly lies. She told us you were never wrecked on a raft in the war. 'You'll not drown that one,' she said. 'He's like his wicked old grandfather.' Yes, she even told us"—her voice broke upon the culminating odium—"what church you go to."

I jumped furiously to my feet. On top of all my troubles, this was the last straw.

"What right have you to preach at me? I only did it for a joke."

"A joke! That makes it more shameful."

"Oh, be quiet," I shouted. "I wouldn't have done it at all if you hadn't run after me, imposed yourself on me

at every turn with your blasted medical papers and your
. . . your inane white cows."

"So that's the way of it." She bit her lip fiercely, but
could not keep back the tears. "Now we're getting the
truth. Oh, you fine gentleman, you hero, you aristocrat
. . . you miserable Ananias, it would serve you right if you
were struck down too." Her colour came and went, she
made the motion of swallowing, then suddenly, passionately, unrestrainedly she gave way to her sobs. "I never
want to see you again, never, never, as long as I live."

"That suits me. I never wanted to see you in the first
place. And for all I care you can go to Blairhill, or West
Africa, or Timbuktu. In fact, you can go to hell. Goodbye."

I walked out of the room and slammed the door.

CHAPTER VIII

Most of that night I lay awake, thinking of my own uncertain future. It was cold in my room. Through the window, which I always kept open, I heard the night trams banging along Pardyke Road. The noise went through my head. Occasionally from the docks came the low wail of a ship, slipping down river on the tide. There were no sounds from next door, none. I lay on my back, with my hands behind my head, gnawing the bitter bone of reflection.

What Usher did not understand was the inner compulsion—call it, if you choose, the inspiration—which motivated my research. How could I abandon it without betraying my scientific conscience, without, in fact, selling myself? The desire to find out the truth concerning this epidemic, this strange bacillus, was irresistible. I could not let it go.

When morning came I rose stiffly. While dressing I burst the knitted sweater that I wore underneath my jacket, an old garment I had kept all through the war and to which I had become attached. Annoyed, I cut myself while shaving. After a cup of tea I smoked a cigarette; then set out for the University.

It was a fine, crisp morning, everyone seemed in the best of spirits. I passed a group of girls with shawls round their heads, laughing and chattering, on their way to work at the Gilmore Laundry. The corner tobacconist was polishing his shop window.

My mood was still hard and bitter, yet the nearer I drew to the Pathology buildings the more my nervousness increased; for alas! to display myself to advantage in a crisis was a feat beyond my powers. When I entered the laboratory and saw that the entire staff was present, I felt that I was pale.

Everyone was watching me. I went to my bench, opened all the drawers and began to empty them of my books and papers. At this, Professor Usher approached me.

"Clearing the decks for action, Shannon?" His manner was brisk, as though my submission were understood. "When you're ready, I'd like to discuss our scheme of work."

I took a quick breath, striving to keep my voice even.

"I can't undertake that work. I'm leaving the Department this morning."

Complete silence. I had certainly achieved a sensation, yet it brought me no satisfaction. I felt a dry smarting behind my eyes. Usher was frowning in a provoked fashion. I saw he had not expected this.

"Don't you realize what it means, if you give up your fellowship at a moment's notice?"

"I've considered all that."

"The Senate will undoubtedly put a black mark against your name. You'll never get another opportunity."

"I'll have to take my chance."

Why was I mumbling? I wanted to be calm and cold, especially since the perplexed annoyance had now left his face and he was considering me with an expression of open dislike.

"Very well, Shannon," he said severely. "You are acting with extreme stupidity. But if you persist, I can't stop you. I simply wash my hands of the whole affair. Your blood is on your own head."

He shrugged his shoulders and, turning towards his office, left me to gather up the remainder of my notes. When the pile was complete, I lifted it in both arms, at the same time darting a glance round the laboratory. Lomax, with his usual half-smile, sat examining his finger nails, while Smith, his back to me, was attending to the cages with apparent indifference. Only Spence showed evidence of concern, and, as I passed his bench, he said, under his breath:

"Anything I can do, let me know."

This, at least, was some slight tribute to my passing. I nodded to Spence, then raised my head, but, as I went through the swing doors, my edifice of books became unbalanced, and despite my efforts, shot from my arms all over the outer corridor. I had to go down upon my knees in the dark passage and grope about for my belongings.

Outside, with the cool air striking upon my heated face, I felt oddly lost to be going home in the middle of the forenoon, an emotion intensified when I almost stumbled over a pail of soapy water in the dark hall of Rothesay. The house had a strange feel about it and an even fustier smell.

I went upstairs, washed my hands from habit, sat down at my table and stared at the dingy wallpaper. What was I to do? Before I could answer that question the door opened and Miss Ailie, carrying a broom and dust pan, wearing an old wrapper and her list slippers, came into my room. She started slightly at the unexpected sight of me.

"Why, Rob, what's the matter? You're not sick?"

I shook my head, while she considered me with anxious kindness.

"Then why aren't you at the University?"

I hesitated for a moment, then blurted out the truth.

"I've chucked my job, Miss Ailie."

She did not press for more information, but looked at me quietly, for a long time, with a beautiful expression, which was almost tender. Blowing the wisp of hair out of her faded blue eyes, she said:

"Well, never mind, Rob. You'll get another."

There was a pause; then, as though wishing to distract me from my own misfortune, she added:

"It never rains but it pours. Miss Law left us this morning. Quite unexpected. Such a nice lass too. She's going back to work for her examination at home."

I received this information in silence; yet, under Miss Ailie's guileless gaze, my face, already downcast, reddened guiltily.

"Tut, tut," she declared. "This'll never do."

Without further comment she left the room, returning presently with a glass of buttermilk and a slice of sponge cake. How she had spirited these precious things out of the kitchen, under the sharp eyes of her sister, I could not imagine. She sat down and with open satisfaction watched me as, unwilling to offend her, I consumed them. Food was Miss Ailie's remedy for most ills, a belief easy to understand in that household.

"*There!*" she exclaimed, when I had finished. No more than that single word. But what a wealth of feeling she put into it! And what heart her kindness put into me!

Now the outlook looked less bad. Slowly, like a sun swimming out of grey mist, a resolution grew within my troubled breast. I would continue my work independently —yes, somehow, somewhere, alone, I would bring it, successfully, to completion. Why not? Others had worked under almost insuperable difficulties. I clenched my fist and banged the table hard. . . . By heavens, I would do it. I'd get a job somewhere, now . . . at once . . . and go on.

CHAPTER IX

WITH MY BELIEF in myself restored, I went out confidently enough, setting my course towards the Northern Infirmary, which lay quite near, on the left bank of the Eldon, within sight of the University Tower. Clearly, my best course—although it might be construed as a "step down"—was to take an appointment as house physician in one of the large city hospitals where I should have at least definite, if restricted, facilities for continuing my research. And I selected the Northern, not only because of its convenience and high reputation, but because I knew the Registrar, George Cox.

The entrance to a metropolitan hospital is apt to be a confusing place, but with the indifference of familiarity I went past the intimidating army of white-clad porters, attendants, and nurses, through a series of tiled corridors, and into the Registrar's office, where I sat down beside Cox's desk and watched him for a few minutes as, amongst the papers which encumbered him, he rapidly signed a batch of diet sheets.

"Cox," I said, when he had finished, "I'd like to join the staff."

Returning my gaze, he grinned heartily, then lit a cigarette. He was a stocky, solidly muscled figure, about thirty-two, with a flat, ugly, good-natured face, a cropped blond moustache, and a coarse, ruddy, greasy skin, full of enlarged pores. He was enormously strong—in fact, he seemed to exude a careless vitality—and the many liberties which he took with himself, from chain smoking to, in his own phrase, "stopping out on the tiles," made not the slightest inroads upon his constitution. Devoted to

65

athletics, he had as a medical student represented the University at every known game and, loth to sever a connection in which he had happily broken practically all the bones in his body, he had dropped breezily into this administrative position in the College teaching hospital.

He answered me at last, with heavy humour. "The Superintendent isn't quite ready to retire yet. When he is I'll let you know."

"I'm not joking," I said quickly. "I really want to come in as a house physician."

He was so surprised he found it difficult to dispose of his smile.

"What's happened to the fellowship?"

"That passed away suddenly . . . this morning."

Cox shifted in his chair, carefully flicked his cigarette ash to the floor.

"It's unfortunate, Shannon. We haven't a single vacancy. You see, we just made our appointments for the next six months, and all the interns look depressingly healthy."

There was a pause, filled by the rattle of a typewriter through the glass partition. I could see that this good fellow was uncomfortable, almost uneasy, that a person of my attainments should be chasing round, at short notice, for a junior's job. Yet I knew his answer to be absolutely honest.

"That's all right, Cox. I'll try the Alexandra."

"Yes, do," he said eagerly. "Shall I ring them for you?"

"Thanks all the same," I said, getting up. "But I'll go over myself."

I did go over to the Alexandra Infirmary. I went to the Great Eastern, the King George, the Royal Free; I made in fact, with increasing chagrin, an exhaustive and fruitless tour of all the city hospitals. The possibility of failing

66

in my quest had never entered my head. I had forgotten that during the war years, to meet the national emergency, the medical curriculum had been so shortened and speeded up that hundreds of young men and women were roughly machined into shape, then disgorged, diploma in hand, off the assembly line, as it were, into the open market. As a result, the profession had become thoroughly overcrowded, and I was now merely one of the crowd.

This fact was borne in upon me even more sharply during the next few days, when, like a candidate for the dole, I presented myself, in line, at the Winton medical agency. There were no available hospital appointments. I might purchase a general practice for a mere three thousand pounds. I might also, if I wished, secure a fortnight's "locum" in the remote island of Skye, but while I debated the desirability of such a stop-gap, the opportunity was snatched from under my nose by the pale, bespectacled youngster behind me. At the end of the week I was constrained, shamefully, to seek out the elder Miss Dearie in her little cubby-hole office under the stairs.

"I'm sorry, Miss Beth. I can't pay you this week. I'm flat broke."

She reared herself, in the shadows, like a pallid boa-constrictor, and fixing upon me a suffering and reproachful eye, with her most prayerful, most ladylike expression, replied:

"I had guessed as much, Doctor . . . not being without a certain experience . . . to my sorrow. Naturally, our rules in such contingencies are strict. But you are an old client of this establishment. You may remain."

As I left her sanctum I felt, with gratitude, that Miss Beth had shown much forbearance towards me. But alas! it was not her nature to display this virtue long, and as my days passed in unsuccessful seeking, she turned up increasingly at table the whites of her eyes, with many mournful and martyred sighs, viewing me from time to time with a saintly resignation as though I were piling faggots round her at the stake, and turning the conversation pointedly to such disconcerting topics as the cost of electric light and the rising price of meat. I noticed also that my portions tended, progressively, with almost mathematical precision, to diminish. Finally, rather than be made to feel a cadger, I began to absent myself altogether from the evening meal, relying upon the hunk of bread and cheese, which Miss Ailie smuggled to my room, to blunt the edge of my hunger.

At the end of the month, although I had dodged Miss Beth as much as possible, I felt in my bones that the crisis was not distant, that presently, in fact, I should find myself upon the pavement, outside Rothesay, with no other lodging than the sky. Then, one Saturday, from the sanctuary of my room, I was called to the telephone by Miss Ailie. Spence's voice came to me over the line.

"Have you fixed up yet, Shannon?" While I hesitated, ashamed to confess my defeat, he went on. "If you haven't, I've just heard of a vacancy at the Dalnair Cottage Hospital. It's a small place, for infectious fevers, and Haines, the doctor there, is leaving rather unexpectedly. Do you remember Haines? Always seemed half asleep. He says there isn't a lot of work. You'd have plenty of spare time. I thought it might interest you . . . especially as it's down Levenford way . . . in your part of the country."

While I began to thank him he rang off, and I hung up the receiver, thinking what a good friend Spence was, in his quiet and unobtrusive way. I had not heard a word from Lomax. I must get this job at all costs, and as Dalnair was near Levenford, I knew instinctively how I must do it. It was time for me to pocket the last vestiges of my pride.

Back in my room, with much heart-burning, I composed

a letter to the one man upon whom I knew I could depend. I borrowed a stamp from Miss Ailie and posted this letter in the hall mail-box. Then, as twilight began to fall, I shrouded my microscope in its green baize cover and carried it across the Park to Hillier's, the pawnshop behind the University, which catered especially for impecunious and bankrupt students. Here, I pledged my instrument for eight pounds, fifteen shillings. It was a Leitz and probably worth twenty guineas, but I was no good at haggling, and took the money without protest.

Ignoring the long-haired young clerk behind the counter whose pencil, protruding from an ear, intensified his general air of sharpness, and who, having driven a hard bargain by deprecating, one by one, the qualities of my microscope, was now disposed to discourse, agreeably, upon the weather, I placed seven pounds, four weeks' rent, in an envelope to give to Miss Beth. Five shillings, the price of a return railway ticket to Levenford, I stowed securely in my top waistcoat pocket. This left a balance of thirty shillings which, as a wave of recollection of my month's privations, my stinted meals, my crusts of bread and rinds of cheese, swept over me, I resolved recklessly to spend, immediately, on a dinner, at the neighbouring Rob Roy Tavern, a noted restaurant, patronized by the University faculty, which offered a native cuisine of the highest excellence.

Then, as I came out of Hillier's, and, already licking my lips, began the ascent of the back avenue—little more than a flagged pathway—which wound up between the sycamore trees towards that summit upon which the University stood, I suddenly discerned a solitary female figure approaching, weighted slightly to one side by her textbooks, descending the path towards the tramway terminus slowly, with a peculiar air of reverie and sadness which, since I immediately recognized the young woman as Miss

Jean Law, caused me a sharp stab of discomfort. Since her head was drooping, her gaze downcast, she did not see me for some seconds; but when about twenty paces distant, as though forewarned by all her instincts of a disburbing presence, an uncongenial protoplasm, she lifted her clouded eyes—which instantly encountered mine.

She started, quite distinctly faltered, then resumed her way, while her face, which seemed apathetic, smudged in places by her day's work, also smaller and more strained than I had ever known it, turned white as her father's flour. She wanted to look away, but she could not, and her dark eyes, compelled against their will, remained upon me, haunted and frightened, almost as though guilty of a sin, while she approached. Now we were level with each other, and so close that the scent of Windsor soap struck upon my nostrils. What was happening to me? At that instant of near contact a sudden palpitating surge gathered and broke within my breast. Then she had passed me stiffly, head rigid in the air, and was immediately beyond my field of vision.

I did not glance behind me, yet the sight of that wan and solitary figure had stirred and upset me beyond belief. Why had I not spoken to her? It would have been so easy, at this moment, with money in my pocket, to make a graceful atonement and ask her to share my meal. Disconsolate, stung by my stupidity, I at last swung round. But she was gone, vanished in the soft dusk swiftly gathering beneath the budding sycamores. I let out a very bad word.

And then . . . I cannot explain my next action, which I regretted immediately I had performed it, nor can I attempt to defend what is so clearly indefensible, yet, since I am sworn to truth, I must shamefully record the facts.

As I went uphill, through the narrow old streets behind

the University, continuing to heap abuse upon myself, I came upon the Church of the Nativity, which in my early student days I had visited every day and where, still, despite the irregularity of my life and the damaging conflicts of my mind, I attended Mass; where, indeed, borne by the irrevocable instinct in my bones, I came occasionally, on a wave of tenderness, to make, in the dimness, an act of reparation, a promise of amendment—an outpouring of the heart from which I arose, comforted.

Now, caught by an irresistible impulse, rather as one is seized by a garrotter from behind, I drew up, blinked, then hurried automatically into the little church filled with the sweet smell of incense, candle-wax, and damp. There, at the door, hastily, as though committing a crime, I stuffed my three crisp ten-shilling notes into the padlocked iron box marked in grey letters St. Vincent de Paul, and without even looking at the altar, stalked out.

"There!" I prayed without satisfaction to whatever saints observed me. "Do without your dinner, you blasted fool!"

CHAPTER X

NEXT AFTERNOON, at two o'clock, I arrived in Levenford. Often I had promised myself a sentimental pilgrimage to this Clydeside borough where I had grown up, where the grey façade of the Academy, the grassy stretch of Common with its little iron bandstand, the elephantine outline of the "Castle Rock" seen through the tall stacks of the Shipyards, with the distant view of Ben Lomond beyond, seemed impregnated with memories of these tender years. Yet, somehow, I had not found the occasion for this indulgence—time had severed so many of the ties which bound me to the town. And now, as I walked up the High Street towards the office of Duncan McKellar, my thoughts fixed on the approaching interview which I had sought, I was conscious of a prosaic drabness, rather than of any romantic quality, in my surroundings. The town seemed small and dirty, its inhabitants depressingly ordinary in appearance, and the once imposing solicitor's office, crouching opposite a sadly diminished Borough Hall, badly in need of a coat of paint.

However, McKellar himself was little changed, perhaps a trifle more veined around the nose, but still clean-shaven and close-cropped, eyes dry and penetrating beneath his sandy brows, manner contained, deliberate, judicial. He did not keep me waiting, and when I was seated before his broad mahogany desk, he began gravely to stroke his full underlip and, against the background of japanned deed-boxes, to contemplate me.

"Well, Robert." His survey completed, he spoke, at last, in a moderate tone. "What is it, this time?"

The question was ordinary enough, but the note of quiet

disapproval running through it made me gaze at him defensively. Ever since those early days when, without a word, he had, while passing me in the street, pressed into my hand tickets for the Mechanics' Concerts, I had been conscious of a current of sympathy, of interest, flowing towards me from this man. He had taken my part when I was a boy, had administered the money left me for my education, a very watchdog of probity, and, as a sort of unofficial guardian, had advised and encouraged me during my student days. But now he was shaking his head in sombre disappointment.

"Come on. Let's have it, lad. What do you want?"

"Nothing," I answered. "If this is how you feel about it."

"Tut, tut. Don't be a young fool. Out with it."

Suppressing my sense of injury, I told him, as best I could.

"You see how important it is. If I'm to go on with this research I must get a hospital job. Perhaps Dalnair isn't a big place, but that would give me all the more spare time to do my own work."

"Do you think I carry appointments, like marbles, in my pocket?"

"No. But you're treasurer to the County Health Board. You have influence. You could get me in."

McKellar studied me again, his brows contracted; then, no longer able to restrain his irritation, he burst out:

"Just look at you, man. Shabby and down-at-heel. You've a button off your coat, your collar's cracked, you need a hair-cut. There's a burst in your boot, too. I tell you, sir, you're a disgrace to me, to yourself, and the whole medical profession. Damn it all, you don't look like a doctor. After all that's been done for ye! Ye look like a tramp."

Under this withering attack, I bit my lip in silence

"And the worst o't is," he went on, lapsing more and more into broad Scots as his anger grew, "it's a' your own perverse and ediotic fault. When I think on the career ye've had, on the way ye've taken medals and honours and fellowships, and then, after folks have built on ye . . . to come to *this* . . . Oh, man alive, it's fair deplorable."

"All right." I stood up. "I'll say goodbye. And thanks."

"Sit down." He shouted.

There was a pause. I sat down. With an effort he mastered his feelings and, in a constrained voice, remarked:

"I just cannot carry the sole responsibility any longer, Robert. I've asked here for a conference a certain person who is interested in you also, and whose sound common sense I value."

He pressed the bell upon the desk and a moment later Miss Glennie, his faithful servitor, respectfully ushered into the room a figure, unchangeable as destiny, fateful as doom, wearing her historic black-beaded cape, elastic-sided boots, and crape-bedizened, white-frilled mutch.

Of all my relatives, the others having wandered far afield, Great-grandmother Leckie was now the sole representative in Levenford. Since her son had died of a stroke shortly after his retirement from the Borough Health Department, she had continued to inhabit his house, Lomond View, now aged eighty-four, yet physically active and in alert possession of all her faculties, unconquerable and indestructible, the last prop supporting the structure of a disintegrating family.

The old woman seated herself, very erect, with a prim bow to McKellar, who had half risen in his chair, then turned towards me observantly, but without visible recognition upon her long, firm, yellowish, deeply wrinkled face. Her purse was still treasured in her mittened hand. Her hair, still parted in the middle, seemed a trifle thinner than of old, but was still untouched by grey, as also were the crinkling whiskers which sprouted from the brown mole upon her upper lip. She still made the same clicking noises with her teeth.

"Well, ma'am," said McKellar, formally opening the inquest, "here we are."

Again the old woman inclined her head and, as though in church and about to enjoy a sermon of excellent severity, she took from her bag a peppermint imperial and placed it austerely between her lips.

"The position simply is," the lawyer continued, that Robert here, with everything in his favour and the best prospects in the world, is sitting before us *without a curdie in his pocket.*"

At this accusation, which was quite true, for, beyond my return ticket to Winton, I had in the way of available currency precisely nothing, my grandmother once more bent forward her head rigidly, to indicate her comprehension of my lamentable situation.

"He ought," McKellar reasoned, getting warm again, "he ought to be in his own practice. There's those would help him to that if he only said the word. He has brains. He's personable. When he chooses, he has a way with him. Here, in Levenford, he could earn his thousand a year in good hard siller without the slightest trouble. He could settle down, get married to a decent lass and become a solid and respectable member of the community, like his friends have aye wished him to. But instead, what does he do? Starts out on a wild-goose chase that will never put a farthing in the bank for him. And now, here he is, begging me to get him a job in a poky, outlandish fever hospital, an old cottage hospital where he'll be lost, buried in the wilds, with no more nor a hundred and twenty pound a year!"

"You're forgetting something," I said. "In this hospital

75

I'll be able to do the work I want to do, work that may take me out of the wilds, and by your own material standards, bring me far more recognition than I could ever earn as a general practitioner in Levenford."

"*Tch!*" McKellar dismissed my argument with an angry shrug. "That's all up in the air. That's the trouble with you. You're too impractical for words."

"I'm not so sure!" For the first time the old woman spoke, gazing at the lawyer inscrutably. "Robert is still young. He's trying for big things. If we make him a general practitioner he'll never forgive us."

I could scarcely believe it. McKellar, who had clearly banked on her strong support, gazed towards her with a fallen expression.

"We must remember that Robert was subject to very mixed influences when he was a boy. He must be given time to shake these off. I don't think it would be a bad thing if he were to have this chance. If he brings it off, well and good. If not . . ." She paused, and I saw what was coming. "He will have to accept our conditions."

The lawyer was now looking queerly at Grandma, darting peculiar, comprehending glances at her, while he pursed his lips and played with the heavy ruler on his desk.

I took advantage of the silence. "Help me get this job at Dalnair. If I don't succeed in what I'm after and have to come back to you for help, I give you my word I'll do what you ask."

"Hmm!" McKellar hummed and hawed, still consulting with the old woman from beneath his brows with a mixed expression, through which, however, there predominated a reluctant respect.

"That seems to me a sound proposal," she remarked mildly, but with a faint, meaningful relaxation of her features towards him.

"Hmm!" said McKellar again. "I dare say. . . . I dare

say. . . . Well——" He made up his mind. "So be it. Mind ye, Robert, I can't promise you the post, but I'll do my best. I know Masters pretty well, the chairman of the committee. And if I get it for you I'll expect you, without fail, to keep your side of the bargain."

We shook hands upon this and, after some further conversation, I went out of the office.

I wanted to leave before the old woman could get hold of me. But as I swung into the street I heard her following close behind me.

"Robert."

I had to turn round.

"Don't be in such a hurry."

"I have a train to catch."

She took no notice of the excuse.

"Give me your arm. I'm not so young as I was, Robert."

I gritted my teeth. I was twenty-four, a bacteriologist who handled with contempt the deadliest germs, who, after the war, had gained a sharp experience of life. But in her presence the years fell away from me and I was again a child. She reduced me. She humiliated me. And I knew, from her possessive touch, that I should have to put up with her for the rest of the afternoon, that she would extract from me, using her tongue like a scourge, the full story of my doings.

As, arm in arm, we rounded, in stately fashion, the bend of Church Street, she leaned towards me, sweeping aside the last of my resistance.

"First thing we do is get that old uniform off your back. We'll go up the town to the Co-operative Stores and get ye into a decent homespun suit. Then, instead of these broken-down bauchles, we'll put a new pair of shoes on your misguided feet. Ay, ay, my man, I'll have ye half-human again, before ye're an hour older."

I shuddered at the prospect of being "fitted," under her

77

eagle eye, by the female assistants of the Boot and Drapery departments.

Leaning closer, exhaling a powerful odour of peppermint, she breathed warmly into my ear:

"Now tell me everything, Robert, about this young woman Law."

BOOK TWO

CHAPTER I

I WAS MET AT Dalnair village station by the hospital chauffeur and handyman, with an old brass-bound Argyll ambulance, the paintwork washed away, but the glass glittering, rather like a hearse. When he had introduced himself as Peter Pim, he placed my bag aboard in sluggish fashion and, after many crankings, started up the machine. We lumbered off, past a jumble of ramshackle houses, a dingy little store, some clay pits, and a disused brickworks; then across a stream, striving valiantly to purify its muddy course, and into a bedraggled semi-urban countryside, upon which, however, the early spring had imposed a fresh green mantle.

From time to time, as I bounced upon the hard front seat, I stole inquiring glances at my companion's expressionless profile, which, beneath his peaked cap, conveyed such an impression of lethargy I hesitated to break into speech. However, at last I ventured to compliment him upon the sound condition of his antique vehicle, which, from his handling of the controls, was clearly a source of pride to him.

He did not immediately reply, then with his gaze fixed on the road ahead he made a sort of considered pronouncement.

"I am interested in mechanics, sir."

If this was so, I felt he could be of service to me, and I expressed the democratic hope that we might be friends.

Again he communed with himself.

"I think we'll get along, sir. I always do my best. I was on excellent terms with Dr. Haines. A nice, easy gentleman, was Dr. Haines, sir. I was sorry to see him go."

Chilled somewhat by this laudation of my predecessor

and by the melancholy intonation with which it was delivered, I lapsed into silence that persisted until we laboured to the summit of a narrow lane and swept into a circular gravel driveway giving access to a little group of trim brick buildings. Opposite the largest of these we drew up and, descending from the ambulance, I became conscious of a short, swart-complexioned woman in uniform, whom I guessed to be the matron, standing upon the steps, protecting her winged white cap from the breeze and radiantly smiling her welcome.

"Dr. Shannon, I presume. Delighted to make your acquaintance. I'm Miss Trudgeon."

While Pim made himself scarce with an astringent expression, she greeted me jovially and, almost before I knew where I was, had shown me to my quarters: sitting-room, bedroom, and bathroom all on the east side of the central building. Then, bustling me along, full of energy and enthusiasm, she took me proudly round the entire institution.

It was quite small, consisting of four little detached pavilions, spaced at the corners of a square, behind the administrative block, devoted respectively to the treatment of scarlet fever, diphtheria, measles, and "mixed infections." The arrangements were primitive, nevertheless, the old-fashioned wards, with their well-waxed floors and spotless little cots, shone with cleanliness. Most of the few patients were children, and as they sat up in their red bed-jackets, smiling as we went past, while the afternoon sun streamed through the long windows, they made me feel that my duties would be agreeable. The ward sisters, too—one presiding over each pavilion—had a reassuringly quiet and sensible air. In short, the general effect of this unpretentious little hospital, which, from its high and wind-swept hill-top, commanded a view of the valley townships it served, was one of efficiency and usefulness.

At the foot of the grounds, some distance from the four

pavilions, there stood a peculiar maroon-coloured edifice of corrugated iron, somewhat dilapidated, and almost entirely surrounded by shrubbery.

"That was our smallpox ward," Miss Trudgeon explained, her small shrewd eyes interpreting my thought. "As you can see, it isn't used . . . so we won't go in. Luckily, the laurel bushes hide it." She added complacently: "We haven't had a case in the last five years."

From here, always with that air of justifiable pride, she conducted me to the nurses' recreation-room, the kitchen, and the receiving-office—all of which exhibited the same immaculate gloss—and finally, to a room with a long wooden counter into which were set gas and electricity fittings and two porcelain sinks. Some varnished desks and a couple of benches were piled against the wall.

"This is our test-room," Matron remarked. "Don't you think it's nice?"

"Very."

I said nothing more, of course. Yet I knew at once that I had found the ideal place for my laboratory. As we retraced our steps along the driveway I was already, in my mind's eye, allocating the available space and making my arrangements.

Back in the main building, Miss Trudgeon insisted on giving me afternoon tea in her own parlour, an airy, charming room facing to the front, with a bow window, chintz-covered chairs and sofa, and a china bowl of flowering hyacinths on the piano, an apartment which, I could not but observe, was even nicer than any we had previously entered. When she had pressed the bell, a red-cheeked country girl in a starched cap and apron, whom she introduced to me as Katie, our "joint" maid, brought in a tea service and a tiered cake stand. Talking all the time, Miss Trudgeon presided officiously behind this equipage, offering me a choice of India or China tea with an excellent cut of plum cake just out of the hospital oven.

She was about fifty, I judged, and before "settling down" at Dalnair, had, she informed me, spent ten years in Bengal as an Army nurse, an experience which had no doubt imparted to her large and prominent features their distinct coppery tinge, and which also, perhaps, had given to her voice and manner characteristics closely resembling those of the sergeant-major. I had noticed particularly her projecting bust, her chesty swagger, and the lateral oscillation of her short but far from inconsiderable haunches, as she preceded me through the wards. And now, her bluff heartiness, the loudness of her laugh, her downright and decisive gestures, seemed to complete the picture of a personality better suited to the barrack square than the sick-room.

Yet what impressed me most was her determined pride in the hospital, a sense almost of ownership. Again, half jocularly, she reverted to that dominant theme.

"I'm glad you approve of our little place, Doctor. It's a bit out of date, of course, but I've tried to get over that with a few Army dodges. I've worked hard to bring things to their present state. Yes, I've really put my back into it."

A brief, odd silence followed, but presently, to my relief, there came a discreet tap upon the door, and in answer to Miss Trudgeon's "Come in," the handle turned noiselessly and a tall, thin, red-haired sister appeared upon the threshold. Upon seeing me, she started, and her pale green eyes, fringed by straw-coloured lashes, sought out Miss Trudgeon's with a deprecating humility which brought to the matron's bronzed face an indulgent smile.

"Come, come, my dear, don't run away. Doctor, this is Night Sister Effie Peek. She usually has tea with me when she gets up in the afternoon. Sit down, my dear."

Modestly, Sister Peek entered the room and, seating herself on a low chair, accepted the cup which was offered her.

"I'm very pleased that you should meet Sister Peek," continued Miss Trudgeon. "She is quite the most helpful member of my staff."

"Oh, no." The pale, red-haired sister repudiated the compliment with a quiver of her unworthy flesh; then turning towards me, she murmured: "Matron is much too kind. But of course a word from her means so much. You see, everyone looks up to her. And she has been here so long, we simply couldn't get on without her. After all, our doctors come and go. But Matron goes on for ever."

Having thus paraphrased Tennyson's "Brook" for my benefit, this blanched creature—even her red hair was pale, and her skin was milky-white—subsided to a respectful silence. In a few minutes, as though not daring to trespass further upon our time, she rose and with a fawn-like glance towards the matron glided from the room to begin her night's duty. I did not long outstay her. I stood up and, having expressed to Miss Trudgeon my appreciation of the warmth of her welcome, excused myself on the grounds that I must unpack.

"That's all right, Doctor. We ought to rub along together. As Sister Peek says, I'm an old-timer here." Bouncing to her feet, her large face wreathed in smiles, she gave me, for an instant, a penetrating glance, adding, with jovial emphasis, "I think you'll find that my ways are the best."

With curiously mixed feelings, I found my way to my own quarters, satisfied by my reception, telling myself, as I pottered round the room, examining its severe yet adequate furnishings with the eye of one who must live and become intimate with these unknown articles, that, although perhaps rather blunt, Miss Trudgeon was a cheery, hearty soul, but at the same time vaguely disturbed by the *brio* of her manner and by impressions and reactions which I could not quite define.

CHAPTER II

Yet nothing, nothing, could depress my spirits, nor damp my satisfaction at the prospect of resuming my research after those weeks of maddening delay.

As I had surmised, my official duties were pleasant and inexacting. The actual capacity of the hospital was small, not more than fifty patients when absolutely full, and now, since no epidemics were prevalent, at this particular season we had only about a dozen children, all convalescent, mostly from simple measles and, no matter how conscientiously I prolonged my round of the wards, I was finished, and free, by noon.

The test-room was better than I had imagined. In the cupboards and drawers I found a variety of equipment which I could convert and use. Material accumulates easily in hospitals—ordered in a burst of enthusiasm, it is put away and forgotten. My own pieces of apparatus were soon installed and, by mortgaging my first month's salary, I redeemed my microscope from Hillier's. Already, on the hospital note-paper, I had initiated a lively correspondence with several doctors in other rural areas affected by the epidemic, and from the specimens which they kindly sent me, together with those which still remained from Dreem, I began again to try to cultivate Bacillus C.

All this, of course, was achieved discreetly. I took care to perform my official duties scrupulously, and I was pleasantly assiduous in my attentions to the matron, who, during these early days, beneath her smiling heartiness, was studying me rather as an experienced pugilist might study an opponent for the first round in the ring.

She was a strange mixture. When she came to Dalnair,

in the "good old days" lamented by Pim—whom I soon found to be a professional grumbler—the hospital had been slackly run. Step by step she had changed the system, worked herself into the good graces of the Hospital Committee, won into her own hands complete authority. Now she managed the place, from attic to cellar, with firmness, economy, and tireless efficiency.

"I'm at her beck and call all day long," Pim confided in me with woeful dignity as, seated on an upturned pail, he was taking all morning to polish the ancient ambulance. "All my little perks have gone. Why, would you believe it, sir, she even checks the soap for my outdoor wash-room!"

Although I took breakfast and supper alone, it was the Dalnair custom for doctor and matron to lunch together. Thus at one o'clock each day she came to my room for "tiffin," as she called it, seated herself at table, and tucked her napkin into her bosom. She was fond of her food, especially of spicy dishes and curries, which appeared frequently upon the menu, served with mango chutney and shredded coconut. Heaping her plate she would mix the ingredients thoroughly, then delve into the savoury mess, using a spoon—the only way to eat curry, she told me—and washing her mouthfuls down with lime-juice and soda. She was proud of her Bengali recipes, and had a fund of anecdotes bearing upon her Army experiences, which went with them, her favourite being a spirited account of how she and Colonel Sutler of the Bengal Medical Service had fought the cholera in Bogra in 1902.

Despite these repetitious stories, she had a sense of humour which, although too boisterous for my taste, had saved me thus far from disliking her. She might be a little martinet, yet her deep chuckle was disarming, and on occasions she could be kind. To those of her nurses who worked well and did not cross her she was, on the whole, good-hearted and fair. Over a period of years she had done her best with the committee—no easy task—to improve the working conditions and inadequate pay of her staff. In a hospital such as Dalnair there was always the serious risk of contracting an infectious fever, and when a nurse was laid up in this fashion Miss Trudgeon, who might very well have slanged her head off the week before, looked after her like a mother.

One of her predilections was a decided fondness for the game of draughts; and occasionally, early in the evening, she honoured me with an invitation to her room to play. Now my great-grandfather, past-master of the art, had taught me, when I was a boy, all the deep and diabolical subtleties of "the dam-brod" and during our innumerable encounters across the chequered board I had acquired from him that particular brand of low cunning which lures an opponent to his doom. At my first meeting with the matron it took me only thirty seconds to discover that she was far from being a match for me—indeed, I was hard put to it to lose. Yet lose I did, with sound diplomacy, upon every occasion, to her extreme delight. When she had beaten me she would lie back in her chair, crowing with satisfaction, taunting me with my inability to get the better of her, and winding up, invariably, with an account of the historic game she had played against Colonel Sutler, during the cholera epidemic, at Bogra, in 1902.

The provocation was severe, yet keeping in mind my main objective, I suffered it with commendable patience. One evening, however, she went over the score, and her taunts got under my skin.

"Poor fellow," she jeered. "Where are your brains? How on earth did you get your medical degree? I'll have to give you lessons. Did I ever tell you the story of my game with . . ."

"I'm beginning to know it off by heart," I snapped. "Set up your men again."

She did so, shaking with laughter at having finally provoked me. The game began, and in five moves I got through her defence and wiped the board with her.

"Eh, what a fluke!" she exclaimed, hardly able to believe her eyes. "Let's have another."

"By all means."

This time she played more cautiously, but she had not the ghost of a chance. Twice I got three men for one, and in four minutes she was beaten.

There was a strained silence. Her face had turned a dusky red. But still she couldn't think that her second defeat was anything but the wildest chance.

"I shan't let you get away with that. One more game."

I ought, at this stage, to have used better judgement, but I was still smarting from her sharp tongue. Besides, these repeated sessions were encroaching upon the time available for my work; I wanted to put an end to them. Using the double shift opening that old Dandie Gow had perfected, I sacrificed four men in rapid succession; then, with two sweeping moves, cleared every one of her pieces off the board.

The triumphant smile which had begun to dawn upon her face stiffened to an angry grimace, while the veins of her neck and forehead swelled. She shut the board and rattled the pieces into their box.

"That will be all for this evening, thank you, Doctor."

Already regretting what I had done, I gave a deprecating laugh.

"Extraordinary how these games turned out."

"Most extraordinary," she agreed stiffly. "There seems to be a little more in you than meets the eye."

"I can't always be so absurdly lucky. I'm sure you'll win next time."

Her exasperation got the better of her. She stood up.

"What do you take me for? A complete fool?"

"Oh, no, indeed, Matron."

With an effort she controlled herself.

"Close the door, then, on your way out."

Back in my room, I began to see how stupid I had been in offending her, and with hands thrust moodily in my pockets I stood staring out of my window, more annoyed with myself than with her.

At that moment, a burst of rapid reports struck my ear, and a red motor-cycle swung round the drive and came to rest outside my room. As the bareheaded rider heaved the heavy machine on to its stand and removed his goggles I recognized him, with a start of surprise. It was Luke Law.

I opened the window.

"Hello, Luke."

"Hello, yourself."

His cheerful smile dispelled my misgivings and, when he had come into the room, by the simple expedient of sliding over the sill, he took off his long leather gauntlets and shook me by the hand.

"I've brought you the bike." He announced and, observing my mystified expression, added: "You remember? I said I would lend it you for a spell."

"Don't you want it yourself?"

"No." He shook his head. "Not for the next few weeks anyway. I'm going to the Tyne Home Bakery in Newcastle. To learn how they fire stone-milled flour. Father knows the manager."

I had not expected this kindness and felt some embarrassment in accepting it, but Luke brushed aside my protests with the most natural air in the world and, stretching himself out in a chair, lit up one of my cigarettes.

"Yours truly isn't allowed to smoke." He grinned. "But I do like a fag—and I have one too, when I think they won't smell it on me. You've no idea what a sell it is, being held in at every turn. I want to be like the other fellows."

He blew smoke rebelliously, yet humorously, down his nose. "And I wish I could do the work I'm set on. Who wants to be a hand baker? Stone-milled flour! Huh! Twenty years behind the times. I want to work with machinery, with bicycles and motor cars, have my own little factory. I'm good at that. . . . I can make things go. If only I could modernize our plant . . . put in mechanical mixers . . . an electric oven . . ."

"You'll do it . . . later."

"Well," he sighed. "Maybe."

I could see that, despite his youth and good nature, he was beginning to chafe at parental restrictions, and to demand the right to his own existence.

After a pause he threw me a glance which, while holding nothing of reproach, while deprecating, in fact, half-humorously, the folly and weakness of the whole female sex, nevertheless conveyed a certain sense of troubled compunction.

"We're a little under the weather at home, Robert. It's Jean . . ."

To hide my feelings, I bent forward and took a cigarette from the box. The very mention of that name had sent a wave of feeling over me. Luke was so absurdly like her, with his open expression, his brown eyes, curly hair, and fresh, brown colouring, that at this moment I scarcely dared look at him.

"Hasn't she been well?" I asked, cautiously.

"She's been awful!" he exclaimed. "At first she went about raging at the terrible scoundrels and blackguards in the world." He chuckled. "That was you, of course. Then gradually she fell into the dumps. And for the last few weeks she's done nothing but cry. She tries to hide it, but I can tell."

"Perhaps she's worried about her exam," I suggested. "Doesn't she sit the final this summer?"

"No exam ever upset Jean like that." He paused and added in a confidential, man-of-the-world tone: "You know what it's all about as well as I do. Here! She asked me to give you this note."

After some fumbling in the inside pocket of his Norfolk jacket, he produced a folded slip of paper, which I accepted with a curious acceleration of my pulse.

"DEAR MR. SHANNON,—Having discovered, by the merest chance, that my brother proposes visiting you on some business of his own, I take the opportunity of sending you these few lines.

"The fact is that I have something to say to you, something quite impersonal and unimportant, and if you should, by any chance, be in Winton next Wednesday, I am wondering if you would care to have tea with me at Grant's in Botanic Road, about five o'clock. Probably you have something better to do. Possibly you have forgotten all about me. In which case, it does not matter. Please excuse my presumption.

"I am,

"Yours as always,

"JEAN LAW.

"PS.—I was walking alone in the High Parks last Saturday and found out why we did not see the White Cattle. There has been an outbreak in the herd and a number of them have died. Isn't it a shame?

"PPS.—I know I have many faults, but at least I speak the truth."

I put down the note and gazed across at young Law's inquiring and ingenuous face, wondering if Jean had not arranged the whole affair—Luke's visit, the offer of the motor-cycle, the invitation to tea upon the following week —with quiet yet definite intention. My earlier moodiness had vanished, currents of elation were tingling all over my skin.

"You'll go?" asked Luke.

"I suppose so," I answered, in a voice which, despite the beating of my heart, I tried to make prosaic and mature.

"Women are a nuisance, aren't they?" Luke said, with sudden sympathy.

I laughed and, in a rush of spirits, pressed him to remain for supper. We had a good meal together, followed by coffee and cigarettes, during which, as superior beings, we loosened our collars and discussed fast motor-cycles, aeroplane design, the brotherhood of man, electric dough-mixers, and the incomprehensible perverseness of the opposite sex.

CHAPTER III

Winton was a drab enough city, grey, beneath a pall of smoke, ringed by belching chimneys, much rained on, oppressed by monumental architecture and some fearful statuary; but its glory, if it could lay claim to glory, was in its tea-rooms. They animated the dreary streets, scores of them, little oases of rest and refreshment where, having traversed the outer premises devoted to the sale of cakes and cookies, the Winton citizens—clerks, typists, shop girls, students, even staid merchants and men of business— gathered at all hours of the day around white-capped tables loaded with scones and shortbread and innumerable pastries, to seek solace in a cup of tea or coffee.

Of these establishments the one most patronized by members of the University was Grant's, where, in addition to a celebrated make of cream buns, one could enjoy the select sense of "tone" conveyed by an interior of dark oak, with real oil paintings, by members of the Scottish Academy, interspersed with crossed dirks and claymores, upon the panelled walls.

Upon the following Wednesday, then, with a strange mingling of eagerness and apprehension, I arrived at Grant's. I had decided to take all the afternoon off work, for I had a special errand which I wished to do in connection with my research. I was early for my appointment, but even so, Miss Law was earlier. As I entered the crowded café, filled with the buzz of conversation and the tinkle of teaspoons, a small figure half rose at the back, beneath the most formidable of the claymores, and, with a nervous gesture, beckoned me to the table which, in the face of considerable opposition, she was bravely reserving for us. Otherwise she did not greet me, and as I crushed my way forward and sat down silently beside her I observed that, in contrast to those easy days of "cool" and sweater, she was dressed with some severity in a dark grey costume and a prim black hat. Also she was pale, extremely pale, definitely thinner, and, though she exerted herself to conceal it, quite painfully agitated.

There was a constrained pause while, by the process of crooking her forefinger and holding it aloft, she at last overcame the difficulty of securing service.

"Lemon or cream?"

These were her first words, and she made the inquiry in subdued tones without daring to look at me, while the waitress stood over us, impatiently fingering her pencil.

I ordered lemon tea.

"And would you care for cream buns?"

I agreed to the buns, adding:

"Of course, this is my treat."

"No," she answered with quivering lips, but a firming of her chin. "I asked *you*."

We sat in silence till the waitress returned, then, in silence, began our repast.

"Very full here, isn't it?" I ventured at length. "Popular sort of place."

"Yes, it is." A pause. "Extremely popular. And deservedly so."

"Oh, yes. Wonderful buns these are."

"Are they? I'm very glad."

"Won't you have one?"

"No, thank you. I'm not particularly hungry."

"I was sorry to hear about your White Cattle."

"Yes, poor things . . . it's been quite bad."

Another pause.

"Rather a wet summer it's been so far, don't you think?"

"Very wet. I don't know what the weather's coming to."

A still longer pause. Then, nerving herself with a sip of tea—and I noticed that her hand shook as she lowered her cup—she turned to me with a look of serious intentness.

"Mr. Shannon," she exclaimed with a gulp, and all in one breath. "I've been wondering if, after all, it would be possible for us to be friends."

While I stared at her, nonplussed, she went on, her colour coming and going, her voice breaking occasionally, as she strove to be calm and reasonable.

"When I say friends, I mean friends . . . nothing less, nothing more. Friendship is such a wonderful thing. And one meets it so seldom. True friendship, that is to say. Of course, you may feel that you don't wish to be friends with me. I'm just nothing. And I admit it was stupid of me to take things so much to heart and quarrel with you. But now I see that you were only joking, and that I was very childish about it. After all, we are practical, adult people, aren't we? We do belong to different religions, but although that's a serious thing, it isn't a crime, at least it's no bar to our having an occasional cup of tea together. It would be a great pity if we stopped being friends, simply for nothing . . . and drifted apart . . . like ships that pass in the night . . . I mean, if we never saw each other again . . . when, if we were sensible we could be meeting often, that's to say, once in a while, as friends . . ."

She broke off, playing with her teaspoon, a bright flush upon her cheeks, her brown eyes bright also, rather frightened, yet resolutely meeting mine.

"Well," I said, doubtfully. "It's a little difficult, isn't it? I have my work. And you're studying hard for your exam."

"Yes, I know you're busy. And I suppose I have to keep at it, too." There was a strange lack of enthusiasm in the voice of this once-eager student of Pathology, and she added quickly, as though pleading for a rational approach

96

to the whole question of the acquirement of knowledge: "We have to take a spell off once in a while. I mean, it's impossible to work *all* the time."

There was a silence. As though conscious of her high colour, she at last lowered her gaze and drew back in her chair, to hide herself from the curiosity of the tea-room. Glancing at her covertly, I was amazed that I should ever have treated her with disdain. Her flush, her lowered lashes, throwing a soft shadow upon the soft bloom of her cheek, gave her a sensitive, yes, a quite angelic air. Nothing, not her prim black kid gloves, nor the old-fashioned round gold watch she wore upon one wrist, not even her absurd hard little hat, could spoil the stinging charm of her beauty.

And suddenly, to my own surprise, I felt a warm tide welling up within me, I found myself answering, with an air of logical decision:

"There's no law against it, I suppose. I dare say we could see each other once in a while."

Her face lighted up. She bent forward with a tremulous and happy smile and in a tone which paid high tribute to my superior wisdom, she exclaimed:

"I'm so glad. I was afraid . . . I mean, it's such a sensible way to look at things."

"Good." I acknowledged her flattery with a generous nod and, spurred by some incomprehensible impulse, gazed into her shining eyes. "What are you doing this evening?"

An imperceptible stiffening of her figure attended this unexpected remark.

"Well . . . I am going to see the Miss Dearies . . . they were so kind to me, you know. Then, I'm taking the six-thirty train home to Blairhill."

The spurt of recklessness expanded in me further. I remarked coolly:

"Come to the theatre with me instead?"

She started, perceptibly, and the faint look of fright came back into her eyes, increasing as I went on:

"I have some business that will take about an hour. Let's meet at the Theatre Royal at seven. Martin Harvey is on there, in *The Only Way*. You ought to enjoy that."

Still she gazed at me in stricken silence as though my invitation had exposed to her all the secret terrors and dangers of the world. Then she gulped.

"Mr. Shannon, I'm afraid you don't understand. I've never been to the theatre in my life."

"Good heavens!" Although I ought to have been prepared for this, I could scarcely believe my ears. "Why on earth not?"

"Well, you know how strict we are at home."

Lowering her gaze, she drew patterns on the cloth with her finger. "In the Brethren, we don't hold with cards, or dances, or going to the theatre. Of course, Father doesn't exactly forbid us . . . but we just never seemed to think of it."

I studied her in wonder.

"Then it's high time you thought of it now. Why," I spoke largely, "the theatre is one of the greatest cultural influences in the world. Mind you, I don't think too much of *The Only Way*. But it'll do for a start."

She was silent, continuing to make designs in painful, downcast indecision. Then slowly, as her Puritan grain refused to yield, she raised her head and faltered.

"I'm afraid, Mr. Shannon, I couldn't go."

"But why?"

She made no answer, but her melting gaze was sorely troubled. Weighing down the scale against her natural inclination, so vivid and ardent, were all the sad and sombre teachings of her childhood, these austere warnings against the world, those apocalyptic prophecies of doom.

98

"Well!" I exclaimed in annoyance. "If that isn't the limit. You waste half the afternoon trying to convince me that we ought to spend some time together. And, when I offer to take you out, to a perfectly innocent entertainment, in fact, a classical performance, based on a famous novel by Charles Dickens, you flatly refuse to come."

"Oh, Dickens . . ." she murmured faintly, as though partly reassured. "Charles Dickens. He was a very worthy writer."

But in my resentment I had buttoned my jacket and was looking round for the waitress to obtain the bill.

Scorched by my displeasure, she observed, with renewed agitation, these signs of imminent departure; then with a little gasp, her breast rising and falling, she tremblingly surrendered.

"Very well," she whispered helplessly. "I'll come."

Despite the entreaty of her gaze, I did not immediately forgive her, not until I had paid the check—an action which now she did not dare dispute—and escorted her to the street. There I turned and, as we said goodbye, I addressed her in a friendly yet warning tone.

"Seven o'clock at the theatre. Don't be late."

"Yes, Mr. Shannon," she murmured submissively and, with a last quivering glance, she swung round and went off.

After standing a moment, I departed for the Pathology Department, where, since I had written him beforehand, I expected that Spence would be awaiting me.

It was quarter past six when I reached the building and, since the last thing I wished was to run into Usher or Smith, I reconnoitred the corridors carefully before entering the laboratory. There, as I had hoped, Spence was alone, bent in close study at his bench.

Since my approach was quiet, I was at his elbow before he became aware of my presence. Then I saw, with some surprise, that he was not working, but examining, meditatively, a photograph.

"It's you, Robert." He looked me over, rather heavily. "I've missed you. How goes it at Dalnair?"

"Pretty well," I answered cheerfully. "I'm scrapping with the matron. But I've cultured my bacillus again—a pure strain."

"Good work. Have you identified it?"

"No, but I shall. I'm working on that now."

He nodded his head.

"I wish I could get out of here too, Robert. If only I could land a professorship at one of the smaller schools . . . Aberdeen or St. Andrews."

"You will," I said encouragingly.

"Yes." His tone was curiously reflective. "I've plodded along pretty hard these last four years . . . for Muriel's sake. She would like it at St. Andrews."

"How is Lomax?" I asked.

Spence gave me his expressionless glance. There was a perceptible pause.

"Handsome and dashing as ever. Quite pleased with life . . . and himself."

"I haven't seen him for ages."

"He appears to have been rather busy lately. Well, it's good to know you're getting ahead. I had your letter. I can give you all the glycerine medium you want."

"Thanks, Spence. I knew I could count on you."

He made a deprecating gesture. There was an odd silence. Awkwardly I shifted my gaze, which came to rest on the photograph before him. His eyes followed mine.

"Take a better look," he said, and handed me the photograph. It was the pleasing likeness of a youngster with well-cut features and a clean, vigorous air.

"Very nice," I commented. "Who is it?"

He began to laugh, a strange sound, for although he

often smiled, in his twisted fashion, I had seldom heard him laugh.

"Could you believe it?" he said. "That's me."

I gave an inarticulate murmur. I didn't know what to say. And I glanced at him uncomfortably. He was so unlike his usual mild and quiet self.

"Yes, I was like that at eighteen. Extraordinary how important a face is . . . I don't mean a good-looking face . . . just an ordinary, even an ugly face. You know what you read in novels. 'His face had a kind of charming ugliness.' But you can't romanticize half a face. Impossible. The Colosseum is quite a spectacle. But only by moonlight, and for half an hour. Who wants to look at a blasted ruin all the time? In fact, if you were to ask me, Shannon, I'd say in the end it would get most hellishly upon your nerves."

No, I had never before seen Spence in this overwrought, this morbid frame of mind. His quiet reserve made one forget that he must always exercise upon himself a rigid discipline against self-pity. Touched, vaguely uneasy, I wondered if I should speak. But at that moment, when he seemed almost on the point of breaking down, he suddenly took himself in hand, jumped up and went over to the storage shelves.

"Come along," he said briskly. "Let's pack up your stuff."

I followed, slowly.

Together we selected a dozen half-litre flasks of the medium, which we packed with straw in a portable hamper, made of stout wicker. Then I left, warmly thanking Spence once more. I was relieved to see that he seemed almost himself again. That odd spell of his had given me quite a shock.

CHAPTER IV

At the foot of the hill I took the red tram to Central Station, and at the Left Luggage Office checked in my hamper. Then I went into the Railway Buffet and fortified myself hurriedly with a cold sausage roll and a glass of beer. I was beginning to have qualms about the evening, and to wonder if Miss Jean's tender conscience might not prove an insurmountable barrier to our enjoyment.

However, when I met her at the theatre she had thrown off her scruples, her expression was eager and responsive, her dark irises held a sparkle of excitement.

"I've been looking at the posters," she said as we entered the foyer. "I can see nothing wrong in them whatever."

Our seats, although inexpensive, were reasonably good, two pit stalls in the third row, and as we occupied them, the orchestra began tuning up. My companion gave me a glance of communicative ardour and burrowed into the programme which I handed her. Then, as though wishing to be free of all encumbrance, she took off and entrusted to me her wristlet watch.

"Please keep this safe for me. It's loose. And has worried me all afternoon."

Presently the lights went down; then, after a short overture, the curtain rose upon a scene of eighteenth-century Paris, and the crashing melodrama of the French Revolution began slowly to unfold its interwoven themes of hopeless love and heroic self-sacrifice.

This was the evergreen play from *A Tale of Two Cities*, with which that superb trouper, Martin Harvey, yielding himself nobly to the scaffold night after night and at Wednesday matinées, had enthralled provincial audiences for at least a score of years.

At first my companion seemed, circumspectly, to reserve her judgement; then gradually she sat up straight, her clear eyes kindling with interest and delight. Without removing her gaze from the stage, she murmured to me in a human undertone:

"What a lovely scene!"

Then she yielded herself to the pale, dark glamour of Sydney Carton, to the frail and sylphlike charm of Lucie Manette.

At the first interval she relaxed slowly, with a sigh, and, fanning her flushed cheeks with her programme, bent a grateful glance upon me.

"It's splendid, Mr. Shannon. So different from what I expected. I can't tell you what a treat it is for me."

"Would you like an ice?"

"Oh, no, I couldn't dream of it. After what we've seen it would be like sacrilege."

"Of course, it's not a really first-rate play."

"Oh, it is, it is," she insisted. "It's lovely. I feel so sorry for poor Sydney Carton. He's so much in love with Lucie and she . . . Oh, it must be a frightful thing, Mr. Shannon, to be terribly in love with someone and not to be loved in return."

"Quite," I agreed gravely. "Of course, they're extremely good friends. And friendship is a wonderful thing."

She consulted her programme to conceal her blush.

"I like them all," she said. "The girl who does Lucie is very sweet, she has such lovely long blonde hair. Miss N. de Silva is her name."

"She," I answered, "in real life, is Martin Harvey's wife."

"No!" she exclaimed, looking up, with animation. "How interesting."

"She is probably forty-five years of age, and that blonde hair is a wig."

"Please don't, Mr. Shannon," she cried, in a shocked voice. "How can you joke about such things? I'm loving every minute of it. Hush! The curtain's going up."

The second act began with green lights and soft, sad music. And more and more, the sensitive features of my companion reflected the emotions awakened in her breast. At the intermission, deeply affected, she barely spoke at all. But, as the last act got under way and she became once more a rapt being, a strange phenomenon occurred, how I could not guess, yet in some manner her hand, small and rather damp, became entangled with my own. So stimulating was the warm current of her blood I did not break the contact. And thus we sat, with fingers interlocked, linked together as though to sustain each other while the drama of Carton's self-sacrifice worked to its heart-rending end. As the noble fellow made the supreme sacrifice, mounting to the guillotine firmly, with pallid countenance and carefully ruffled raven locks, his speaking eye soulfully sweeping the gallery and pit, I felt a convulsive tremor pass through my companion's body, which was very close to mine; then, one by one, like pattering raindrops in springtime, her warm, tender tears fell upon the back of my hand.

At last, the end, with a clamorous house and many, many curtain calls for Miss de Silva and Martin Harvey—now looking, in fact, happy and handsome in his silk shirt and varnished top-boots, marvellously resurrected from the tomb. Miss Jean Law, however, was too overcome to join in such banal applause. Silently, as though crushed by feelings too deep for words, she rose and accompanied me from the theatre. Only when we reached the street did she turn to me.

"Oh, Robert, Robert," she whispered, with brimming eyes. "You can't believe how much I've enjoyed myself."

It was the first time she had used my Christian name.

We walked to Central Station in silence and, since her train, the last of the day, did not leave for fifteen minutes, we stood somewhat self-consciously together under the bookstall clock.

Suddenly, as though awakening from a dream, Miss Jean gave a little start of recollection.

"My watch!" she exclaimed. "I was almost forgetting it."

"Oh, of course." I smiled. "I had quite forgotten too." And I felt in my jacket pocket for the trinket she had entrusted to me.

But I could not find it. I searched unsuccessfully through all the pockets of my jacket, inside and out. Then, with growing consternation I began to fumble in my waistcoat pockets.

"Good heavens," I muttered. "I don't seem to have it."

"But you must have it." Her voice sounded stiff and queer. "I gave it to you."

"I know you did. But I'm such an absent-minded beggar. I mislay everything."

I was now searching, vainly, and somewhat desperately, in my trousers when, chancing to glance up, I caught sight of the look upon Miss Jean's face, the look of a pure young woman, who finds, after all, that she is indeed dealing with a blackguard and has been deceived, duped, and deluded by him, such a look of pain, doubt and consternation I stopped my futile fumblings in dismay.

"What's the matter?"

"It isn't my watch." Her lips had turned deathly white, her voice was smaller than ever. "It's my mother's watch, given her by my father. I borrowed it, out of vanity, to impress you. Oh dear, oh dear." The inexhaustible fountains of her eyes overflowed again. "After this lovely evening . . . when I was trusting you and . . . liking you . . ."

"Good Lord," I shouted. "Do you think I've stolen the blasted thing?"

By way of answer she broke down completely. Then, as she opened her handbag to find her sodden handkerchief, a sudden gleam of gold illumined the dimness of the station arches. Even as she started, I remembered that, while she sat entranced—fearing, indeed, that I might lose the thing—I had slipped it for safety in her bag.

"Oh!" she gasped, petrified. "Oh, dear, goodness . . ." She stared at me in horrified contrition and stammered: "How can I . . . ever apologize . . . for doubting you?"

Stony silence on my part.

From behind us came the shrill blast of a guard's whistle, followed by the warning shriek of an engine.

"Robert!" she cried wildly. "What can I say . . . oh, my dear, what can I do?"

I gazed upon her coldly. Again the engine shrieked.

"Unless you wish to spend the night on the Winton pavements, I advise you to catch your train."

Frantically, she gazed from me to the platform where, with slow, reverberating chuffs, her train was beginning to move. For an instant she hesitated, then, with a little moan, she turned and ran.

When I saw that she was safely aboard I turned, collected my hamper, and, a few minutes later, took the last train for Dalnair, not altogether displeased with myself. That I was a bit of a fraud, I fully realized; but somehow, like Sydney Carton, I had acquired a halo, at least for the time being, and I rather liked the cosy feel of it.

CHAPTER V

I GOT BACK TO THE hospital shortly before midnight and, to my surprise, observed that a light was still showing in Miss Trudgeon's window. As the slate in the hall indicated that there were no new admissions, I locked up, meaning to turn in at once. But I had no sooner entered my own quarters than I heard, from the corridor, those ingratiating tones which belonged only to Sister Peek.

"Doctor . . . Dr. Shannon."

I opened my door.

"Doctor." She gave me her meek, downcast smile. "The matron wishes to see you."

"What?"

"Yes, at once, Doctor, in her office."

This peremptory summons, delivered secondhand, at such an hour, struck me as an impertinence. For an instant, anxious to preserve the peace, I thought of complying. Then I felt it was too much to swallow.

"Give the matron my compliments. If she wants to speak to me, she knows where to find me."

Sister Peek turned up the whites of her eyes in dismay, yet from the manner in which she scurried off, I could see that she was not sorry to act as the virtuous intermediary in promoting the difference between the matron and myself. She must, indeed, have delivered my message with considerable *empressement* for, a minute later, Miss Trudgeon bore in upon me, wearing her dark uniform but without her cap, cuffs, and collar. Shorn of these embellishments of white linen, her face looked yellower than ever.

"Dr. Shannon. On my monthly inspection to-day I went

into the test-room. I found it in the most atrocious disorder, littered with all sorts of rubbish—untidy, messed up and muddled."

"Well, what about it?"

"Is it your doing?"

"Yes."

"You had no right to do such a thing, no right whatsoever. You should have asked me first."

"Why?"

"Because you should. It's my department."

"Isn't the whole hospital your department?" I was beginning to lose my calm. "You want to run the entire show. You're not content unless you have everyone bowing and scraping to you. In fact, you treat this place as though it were your own private property. Well, it isn't. I have my rights, as well as you. I happen to be doing some important scientific work at present. That's why I took the test-room."

"Then you'll kindly give it back."

"Are you suggesting that I stop my work?"

"It's a matter of indifference to me what you do, so long as you carry out your job. But I want my test-room back, clean and tidy again."

"Why? The room's never used."

She gave a short laugh.

"That's where you're wrong. It's used at this time every year. For my nurses' lectures. Didn't you notice the desks? The session begins on Saturday."

"You can use some other room," I protested, feeling as though my feet had been swept from under me.

She shook her head deliberately.

"There are no other rooms with proper accommodation. Only the isolation ward. And that's much too damp and miserable. Apart from the nurses, I wouldn't wish you to be uncomfortable, Doctor. You see," with acrid humour she launched her final shaft, "*you* are the one who gives the lectures."

Outmanœuvred—in fact, completely cornered—I could only glare at her in helpless silence. The flicker of derisive amusement in her eyes, as she moved to the door, showed her satisfaction at having evened the score between us and put me in my place.

I went to bed threshing out this new difficulty in my mind. Seasoned by a life of brawls and bluster, toughened by interminable rows with servants, tradesmen, nurses and sisters, waddling forward, victoriously, with a gory trail of doctors in her wake, she was a hard nut to crack. Much as it galled me, there was nothing for it, at present, but a strategic retreat.

At lunch next day, after a period of silence, I told her formally that I would clear out of the test-room.

In reward for my capitulation she gave me a grim smile.

"I thought you'd see reason, Doctor. May I have the chutney, please? Now, I recollect when I was in Bogra . . ."

I felt like breaking the bottle on her head. Instead, I passed it to her with a smile of equal grimness.

An hour later, at half-past two, I walked down casually to the old smallpox isolation pavilion, then quickly dodged into the protection of the shrubbery which concealed it. Miss Trudgeon was busy in the linen-room; nevertheless, I wanted to be careful.

The isolation pavilion was a ruin—no other word is possible—I effected an entry only by breaking in a decayed corrugated iron panel. Darkly shuttered, chilly as a sepulchre, and empty of everything but dust and cobwebs, it obviously hadn't been opened for years. Striking matches, which burned my fingers, I surveyed the abandoned ruin. There was a hole in the boards where the stove had been ripped out. A chipped enamel basin, yellow and corroded, lay on the floor. Even the water was cut off, and the tap had almost rusted away.

Disconsolately, I came out, found Pim at the garage, and explained my situation to him.

"I'm going to move into the old smallpox pavilion."

He laughed incredulously.

"That place! It's no use for anything."

"We could recondition it."

"Never."

He continued to insist that it was impossible; but, when I pressed ten shillings into his palm, he finally consented, although with a bad grace, to my plan.

That same evening, when it was dusk, we moved all my gear from the test-room to the derelict pavilion. Then Pim, grumbling all the time, began to restore the place to a primitive sort of order, fitting a new faucet for me, connecting up the cut-off electric wires, restoring the worst of the rotted woodwork. Dirty and tired, we stopped at ten o'clock, when he had to fetch some of the sisters from the station.

It took two more nights to complete the job, and the result was poor enough. Still, it was my own place, draughty and unheated, but with a stout bench, water, electricity, four walls, and a roof. Sister Cameron, who was in charge of the scarlatina ward, had made for me, from old bed-jackets, three curtains of red flannel which, rigged up behind the shutters, permitted not a blink of light to escape. A new lock, fitted to the door, gave to me the sole right of entry and of egress. And by running an invisible wire from the bell-push on the door of my living quarters, Pim had arranged an indicator which would give me warning when I was wanted. I had, in short, a secret laboratory, a fort, an arsenal of research, from which no one could dislodge me. Every evening, after my final round of the wards, I made a detour to the shrubbery and, in the falling darkness, I slipped into the thick laurel bushes and gained the sanctuary of the pavilion. I was hard at work by nine o'clock.

Keeping myself going with black coffee, which I brewed myself, I worked usually until one in the morning; and sometimes, in the absorption of my quest, I kept on until dawn and did not go to bed at all, relying on a cold shower and hard rub-down to freshen me for breakfast, and the duties of the coming day.

I progressed rapidly, but this constant application was taking toll of my nerves, and in the afternoons I began to make use of Luke's motor-cycle. Nothing was more sooth-ing than a swift rush along the empty country roads, this whizzing anæsthesia of speed. And the bike, as though imbued with a homing instinct, brought me always to the vicinity of Blairhill, bearing me, with a roar and a crackle, past the gate of the villa Siloam.

One afternoon, instead of flashing past, I slowed down, ran the machine up the little back lane, and stopped behind the garden wall. It was not a high stone wall, and I scaled it easily. And there, in the latticed summer-house, almost at my feet, was the daughter of the baker of Blairhill.

Still unconscious of my presence, she was seated at a rustic table, bareheaded and wearing a short jacket, with her chin in her cupped hand, a medical textbook and a paper bag of plums before her. She was studying, of course. Yet so pensive was her air, so absent her manner, so remote her gaze, and so frequently did her fingers dip into the paper bag, I began to fear that her application to Osler's *Practice of Medicine* was not all that it might be. She had indeed, since my arrival, without once turning a page, consumed, in a melancholy fashion, three ripe plums; and now, sadly selecting her fourth, had, with a faint sigh, plunged her white teeth into its succulent flesh, so that little drops of ruddy juice ran down her chin when, glancing up suddenly, she caught sight of me upon the wall. She started, and almost swallowed the plum-stone.

"It's all right," I said. "I haven't come to steal anything."

She still choked on the stone.

"Oh, Mr. Shannon . . . I'm so glad to see you . . . I was just thinking . . . about our awful misunderstanding . . . and wondering how on earth I could put it right."

"I thought you were working."

"Yes, I was," she admitted, but with a faint blush. "In a sort of a way. My exam's in four weeks' time." She sighed. "I don't seem to be getting on."

"Perhaps you need some fresh air," I suggested. "I have Luke's bike here. Will you come for a spin?"

Her eyes sparkled.

"I should love it."

She got to her feet and, reaching down, I helped her, quite unnecessarily, for she was light and agile, to the top of the wall. We dropped down on the other side. The next minute she was seated on the pillion, I had kicked at the starter, and we were off.

It was a brilliant August day and, as we escaped from the winding streets of Blairhill, encouraged by the sunshine and the delightful rapidity of our motion, guided, also, by some strange, nostalgic compulsion, I set our course for the village of Markinch upon the southern shore of Loch Lomond. The countryside was superb, the Darroch foothills agleam with wheatfields in full ear and starred with patches of scarlet poppies. On the fertile slopes of Gowrie the orchards of pear, apple, and plum lay heavy with ripe fruit, and the pickers, filling, with seeming indolence, the pannier baskets strapped about their waists, waved to us as we sped past. Defying the rush of air, I shouted over my shoulder to my companion.

"Fine, isn't it?" We survived a series of exhilarating bounces and dodged, by inches, a stationary farm-cart. "You hang on well. I suppose you often go out with Luke?"

With her lips close to my ear she shouted back:

"Oh, yes, quite often." But in her tone there was that which disparaged all previous excursions, which put Luke severely in his place as a mere brother, which exalted this present moment to an incomparable plane. More and more I became conscious of the circlet of her arms about my waist, the light contact of her form behind me, the pressure of her cheek against my ribs, as she burrowed for protection against the wind.

About five o'clock we swept over the crest of Markinch Brae; and there, before us, was the Loch, cool and unruffled, bearing the deep blue of the unclouded sky, with richly wooded slopes rising from its edges to the sharp, ridged mountains of a paler blue, beyond. Breaking the surface of the still expanse, a chain of small green islands lay mirrored, like a jade necklace, and, upon the nearer shore, there was clustered a little clachan of white-washed cottages, embowered in honeysuckle and wild dog-roses.

This was Markinch, the most favoured of all my boy-hood haunts, whither I had so often come, alone, or with my friend Gavin Blair, to find solace for my wounded soul. And now, as we descended the steep, winding hill, I experienced again, and more intensely, that inner glow always awakened in my breast by this sleepy, forgotten little spot, steeped in summer quiet, drenched in the scent of honeysuckle, with no sounds but the drone of bees, the splash of a fish in the shallows, and no sign of life but a single collie dog, a drowsy sentinel, stretched in the white dust by the little pier at which the toy red-funnelled steamer of the Loch called once a week.

At the end of the short village street I drew up and we detached ourselves stiffly and somewhat self-consciously from the machine, which, although fuming and smelling of hot oil, had nobly withstood the heat and burden of the day.

"Well . . ." I said, finding it strangely difficult to meet her eye after the close communion of our journey. "That was a glorious run. I expect it's given you an appetite for tea."

She glanced around appreciatively, but, having failed to discover even a single village store, she turned to me smiling, and with an air of intimate comradeship.

"It's beautiful. But we'll never get anything to eat."

"I can't let you starve." I led the way to the last little white cottage of the row, where, above the porch, almost concealed by climbing scarlet fuchsias, there was a weathered sign bearing the cryptic word: *Minerals*—which in that Northern district is to be interpreted as meaning "soft drinks."

I knocked at the door, and presently there appeared a small bent woman in a dark tartan dress.

"Good afternoon. Can you give us some tea?"

She gazed up at us with a discouraging shake of her head.

"Na, na. I dinna sell aught but the aerated watters . . . Reid's Lemonade and Barr's Iron Brew."

My companion shot me a justified glance, but I continued:

"You surprise me, Janet. Many a time you've given me a lovely tea. Don't you remember when we used to come fishing . . . Gavin and I . . . and the salmon we caught for you . . .? I'm Robert Shannon."

At my use of her Christian name she had started and now, peering closely at me like a little old witch, she uttered an exclamation of affectionate recognition, that cry which springs instinctively from the Highland heart, so slow always to recognize strangers but warm, ever warm to a friend.

"Guid sakes alive. If I'd had my specs I would have kenned you. It's you, yourself, Robert."

"Indeed it is, Janet. And this is Miss Law. And if you turn us from your door we'll just fade away and never come back."

"I'll no do that, though," cried Janet vigorously. "Na, na. Heaven forbid. Ye'll have the finest tea in Markinch inside ten minutes."

"Can we have it in the garden, Janet?"

"Ye can that! Well, well! It beats a'. Robert Shannon, grown up now, and a doctor . . . Ay, ay, ye canna deny it. I read a' about ye in the *Lennox Herald* . . ."

With these, and many other ejaculations, Janet ushered us through to her back garden, then scurried off to the dark little kitchen where through the fixed window we caught glimpses of her bent figure bustling about with a big iron griddle.

As a result of her willing labours we were soon seated, under the wooden trellis, before that plain but delicious fare I had savoured, here, in the past—new baked scones and home-churned butter, boiled fresh eggs, heather honey in the comb, and strong black tea. Jean said grace gravely, with closed eyes, then, naturally, and with good appetite, she began the wholesome country meal.

At first, old Janet hung about, eager for all my news, and glancing at us with native shrewdness, embarrassing us considerably by her questions. After a while, however, when she had replenished the tea-pot, she left us. And, with a sigh of contentment, Miss Jean turned towards me.

"This is so lovely," she exclaimed, happily, guilelessly. "And to think that we nearly missed it all. If I hadn't asked you to be friends, that day in Grant's . . . You've no idea what a lot of nerve it took . . . I was shaking all over."

"Do you regret it?"

"No." She blushed faintly. "Do you?"

I shook my head silently, still looking at her, causing her gaze to fall, a gesture of timidity, which, as on that occasion when I had passed her, sad and solitary, outside Hillier's on Fenner Hill, sent over me a throbbing wave of tenderness. How pretty she was, in this country setting, wind-swept and glowing, virginal and sweet. A gipsy, perhaps. Her clustered hair was brown, held by a brown ribbon, brown also were her eyes, and her face, which had tiny freckles of a deeper brown dusted upon it.

Playing nervously with her teaspoon, she remarked, as though attempting to return the conversation to an ordinary level:

"Can you smell the honeysuckle? I'm sure it's somewhere in the garden."

I did not answer, though the scent of the flower, or of something sweeter, was mounting in my blood. Beset by an emotion that was strange and new, I tried to direct my thoughts into the plane of reason, to my research experiments, towards the innumerable dissections which I had coldly performed in the Department mortuary. How, in the light of these, could I ever find beauty in the human form? But, alas! I could. I thought then, in desperation, of those amœbæ, lowest form of all cellular life, which, when placed together beneath the microscope upon a slide, are instinctively attracted. Had I not a mind, an understanding, and a will to save me from that blind reaction? I heard myself saying, independent of my own volition:

"Shall we take a stroll? It's not late yet. We'll not go far."

She hesitated. Yet she also was reluctant to break the spell that lay upon us.

116

"Do come," I urged. "It's still early."

"For a little way then," she consented, in a low voice.

I left a generous present upon the table, and we took our leave of Janet. Then we set out slowly over the narrow pathway to the winding shore of the Loch. Twilight was beginning to fall, a crescent moon swung high in the eastern sky and was bosomed in the mysterious depths of the dark water beneath. The air was soft, gentle as a caress. Away in the distance a grey heron cried and was answered remotely by its mate. Then the low lapping of the lake became part of the stillness of the night.

In silence we followed the muted water's edge until, reaching a little sandy cove, sheltered by banks of meadowsweet and mint, we stopped, suddenly, and turned towards each other. An instant of expectation. Her lips were warm and dry, parted as though in sacrifice, offering themselves in the pure and perfect knowledge that never before had they been kissed by any man.

Not a word was spoken. I held my breath, my heart was beating in my breast, as though fearful of a kind of death. But no, the enchantment was prolonged, there was nothing but that sweet, that single kiss. Her innocence had conquered.

As we walked back slowly, a pure white mist crept over the water like breath upon a mirror. Veils of vapour loomed over the land, filling the valleys with a rimed and ghostly air. And although for me the moon shone with a brighter radiance, strangely, my dear companion shivered.

CHAPTER VI

ON THE AFTERNOON of September 29, in my laboratory day-book, which I used as a diary and a record of my work, I made this elated entry:

"This morning at 2 a.m. I finally identified Bacillus C.

"It is none other than *Brucella melitensis*, an obscure cocco-bacillus which David Bruce isolated in 1886 during an outbreak of fever in Malta caused by the milk of infected goats.

"This bacillus, confined, apparently, to the Mediterranean littoral, and, according to the text-books, transmitted only by goats, had always been regarded as of mere historical interest or at least of minor importance in the field of general medicine. This belief is wholly incorrect.

"On the contrary, *Brucella melitensis* is the causal organism of the recent severe epidemic here, and almost certainly, of other clinically similar epidemics currently reported in Europe and the United States. From careful checking of the data at my command, I am convinced that, in the present instance, transmission by goats' milk may be ruled out as an impossibility. I suspect, in fact, as the infective agent, the milk of cows. Should this be so, the importance of this discovery cannot be overestimated."

I threw down the pen and, with a glance at the clock, snatched up my cap and hurried from the hospital to Dalnair Station to catch my train. I was meeting Jean in Winton at three o'clock and, glowing with excitement, I could scarcely wait to give her my wonderful news.

118

All that lingering summer, which, by the dreamlike beauty of its days, conspired to defeat the force of reason, we had drawn more closely to each other. I, perhaps, was a willing victim, but my companion, by her temperament and denomination, by every intimate beat of her family life, was better able to appreciate the barrier to our attachment which, on that evening at Markinch, had been blindingly revealed to her. Bound by the web of parental ties, enclosed by the inexorable limits of her creed, no nightmare was more fearful to her than the grim phantom of my religion. More than once she had, with tears, protested that our relationship was impossible. But when, after a sad goodbye, I returned to Dalnair, the telephone in my room would ring and her voice would tremble across the wire.

"Oh, no, Robert, no . . . we can't give each other up."

Rent by the wonder of this new emotion, swept away as by a cataract, we were hopelessly in love.

In Winton, half an hour later, an autumn rain was falling as I left the train and hastened to the quiet café which we had discovered near the Central Station. She was already there, a lonely figure, at the far end of the almost deserted lounge.

"Jean," I exclaimed, going forward and taking both her hands, "I've got it at last."

Seating myself beside her on the wall settee, I poured out the account of my success.

"Don't you see the tremendous significance of it? Not just goats' milk . . . on the island of Malta. But cows' milk, everywhere. Cows' milk, cheese, butter, all dairy produce . . . the most generally used foods in the world . . . that's how this germ is transmitted. And there's more. I telephoned Alex Duthie this morning. He told me they had a lot of trouble with their dairy herd just before the epidemic. Several of the animals died. That's no coincidence

. . . must be some relationship. In fact, he said there's been severe outbreaks among cattle herds all over the country . . . 35 per cent. affected. If they get another sick animal at Dreem, Alex's going to let me have milk samples. Don't you see the possibility, Jean . . . heavens, if there should be a connection between the two . . ."

I broke off, in a ferment of feeling, while she gazed at me with quiet sympathy.

"I'm so glad, Robert." She hesitated, and her smile became subdued. "I wouldn't mind if they gave me that question at my exam to-morrow."

There was a pause, during which my effervescence slowly ebbed. I had actually forgotten that it was the eve of that important event, her degree examination, and her anxiety for the ordeal which would begin upon the following morning and endure for five days was now so apparent it awakened in me a sudden stab of contrition. I had pushed ahead with my research, every night, pressing on, full of inexhaustible energy, avoiding pitfalls by a kind of magic. But what of her? When she spoke palely of hours filled with anxiety for the future I had remonstrated that she also had her work, and I had, it is true, from time to time, at Dalnair, taken her over certain subjects which I thought likely to crop up in her papers. Yet could I not have coached her more thoroughly, more patiently, instead of proving a perpetual distraction?

"You'll be all right," I said encouragingly. "You've studied pretty hard."

"I suppose so," she answered, wanly. "I don't seem to have much confidence. Professor Kennerly's the examiner . . . and he's very strict."

Again my heart and conscience smote me. Was this the same bright and bustling neophyte who, fervent for her mission, with enthusiasm to heal, had come to my room to probe the exciting mysteries of trypanosomes?

"Jean," I said in a low voice, "I've been a selfish brute."

She shook her head listlessly, with drooping lip.

"I'm as much to blame as you."

In silence I bent forward and pressed her fingers tight. She whispered:

"At least we have each other."

When we left the café I was still accusing myself and, on our way to the station, in an effort to cheer her, also, perhaps, to appease my sense of guilt, I stopped at a little antique shop at the corner of Woolmarket. In my journeyings through this back street I had observed in the window a green necklace, extremely simple, for the beads were only of glass, but pretty, in good taste, and genuinely old. Before my companion knew what I was about I asked her to wait, went in and purchased it. A moment later, as we entered the station and stood at our usual place of leave-taking, under the bookstall clock, I gave the beads to her.

"That's for good luck," I said. "Green is my lucky colour."

She flushed with surprise and her face, losing its despondency, slowly lit up with pleasure. I had never given her anything before.

"They're beautiful," she said.

"No, no. They're nothing. But let me put them on."

I took the beads and fastened them around her neck, then, carried away by this new tenderness, careless of the passing crowds, the public place, I held her in my arms and kissed her.

She had to leave immediately for her train. As I turned away, I suddenly caught sight of a tall and ladylike figure, standing as though petrified, her eyes fixed upon me in a shocked and unbelieving stare. With a sinking of my heart, I recognized her, knew instantly that she had witnessed the gift of the necklace, the close embrace. I took a step towards her, but with the glassiest of glances, and a frigid, an imperceptible inclination of her head, she had begun already to move away. It was Miss Beth Dearie.

For the rest of that week, according to our arrangement, I made no attempt to communicate with Jean. But while I worked hard at Dalnair, I thought of her, and on the following Monday morning I rose early and hurried down to the lodge to get the *Herald* before it was sent into Miss Trudgeon's parlour. The medical passes appeared always at the top of the last page, and standing in the drive in my pyjamas and overcoat, I ran my eye hastily over the printed list. Then again, more carefully, but with a growing sense of misgiving, I scanned it.

Jean's name was not there. I could not believe it. She had failed.

Although she had warned me not to do so, swept by a deep commiseration, I felt I must telephone her at once. I went to the switchboard in the hall and, while Sister Peek scurried around with her ears alertly cocked, I called the number in Blairhill.

"Hello. I want to speak to Miss Law."

It was a woman's voice that answered, not Jean's, alas! but almost certainly her mother's.

"Who is speaking?"

I hesitated.

"A friend."

There was a pause, then the voice came back.

"I am sorry. Miss Law is not here."

"But please listen," I said. Then I broke off, for the sharp crackle against my ear-drum told me that the other party had hung up.

All that day, scarcely knowing what to do, I laboured under a dismal oppression. After supper, when seven o'clock struck, I was preparing to restore myself by my nightly session in the laboratory when Katie, the maid, who had already cleared away the dishes, tapped upon my door.

"There's a gentleman to see you, sir."

"Is it a patient?"

"Oh, no, sir."

"Relative?"

"I don't think so, sir."

I gazed at her in perplexity: I wasn't used to visitors at this hour.

"Well . . . you'd better show him in."

There must, that evening, have been a blind spot upon my intelligence. I got the shock of my life when, with a firm tread, Daniel Law came into the room.

As the door closed behind him, he bestowed upon me his grave and steady gaze.

"I hope I am not intruding at an awkward time, Doctor? If convenient, I should greatly like to have a word with you."

"Why . . . certainly," I stammered.

At this he bowed and removed his heavy black coat, which he folded methodically and placed, with his hat, upon the couch. Then, pulling a hard chair near to me, he sat down, very formal in his best dark suit, white dickey, and string tie, laid his hands upon his knees, and again transfixed me with unhesitating eyes.

"Doctor," he quietly began. "It was not an easy step for me to come to you like this. Before doing so I wrestled long in prayer." He paused. "You have been seeing much of my daughter lately?"

I turned extremely red.

"I'm afraid I have."

"Might one ask why?"

"Well . . . as a matter of fact . . . I'm very fond of her."

"Ah!" There was neither irony nor condemnation in the simple exclamation, merely a sombre, somewhat cold concern. "We are fond of her too, Doctor. Indeed, ever since she became a child of light, she has been to us as the lamb to the shepherd. You will appreciate, therefore, how great was our disappointment when we learned to-day that she had failed to obtain her medical degree. And I fear the main reason was that, instead of working, she was wasting her time in frivolous pursuits."

I was silent.

"Of course," he went on, with a visionary air, "I have every confidence in my daughter. We must bear the hand of the Lord when it presses upon us, and she will be sanctified by this affliction. My sainted wife and I have taken counsel with her and she will try again, after some months of uninterrupted study. What concerns us is a much more serious issue. I do not know how far your acquaintance has gone, Doctor—I can get no word of this from my daughter and am indebted to Miss Dearie for the little information I possess—nevertheless, I fear you must agree that, under the circumstances, it has gone far enough."

"I don't understand," I said quickly. "Why do you object to my knowing your daughter?"

He made no immediate answer. Pressing his finger tips together, he meditated intently.

"Doctor," he said suddenly and with greater firmness, "I hope my daughter will marry. One day I hope she will be a happy wife. But she will never find that happiness except with one of her own religious persuasion."

We were in deep water now, but, uncaring, I plunged forward.

"I don't agree with you," I said. "Religion is a private affair. We can't help what creed we're born into. It's quite possible for two people to be tolerant of each other's belief."

He shook his head, darkly, with a cold and strangely baffling smile which seemed, if anything, to indicate his exclusive familiarity with the ways and ordinances of an Omniscient God.

"I make allowance for your youth and inexperience. There can be only one true testimony to the Blood, one true congregation of the saints. In that true congregation of the Lord's anointed my daughter has been reared. She can never commingle with the waters of Babylon."

As he spoke, by some strange antithesis, my thoughts flew suddenly, and heavily, to the lovely waters of Markinch, beside which Jean and I had wandered, to exchange, under the soft, indulgent dome of heaven, our first sweet kiss.

"Young man." Observing my bitterness, and the signs of rebellion in my face, his tone grew harsh. "I wish you well, and hope that light will one day break upon you. But it is only just that you should understand, finally, that my daughter is not for you. There is, in our communion, a ministering brother to whom she is virtually affianced. I refer to Malcolm Hodden. You have met him under my roof. At present he is a teacher, but he aspires one day to be a minister of the Gospel and to bear the torch into the wilderness. By every affinity of mind and spirit he has shown himself worthy to lead and guide her along the pathways of this earthly life."

There was a silence. He seemed to wait for me to speak but as, sunk in my chair, I said nothing, he rose, quiet as ever, and methodically put on his coat. When the last button was in place he gazed at me between sad forbearance and frigid admonition.

"I am glad that our conversation has been salutary, Doctor. We must all learn to submit to the Lord . . . to come to a true knowledge of His will. . . . In parting, I commit you to His care."

Taking up his hat, with firm footsteps, and that air of serene and steady discipline, he passed from the room.

I did not move for a long time. Despite his rigid and narrow views, I was constrained, in honesty, to admit that he was acting according to his lights. This did not help me. The tone of his discourse, as though every word were sacred and prophetic, drawn from Revelation, had cut me to the quick. And Hodden . . . ah, that was a bitter pill to swallow.

Full of hurt and angry love, I thought of Jean. I set my jaw firmly. At least I had not promised not to see her.

CHAPTER VII

IN THIS RESTLESS and uneasy mood I made my night round of the wards. When I had given Sister Peek her instructions, I went, as usual, to the isolation pavilion, but I could not concentrate. The pursuit of pure science, to which I was dedicated, demanded complete detachment from all the entanglements of life. Yet now I cared nothing for that solemn covenant. The vision of Jean was before me, slim and fresh, her brown eyes misted with the bloom of youth. I loved her. I must see her.

On the following afternoon, the moment I was free, I hurried to the garage. Twice already I had telephoned to the villa Siloam, but on each occasion the voice of Mrs. Law had answered, and without a word, as though it were a hot iron, I had dropped the receiver back upon its hook. Now, despite the drizzle, I set off upon the motor-cycle for Blairhill.

At the rear of Siloam, with beating heart, I made my way to the summer-house. I found it empty, the chair untenanted, the rustic table bare of Osler's *Practice of Medicine*. Uncertainly, I sat on the wall watching the rain drip from the green-painted lattice-work; then, dropping down on the near side, I skirted the garden and gained the front of the house. For almost half an hour, I hung about in the bushes, straining my eyes towards the mysterious lace-curtained windows. But although I several times caught sight of her mother, moving about in the dim interior of the "front room," I was not once rewarded by a glimpse of Jean.

Suddenly I heard the sound of approaching footsteps in

the avenue. At first I thought that it was Daniel Law, but a moment later Luke's figure swung into view. I came forward.

"Luke!" I exclaimed. "I didn't know you were back."

"Yes, I'm back," he admitted.

"Why didn't you let me know? You're the very one who can help me."

"Am I?"

"Yes, Luke. Now listen." I spoke with painful urgency. "I must see Jean, at once."

"You'll not do that," he answered, hesitantly, glancing from me to the silent front of the house. Then, taking apparently a decision in my favour, he added: "We can't talk here. Come on down the street with me."

He led the way back to the town, gazing occasionally over his shoulder, then at a rather disreputable corner near the Market Square, dived into a gaudily painted saloon which bore the sign: BLAIRHILL SPORTS BAR. Seated in a booth at the back of this depressing emporium, which from its convenient array of pin-ball and fruit machines, I saw to be the resort of Blairhill's gilded youth, Luke ordered two glasses of beer. Then he gave me a long, equivocal stare.

"You've done it this time," he said at last. "If you ask me . . . it's all *up*."

I leaned forward quickly.

"What happened?"

"The worst I remember. When Mother heard from Miss Dearie, about you I mean, she took Jean aside, very quiet and sad, and had her crying all over the place. When Father came in at tea-time there was a long consultation. Then, while Mother went and fetched Malcolm, Father went up and prayed with Jean, for about an hour, in her room. Even in the kitchen, I could hear her sobbing, as if her heart would break. When they came down she had

128

stopped. She was white-looking, but quiet. You see, it was all over then."

"Luke! What do you mean?"

"I think they made her promise she would never see you again."

It took me a minute to fully grasp his meaning, but presently there fell upon me an iron conviction that he spoke the truth. Although in this age of progress one could barely credit the fact, there existed in this family an authority which went back to those days of the Old Testament, when the tribes of Gilead and Gad followed their destiny across the plains of Moab, tending their flocks and herds, submitting to the elders, trusting blindly in the Lord.

Daniel Law was such a patriarch. He still lived in and by the books of Kings, Numbers, and Deuteronomy. And amidst the roar of the machine age, the distracting blare of jazz, and the enticing flicker of the cinema, he had raised his children in that tradition, not by fear, for he was no tyrant, but by a rule of tempered firmness, above all by the inflexible display of his conviction, the unwavering light of his example. The popular, slightly comic conception of the street-corner evangelist was as remote from Daniel Law as a sickly weed from a stalwart oak. He was no weak-kneed tract-passer, no whining intoner of the Psalms. He was, indeed, a veritable Paul, righteous and valiant, with a gleam in his eye which cowed the evil serpent before he crushed it beneath his heel. He had, of course, the defect of his qualities. His gaze was steady, yet he could see only straight ahead. Compromise was beyond him—a thing, to him, was either black or white. Outside the shining orbit of his own interior light, there existed only darkness, beset with temptations for the elect and, like twisted roots in a dark forest, the snares of Satan. Tolerance was a forbidden weakness, indeed, a word he did not understand. If one were not "saved" then, alas! one was eternally damned. This it was which for years had kept his daughter upon the stony path, saved her from the iniquities of dances, card playing and the theatre, reduced her reading to *Good Words* and *Pilgrim's Progress*, and now, by the exercise of prayer and pressure, had wrung from her that tearful promise to renounce her unworthy lover.

All this flashed across my mind as I sat opposite Luke in the cheap and chilly beer parlour, and although my reflections gave me the dizzy sensation of having run into a stone wall, although also I felt a smouldering resentment against Jean for having surrendered me, nevertheless, I could not, simply could not, give her up.

"Luke," I said, tensely. "You've got to help me."

"Yes?" he queried, without much conviction.

"I simply must see your sister." I made the statement with a certain desperation.

He did not answer. Wiping his lips with his floury cuff, he gazed at me with a sorrowing smile.

"You can do it, you know," I went on. "I'll wait here while you go back to the house and tell Jean to step out and meet me."

Still quiet and pitying, he shook his head.

"Jean's not at the house. She's away."

I stared at him, motionless, while slowly he nodded his head.

"It's well seen you don't know Father. She was sent off last night to our Aunt Elizabeth in Bethnal Green. She's to stay there, studying, for the next four months, until she sits her exam again." He paused. "And Mrs. Russell, that's our aunt, has instructions to open all her letters."

Bethnal Green, a suburb of London, more than three hundred miles away—destination impossible of achievement by the villain Shannon. And no letters, by request! Oh, wise, resourceful Daniel. In fact, a Daniel come to judgement. I sat there, quite still, but my eyes fell wretchedly.

There was a protracted silence from which I was roused by the voice of Luke as, in a sympathetic manner, he inquired:

"Would you like another beer?"

I lifted my bowed head.

"No, thanks, Luke." At least he meant well. "And that reminds me. You want your bike back."

"Ah, there's no hurry."

"Yes, you must." I saw he was protesting only for politeness' sake. "It's in the lane at the back of your house. I took good care of it. Here's the key."

He accepted the ignition key without further demur; then we got up and went out. In the street, after a glance up and down, he shook my hand with a kind of melancholy comradeship. I set out to walk to the station.

The rain was falling more heavily now, running in the gutters, plastering the narrow thoroughfare with mud, making everything grey and miserable.

Oh, God, I thought to myself, in a sudden access of heartache, what am I doing in this dreary and forsaken little town? I want to be in the sunshine, away from this mess, uncertainty, and endless striving. I'd like to be on a *dubbeh*, floating down the Nile, or on the bright hills of Sorrento, basking above the blue Tyrrhenian Sea. No, damn it, I'd rather be in the fog and grime of Bethnal Green.

But I knew I could not be there.

CHAPTER VIII

AFTER THAT, EVERYTHING fell on me at once . . .
but I will try, calmly, to keep the sequence. I don't intend
to harp on my state of mind. It was like the weather, which
continued with incessant rain and blustering equinoctial
gales that tore from our trees leaves and twigs not yet
dead, strewing a sodden litter upon the drive.

We were now extremely busy in the wards, mostly
with diphtheria cases—an epidemic of this disease had
developed in the western district of Wintonshire. I'd had
this infection myself, a circumstance which, I dare say,
gave me a fellow feeling for the children who came in
with it. So far, we could boast of a clean sheet, not a single
death, and Miss Trudgeon proudly paraded about the
place as though she, personally, were responsible. And
perhaps she was—her efficiency impressed me more and
more, and in my heart I had begun, unwillingly, to
admire this conscientious, capable, indomitable little war
horse, whose hidden qualities far outweighed her obvious,
and less attractive, attributes. But I took care not to tell
her so. In my present mood I was sullen and rude to
everyone.

Then, on the night of the third of November—this exact
and fatal date is inscribed indelibly upon my recollection
—I came back with bent head and flagging steps from the
pavilion to my quarters and flung myself into a chair.

I hadn't been there ten minutes before a persistent buzzing struck my ear. It was the telephone on my bedside
table, the bell sounding faintly because I had forgotten to
throw back the switch before leaving the pavilion. I went
into the bedroom and wearily picked up the receiver.

"Hello."

"Hello. Is that you, Doctor? I'm right glad to have reached you." Despite the bad connection, the relief in the voice was evident. "This is Duthie, Alex Duthie, at Dreem. Doctor . . . Robert . . . you must do something for me."

Before I could answer he went on:

"It's our Sim. He's been sick for a week with diphtheria. And he's not getting on. I want to bring him over to you at the hospital."

I did not hesitate an instant. We were already full and Alex, living across the border of the county, had no call upon our resources. Yet I couldn't dream of refusing him.

"All right. Get your doctor to sign a certificate and I'll send the ambulance over, first thing in the morning."

"No, no." His voice came back quickly. "The boy's right bad, Robert. We have a car at the door, and he's all wrapped in blankets. I want to fetch him to you now."

I wasn't sure that it was correct to make this irregular admission, on short notice. However, because of my deep regard for Alex, I had to take the risk.

"Go ahead then. I'll expect you in about an hour. See you keep him warm on the way."

"I will. And thanks, lad . . . thanks."

I replaced the receiver and went along the corridor to the matron's room. Here, however, the lights were out and I was obliged to press the night bell, which summoned Sister Peek. When she arrived I gave her curt instructions to prepare a cot in the side room of Ward B, a comfortable little annex usually reserved for private patients and now the only space remaining unoccupied. Then I sat down to wait.

It was not a long vigil. Shortly before midnight a closed hired car drove up to the front entrance, and as I pushed open the door against the wind and heavy, driving rain,

Alex appeared carrying his son, all bundled up in blankets, in his arms. I showed him into the reception-room. His face was white and drawn.

When he had deposited the boy upon the couch, where Sister Peek began to prepare him for examination, Alex wiped his forehead with the back of his hand and stood aside in silence, fixing upon me a look of haggard inquiry.

"Don't look so worried. When did Sim take ill?"

"The beginning of the week."

"And he's had his antitoxin injections?"

"Two lots. But it hasn't helped him much." Duthie spoke faster. "It's deep down in the throat. When we saw that every minute he was getting worse, I just had to bring him over. We have faith in you, Rob. Take a look at him, for pity's sake."

"All right. Don't get excited."

I turned towards the couch and immediately the reassuring expression which I had assumed for Duthie's benefit left my face. In fact, as my gaze fell upon the livid child who, with closed eyes and clutching hands, was fighting for every breath, I received a painful shock. Silently, I went on to examine him. The temperature was 103, the pulse so thin as to be almost imperceptible. I did not try to count the respirations. A tough yellow membrane covered the back of the throat and extended viciously into the larynx. The child was clearly *in extremis*, already almost moribund.

I glanced at Duthie, who, standing mutely by, was trying, with even greater anxiety, to read my face; and although moved by pity, I felt a sharp anger against him for the predicament in which he had placed me.

"You should never have brought him out. He's desperately ill."

He swallowed dryly.

"What like's the matter?"

134

"Laryngeal diphtheria. The membrane is blocking the windpipe . . . keeping him from breathing."

"Can't anything be done?"

"Tracheotomy . . . and at once. But we can't do it here. We've no theatre, no facilities. He should have been moved to one of the big city fever hospitals long ago." I moved across to the telephone. "I'll ring up the Alexandra now and make arrangements to get him in at once."

I had begun to dial the emergency number when suddenly the child began to crow, a thin, desperate stridor which rasped and echoed in the room.

Alex pulled at my arm.

"We'll never get him to another hospital. God knows it was bad enough coming here. You do what's necessary yourself."

"I can't. It's a job for an expert."

"Go on, do it, do it."

Arrested, I stood staring at him, in a startled and helpless manner, like a fool. As I have explained elsewhere, I had the most limited experience in the practice of medicine, and had never attempted a serious operation in my life. From the clear heights of pure science I had always affected to despise the bustling practitioner who, in a pinch, would tackle anything. Yet there was no denying the dreadful urgency of this case. It was, indeed, a question of minutes—for I now perceived that if I evaded the issue, on the pretext of transferring the case to the Alexandra, the child would never reach that hospital alive. Aware of my own hopeless inadequacy, I groaned inwardly.

"Get Matron up." I turned to Sister Peek. "And move the patient over to the side room at once."

Six minutes later we were in the side room, Miss Trudgeon, Sister Peek, and myself, gathered round the plain deal table upon which, in a clean hospital nightdress, lay the gasping form of the unconscious child. Apart from that convulsive breathing there was dead silence in the cramped little room. I had rolled up my sleeves, washed my hands hurriedly in carbolic solution, and now I was in such a mortal funk, I glanced instinctively, incredibly almost, towards the matron for support.

She was admirably calm, impersonal, efficient, and, although she had just awakened from sleep and thrown on her uniform at short order, correctly dressed. Even her starched headdress was adjusted so that not a hair seemed out of place. Despite the feud between us, I couldn't suppress a surge of admiration, and of envy too. She knew her job inside out, and her courage was superb.

"You won't want an anæsthetic?" she asked me in an undertone.

I shook my head. The state of the breathing simply wouldn't permit it. In any case the child was too far gone.

"Very good, then," said Miss Trudgeon, cheerfully. "I'll take the head and arms. You steady the legs, Sister Peek."

As she spoke she handed me a lancet from the square of white gauze in the enamel basin and, staunchly setting herself at the head of the table, took a firm grip of Sim's arms. The night sister, in a wobbly fashion, grasped the boy's ankles.

Although doubtless it was only for an instant, it seemed to me that I stood there, with the knife in my inept and nerveless hand, for a timeless eternity.

"We're all ready then, Doctor," the matron reminded me and, believe it or not, there was again a firm encouragement in her tone.

I took a deep breath, clenched my teeth, and, holding the skin tense, made an incision in the child's throat. The blood oozed thick and dark, obscuring the wound. I swabbed, again and again, and cut deeper. Sim was unconscious, and felt nothing, I am sure; yet at every touch he writhed and squirmed on the table in a kind of feeble agony. At the same time there came, intermittently, that frightful heave for breath, which convulsed all his body, as though he were a fish, gasping upon a slab. These sudden uncontrollable movements increased my difficulties. I tried to get a retractor into the opening. It went in, but immediately fell out and went clattering to the floor. Then the blood welled thicker, not a bright, spurting stream which I could have controlled, but a slow treacly flow which choked up everything. I couldn't use the lancet any more. I was too near the great vessels of the neck. One false snick and I would sever the jugular vein. I tried with my forefinger to part the tissues, muddling about in the mess, seeking desperately for the trachea. If I didn't find it quickly it was all up with Sim. He was almost black in the face now. His efforts to get air, which sucked in all his ribs, and breastbone, till his small white chest was hollow, had a more frantic quality, but were less frequent and more feeble. There were long intervals when he didn't breathe at all. Already his body had a cold and clammy feel.

The perspiration burst in great beads upon my forehead. I felt so sick I thought I was going to faint. I couldn't find the windpipe, I simply couldn't, and the child was almost gone. Oh, God . . . for Christ's sake . . . help me find that trachea.

"No pulse, now, Doctor." It was a soft, reproachful bleat from Sister Peek who, from time to time, had laid her fingers on the boy's wrist. But still, at the head of the table, the matron never said a word.

I don't know what came over me—with the courage of despair I took the lancet and cut deep. Suddenly, as by a kind of magic, there sprang up in the wound, thin, white, and shining, like a silver reed, the object of my blundering, frantic search. My own breast gave a great convulsive heave and, dashing the perspiration from my eyes, I slit the exposed trachea. Instantly, there was a whistling inrush of free air, a blessed draught which filled those choked and suffocating lungs. Once, twice, the starved chest heaved deeply, to its full extent. Again and again, in a kind of ecstasy of relief. Then, slowly, at first, but with increasing force, the moribund child began regularly to breathe. The dusky tinge faded from his skin, the bluish lips slowly turned to red, he ceased to struggle.

Quickly, with trembling fingers, I slipped in the double tracheotomy tube, sutured a few small bleeding points, stitched up the wound and bandaged it so that the narrow metal orifice of the tube protruded. My knees were knocking under me, my heart bumping against my ribs, and the worst of my agitation was that I had to hide it. I stood limply by, damp and dishevelled, with bloodied fingers, while Matron expertly tucked Sim into the side-room cot, with hot bottles round him and his head well-pillowed.

"There now," Miss Trudgeon remarked at last. "He ought to do very nicely. You'll take over this case, Sister, and special on it all night."

As she swung round to go out, she gave me a quick half-glance, neither of approval nor disapproval, as though to say: It was touch and go, but you came out of it better than you deserved. For the first time we understood each other.

Even when Matron had gone I could scarcely bring myself to leave. Sister Peek had drawn up a chair to the cot, with a tray of swabs handy to clear the mucus which occasionally bubbled in the mouth of the tube, and behind her I remained watching the boy, now resting, a good colour in his cheeks. From sheer exhaustion he had begun to drowse, but suddenly, briefly, his eyes opened and, by a strange chance, encountered mine. For an instant he smiled, at least a shadowy suspicion of a smile faintly moved his lips. Then his lids drooped and he was asleep.

Nothing could have so deeply moved me as that tremulous and childish smile. I could have wished no greater reward.

"I'm going now, Sister," I said in a matter-of-fact tone. "You know what to do?"

"Oh, yes, Doctor."

Only as I went out did I remember Alex Duthie, still waiting in the reception-room, and at the prospect of ending his suspense I increased my pace, under the bright and singing stars. Yes, he was there, seated stiffly in a hard chair, facing the door, holding his cold and empty pipe, as though he had not stirred since we had left him. When I entered, his attitude became more rigid, then he rose, confronting me in silence, his eyes burning with the question he could not bring himself to utter.

"He's all right now."

So set was his expression, he could not immediately relax it. I could see the sinews of his jaw muscles drawn taulty under the skin. Then, all at once, his mouth began to twitch. He said, at last, in a low voice:

"You did it?"

I nodded.

"Now he can breathe. In fact, he's asleep. When he's got over his diphtheria, in ten days or so, we'll take out the tube and the wound will heal up. There'll hardly even be a scar."

Duthie took a step forward and seized my hand, wrung it so gratefully, with such fervour and feeling, he made me flinch.

"I'll never forget what ye've done for us this night. Never, never. I told you we had faith in ye, the wife and me." Mercifully, he relinquished my crushed fingers. "Can I ring her up? She's waiting at the farm manager's house."

A moment later he was in the hall, relating the good

news, inarticulately. When he had finished I rejoined him, went out with him to the hired landaulet, beside which the forgotten driver, his cap pulled over his ears, patiently paced up and down.

"All's well, Joe!" cried Duthie in an uplifted tone. "The young-un's ower the worst."

In his gratitude the good fellow leaned through the window, his voice tense with feeling.

"I'll be over to-morrow, lad, and bring the missus. And again . . . from the bottom of my heart . . . *I thank ye.*"

When the car had gone I lingered in the cool, windy darkness. Then, as I heard the clock in the vestibule strike one, I made my way rather dizzily to my bedroom. I was so confused I didn't want to think about anything. I only knew that amidst my disappointments and perplexities there was a queer peace in my heart. I fell asleep almost at once, thinking, of all things, of Sim's smile.

CHAPTER IX

I MUST HAVE SLEPT for about four hours when I was again aroused, and forcibly, by someone tugging at my arm. I opened my eyes to find the light full on and Sister Peek at my bedside, with a stricken face, exclaiming hysterically in my ear:

"Come at once . . . at once."

She almost pulled me from the sheets and, as I struggled into my coat and slippers, I realized, though half awake, that only a catastrophe could have caused this shrinking creature to burst into my room in such a fashion and at such an hour. Indeed, she seemed almost at her wits' end, and as I set out beside her, half running, towards Ward B, she kept on repeating, like a lesson she had learned, while she scurried along:

"I didn't do it. I didn't do it."

In the dim, warm side room Sim was lying back upon his pillows, propped up as I had left him, very peaceful and quiet. Yet he seemed unnaturally still, and as I knocked the shade off the night-light and peered closer I saw, with a start, that the shining orifice was missing from his bandages, the tube was no longer in his throat. Hastily, I snatched up a pair of forceps and cleared the plug of mucus from the wound, then, taking hold of his slack arms, I began to apply artificial respiration.

I worked on Sim, like one demented, for over an hour. But even before I arrived, he had been dead, quite dead. I stopped, buttoned up the crumpled nightdress, composed that inconsiderable frame which had struggled so hard and endured so much, laid back the head upon the pillow.

Suddenly, as I straightened out the bed, I uncovered, in a fold of the wrinkled sheets, the tracheotomy tube, all choked and foul with membrane. I stared at it stupidly, then I turned towards Sister Peek, who all this time had remained pressed against the door.

"It's blocked," I said in a tone of wonder. "He must have coughed it out."

Then I saw everything, and even before I could accuse her, the expression upon her face told me that my suspicion was correct. Another thought struck me. I walked slowly past her into the ward kitchen. Yes, on the table— that same deal table on which had been fought out the battle for Sim's life—there stood a tea-pot, a plate of sardine sandwiches, and a cold, half-finished cup of tea. Tempting little repast.

"Oh, Doctor." She had followed me, wringing her hands. "I never thought . . . he was sleeping so comfortable . . . I only left him for a minute."

I couldn't bear it. I thought my heart would burst. I went out of the kitchen, through the ward and into the open. Outside the few stars were fading and the first faint fingers of dawn had erased the darkness from the eastern sky. Beating my forehead with my clenched fists, I reached my sitting-room, where I fell into a chair by the table. It was not that my own slight achievement had been torn from me. What burned and rankled in my breast, and poisoned all my being, was the senseless turning of victory to defeat, the selfish, criminal waste of life. Sunk in a blind stupor, I surrendered to despair.

I must have sat without moving for a long time, for I was still there, in my overcoat and my pyjamas, when Katie appeared at nine o'clock to lay the breakfast table. Unable to bear her solicitous glances, I went through my bedroom to the bathroom, shaved automatically, and dressed. When I came back an extra good breakfast was awaiting me, toast, coffee, bacon and eggs under the metal cover. But although I needed food I could eat nothing, my stomach revolted even at a few sips of coffee. I went to the window and looked out. It was a cold and foggy morning, forerunner of the overcast damp of winter.

A knock on the door. As I turned, slowly Miss Trudgeon came into the room, composed, as usual, but showing in her eyes some signs of strain. Her manner was friendly. She crossed over to the fireplace where a few green sticks were spluttering and throwing out eddies of damp smoke.

"Sister Peek has been to see me." Her voice, when she did speak, was serious and restrained. "She is very much upset."

"I'm not surprised," I said bitterly.

"I know how you must feel, Doctor. Especially after all your efforts. The whole thing is highly regrettable." She paused. "For my own part, I regret it exceedingly, for no one could take the interests of this hospital more to heart than I. But these accidents do occur, Doctor, even in the best-regulated institutions. And, in a long experience, I have found that there is only one thing to do about them."

"And what's that?" I couldn't help asking.

"Overlook them."

I caught my breath sharply.

"You can't overlook this. It wasn't an accident. It was a case of gross negligence, which must be punished."

"Suppose we do as you suggest. What happens? Sister Peek is dismissed, there is a deal of talk and scandal, the hospital gets a bad name, and nobody is a bit the better for it."

"She'll have to go," I answered doggedly. "She's a bad nurse and she cost that child his life."

Miss Trudgeon made a soothing gesture.

"I understand your point of view, Doctor. And I sympathize with it. But . . . in this hospital . . . there are other

143

considerations of a practical nature to be borne in mind."

"She can't be allowed to stay here to do the same thing over again."

"She won't," Matron said quickly. "This will be a lesson she'll never forget. I'll guarantee that. I can assure you, Doctor, that Sister Peek has many good points, and it would be altogether unwise, I won't say unjust, to ruin her career, for that's what it would amount to, because of this single incident."

I gazed at her heavily, recollecting how she went out of her way to make a favourite of the night sister. I wondered if a vague sense of privilege did not attach to Effie Peek. I was about to speak when there came a subdued knock upon the door and Katie again presented herself upon the threshold.

"Mr. and Mrs. Duthie waiting to see you, in the reception-room, sir."

I felt myself turn cold, indeed an involuntary shiver passed through all my limbs. My reply to the matron was frozen upon my lips. I looked dully at the floor for a moment; then, by an effort, forced myself to move towards the door.

As I went out Miss Trudgeon came close to me and urged, in a voice of unmistakable sincerity:

"Be careful, Doctor. In your own interests . . . and mine."

My vision was so blurred and uncertain, the corridor seemed full of fog; but as I stumbled into the reception-room I could see clearly enough that Duthie and his wife were smiling as though unable to contain a deep and inti-mate happiness. In fact, when I entered Alex got up, with a beaming face, and gripped me by the hand.

"I hope we're not too early for you, lad. But there's no holding the missus and me this morning. We felt like singing on the way down here."

"That's right, Doctor." Alice Duthie had risen and was standing beside her husband, her simple careworn face quite radiant. "And we owe it all to your skill and cleverness."

I steadied myself against the table. My legs were failing me, my head seemed stuffed with cotton wool and, worst of all, I felt every second that I was going to break down and cry.

"Eh, lad!" Alex exclaimed. "Ye're quite done up. And no wonder either, after losing your sleep on our behalf. We'll not be bothering you a minute longer. We'll just gang over and take a look at Sim."

"Stop . . ." In a weak and broken manner I brought out the word.

They looked at me, at first amazed, then with concern, finally in sharp anxiety.

"What's like the matter?" Alex said in an altered voice. Then, after a pause, as though it were dragged from him: "Is our boy bad again?"

I nodded my head, blindly.

"Much worse? Good God, man, don't stand like that. Tell us how he is."

I couldn't look at Alice; the sight of Alex's face, emptied of its light, turned grey and pitiful, was as much as I could bear.

"God in Heaven," he said in a low extinguished tone. "It's not *that*."

There was a long silence, how long I don't know. Time ceased to have any meaning, everything was blurred and blank. But I could see that Alice was weeping and that Duthie had his arm round her. When at last he did speak, his voice was cold and hard.

"Can we go over and see him?"

"Yes," I muttered. "Shall I come with you?"

"If you don't mind, we'll go alone."

On his way to the door he turned to me as to a stranger.

"This would have come easier if last night ye hadna let me think ye'd saved our boy. I never want to set eyes on ye again."

I went back to my room, where I wandered about, without purpose, picking up things and laying them down again.

And then, as I gazed through the window, I saw Alex and Mrs. Duthie come round the corner of the building and proceed slowly down the drive. His figure looked bowed and crushed, his arm was still about his wife's shoulders, holding her closely and supporting her as she moved forward, blind and helpless with weeping.

Then everything boiled over inside me. I swung round and went down the corridor to the sisters' sitting-room. As I had guessed, Sister Peek was there alone. She was seated in a comfortable chair before a good fire, her eyes red, but her expression vaguely relieved, as though, having had "a good cry," she now felt that the worst was over. She had just finished her lunch, that early meal which she took before retiring, and on her plate I made out two chop-bones, picked clean.

A spasm of rage, of wild and senseless fury, choked me.

"You cheap, useless, callous slut! How dare you sit there, swilling and guzzling and warming yourself, after what you've done? Don't you understand that your selfish carelessness cost that poor kid his life? It's your fault, your cursed rotten fault that he's lying there, dead, at this minute."

The look on my face must have frightened her. She slid from the chair and retreated to the corner of the room. I followed her, caught her by the shoulders, and shook her till her teeth rattled.

"Call yourself a nurse. Hell and damnation, it's enough to make a cat laugh. If you stay on here, I'll see you get it

146

in the neck. You ought to be hanged for what you've done. Think that over the next time you want to slink away from your patient for a cup of tea."

She did not attempt to answer. As she cringed there, limp and shaken, her green eyes glinted up at me.

I turned and went out. Although I didn't regret it, I was painfully aware that my outburst had been mistaken and stupid. But I didn't realize how stupid until later.

CHAPTER X

THREE WEEKS LATER, while we sat drinking our coffee after lunch, Miss Trudgeon, with a companionable air, produced a letter. That night of the tracheotomy had marked the end of our strife. She no longer put my back up, I was prepared to swear by her honesty and dependability. Indeed, I had almost begun to feel that she was, reluctantly, taking a liking to me.

"We'll be having our annual visit from the management committee this afternoon."

I studied the typewritten notice which she handed me.

"I'd better put on a clean collar in honour of the event."

"It might be advisable." Her small eyes twinkled. "There are only three members . . . Masters, Hone, and Gloag. But they're quite particular. They're earlier than usual this year."

"What's the procedure?"

"We feed them—that's half the battle—then take them round." She glanced at me wryly. "You don't have to worry. I'm the one who gets rapped on the knuckles."

I did not give much heed to the impending visitation. I was still oppressed and suffering from reaction, and only recently had begun to pick up the thread of my research. No word at all had come from Jean, and two letters which I wrote her had been sent back, redirected in a strange hand. Vaguely, throughout the afternoon, I was conscious of an air of preparation, of sweepings and scurryings in the corridors, of a final polish being laid upon floors and walls already spotless. Also, in my room, a tantalus of spirits arrived upon the sideboard, while extra leaves were put in the table, which was then ornamented with a centre-piece of flowers and set for a massive repast.

At half-past four, a closed car drove up to the front door and, after a few minutes of conversation and laughter in the hall, Matron appeared, all smiles, in her best uniform, bringing into the room the members of the committee.

"Dr. Shannon . . . this is Mr. Ben Masters . . . Mr. Hone . . . and Mr. Gloag."

She introduced me with a genial sparkle in her eye, almost coyly, as though we had never been anything but the best of friends and had always lived together in perfect harmony, then immediately proceeded to pour out for the newcomers large tumblers of whisky which, with an air of dignity and responsibility, they accepted as their due.

The leader of the party, Mr. Masters, was a tall, spare, rough-looking man of about fifty, with hard, weather-beaten features, deepset eyes, and the loud, harsh voice of one accustomed to shouting orders in the open air. He looked to me like a gang foreman and was, I afterwards discovered, a jobbing builder and contractor in the nearby town of Prenton. As he drank his whisky, listening without comment to the matron's stream of small talk, I felt him gazing at me speculatively over the rim of his glass.

Meanwhile, I had been buttonholed by the second member of the committee, Mr. Hone, a plump, natty figure with a waxed moustache, a tight blue suit, and spats. He seemed fussy and loquacious, yet his manner, though commercial, was agreeable.

"You know, Doctor," he confided in me, "nothing fits a man better than to serve his fellow creatures on a hospital committee. It takes time, mind you, and time's money these days, especially when you have your own business— I'm in the drapery and upholstery line myself—but look at the good you accomplish. . . . Thank you, Matron, I don't mind if I do. The labourer is worthy of his hire. Very fair whisky this. I wonder what it costs us. . . . And the interest, Doctor, you've no idea the things I've learned about medicine. Only the other day the wife showed me a rash on our youngest—a bonny baby, though I say it as shouldn't— and when I told her not to worry—it was only from the blood, you understand—why, Albert, she says, I have to compliment you, even though you are my husband, you know all the fevers, you're as good as a doctor any day! I'll leave this card with you!" Producing a trade card from his top waistcoat pocket he pressed it confidentially into my hand. "As you observe, I do a little undertaking on the side. In case any bereaved relatives of your better-off patients should require my assistance it's nice to be prepared. We do everything very dignified, Doctor. And reasonable."

So far, Mr. Gloag, the last member of the party, a small, sharp-eyed man of middle age, had remained dumb; nevertheless, he had a way of cocking his head towards the conversation as though determined to let nothing go past him, and from time to time, as a sign of his agreement with his colleagues, he emitted a half-grudging exclamation of assent.

"Well, gentlemen," Miss Trudgeon remarked, in her most dulcet tones, "I hope you've brought good appetites. Shall we sit in?"

Our guests showed little hesitation in accepting the invitation. They had undoubtedly come prepared to do justice to this annual, free repast, and although occasionally Mr. Masters, at the head of the table, threw out a rough witticism, for most of the meal nothing was heard but the clink of knives and forks, the steady grinding of jaws.

Yet, at last, despite Miss Trudgeon's hospitable pressings,

the efforts of the committee flagged and failed. After a pause, Mr. Masters pushed back his chair and rose to his feet, dusting the crumbs from his waistcoat, with a businesslike air.

"Now, Matron, if convenient we'd like to go round with you. And the doctor."

His official manner set the general tone as they began their tour of inspection, and I soon perceived, from the matron's air of tension and slightly heightened colour, that this was rather more of a trial than she had been prepared to admit to me.

In the administrative building the visiting members systematically viewed the office, the laundry, and the kitchen, where Mr. Gloag, in particular, showed a remarkable talent for prying into cupboards, sniffing in dark corners, and lifting the lids of pots and pans, to sample the flavour of the staff's supper.

Next our party passed to the wards, where, facing their main task, the committee-men began a slow and almost royal progress. Determined to miss nothing, Gloag went everywhere, even peering under the beds in his efforts to find illicit dust. Once we lost him in the lavatory of Ward B, but he reappeared with an expression of defeat, having found everything in working order. Masters was equally thorough, interrogating the patients, inquiring of each in hoarse whispers, which could be heard all over the place, if there were any cause for complaints. Hone, meantime, made it his duty to sound out the members of the staff, especially the younger nurses, inquiring with unctuous familiarity into their health and habits. Once he paused and, pointing to a well-marked case of measles, remarked to me over his shoulder, in a stage whisper, with the air of a connoisseur:

"Beautiful rash, Doctor. Chicken pox, eh? I could tell it a mile away."

I did not contradict him. In fact, I effaced myself as much as possible. This was obviously the matron's responsibility and, while I couldn't but sympathize with her, I had no wish to draw the enemy's fire upon myself.

Perhaps I was prejudiced, and the committee was carrying out its task from the highest motives, yet I couldn't suppress the thought that these three were uninformed and ill-mannered busybodies, each in his own way a small-town politician of the type which pushes forward in public affairs to secure some personal advantage and, invested with a petty authority, takes good care to exercise it to the full.

At last it was over; we emerged from the end ward into the crisp November air and, with a sense of relief, I was preparing to see our unwelcome guests depart, when suddenly, in a tone of purpose, Masters exclaimed:

"Now we'll take a look at Pavilion E."

For an instant I was puzzled and, indeed, a general air of surprise fell upon the party; then, with a start, I observed the direction of his gaze.

"You mean the old smallpox ward?" Matron asked in a doubtful tone.

"What else?" Masters replied testily. "It's part of the hospital buildings. I want to see it like the rest." He hesitated for a moment. "I'm thinking we might reconstruct it."

"Of course"—Matron spoke without moving—"it hasn't been used for some time."

"Yes, indeed," I broke in hastily. "It's quite derelict."

"We'll be the judge of that. Let's get a move on."

I allowed myself to be swept forward with the others, at a loss as to how this had been sprung upon me. From her ill-concealed surprise and annoyance, I was perfectly convinced that Matron had no hand in it. Masters was at the door now, turning the handle, thrusting with his shoulder against the panel. As this held fast, I took a completely wrong decision.

"It's probably nailed up. We'll never get in."

There was an odd sort of silence. Then Hone remarked softly:

"Don't you want us to get in, Doctor?"

Meanwhile Masters had struck a wax vesta and, bent down, was fiddling at the keyhole. In a tone of discovery he exclaimed:

"This is a new lock . . . a brand-new lock." He straightened himself. "What's going on here? Gloag, go and tell Pim to bring a crowbar."

I saw then that I had to face it. I did not wish Pim to be involved, and Matron was looking worried, so I fumbled in my inside pocket, and brought out the key.

"I can let you in." Making the best of a bad job, I unlocked the door and switched on the light.

With their instincts of detection fully aroused, all three of them pushed forward and stared in an outraged fashion at my equipment. After their hitherto fruitless excursion it was meat and drink to them to discover this iniquity.

"God damn it!" Masters exclaimed. "What's all this?"

I smiled at them propitiatingly.

"It's very simple, gentlemen. I am doing some research work, and as this pavilion was completely unoccupied I ventured to make use of it as my laboratory."

"Who gave you permission?"

In spite of my resolution to be meek, I reddened at Masters's tone.

"Was it necessary to have permission?"

Masters's brows drew down. He glared at me.

"Don't you realize that you are responsible to the committee for everything? You had no right whatsoever to take such a liberty."

"I don't understand your point of view. Am I taking a liberty in applying myself to scientific research?"

"Certainly you are. You're the doctor of this fever hospital, not a bloody experimenter."

Hone coughed gently behind his hand.

"May we inquire whose time you utilized for this so-called research of yours? I presoom you were doing it when you should have been in the wards, caring for our patients."

"I worked in my own time, at night, when my official duties were over."

"Your official duties are never over," Masters cut in rudely. "This is a whole-time job. We pay you to be on your toes twenty-four hours of the day, not to sneak off and shut yourself up with a lot of germs. What the hell have you been doing with them?"

Forgetting the wise example of the matron—that the only way to deal with a self-important official is to flatter and cajole him—I lost my temper.

"What the hell d'you think I've been doing? Keeping them as pets?"

Genuinely shocked, Hone interposed.

"Insolence won't help you, Doctor. Most improper. It's a nasty business this, a very nasty business. Who do you think pays for the electricity you burn, and the gas to light these burners? We represent the ratepayers of the district. You can't run a private business on public time and public money."

"We'll have to report the whole thing to the main committee," Masters declared. "I'll bring it up myself."

"Uh-huh," added Gloag.

I bit my lip impotently. The grain of truth in Hone's remarks made them even more unpalatable. Although I had never dreamed that it was necessary, I saw now that it would have been wiser for me, in the first instance, to have secured permission. I could only grind my teeth in silent rage, my misery enhanced by the odd glance of commiseration which Miss Trudgeon gave me, as I shut the door of that fatal pavilion and followed the others to the main building where, after a quick nip of spirits to fortify themselves against the cold, my three oppressors bundled into their coats and scarves and prepared to take their departure.

Their leave-taking of the matron was cordial, but they barely said goodbye to me, and that with the chilliest of glances.

Glumly, I wandered back to my room. My ill-luck was colossal; still, I couldn't believe that they would come down upon me severely. It wasn't a crime I had committed, and when, in calmer mood, they considered the matter, they must surely see the honesty of my motives. Resolved to leave nothing to chance, I went there and then to my desk and wrote them a full account of all that I was attempting in my research. I felt more confident when I had posted it.

That night, when I returned from my last round, I met Sister Peek in the corridor. She hadn't gone on duty—the night report book was clutched under her arm. Apparently she had been waiting for me. Whenever I appeared she took a quick breath.

"Good evening, Dr. Shannon. I hope you enjoyed yourself this afternoon."

"What do you say?" I asked her.

"I hope you liked the visit this afternoon."

Her voice was strangely shrill, indeed, the very fact that she should address me directly was, in itself, odd enough to arrest my attention. Lately she had kept out of my way, and when we did meet had passed me without raising her eyes. Peering at her in the dim corridor, I saw that she was crouching, almost, against the wall. Yet, for all her shrinking, she went on, with a gasp and a rush:

"It must have been nice for you when they walked into the isolation pavilion. And found out about your fine laboratory. I'm sure you enjoyed it thoroughly."

I kept watching her face. It surprised me how much she hated me.

"Oh, yes, indeed, my fine Dr. Shannon, I'm not the one that's going to be kicked out. So there! Perhaps that will teach you not to insult a lady. For in case you may not know it," she gulped with fearful triumph, "*the chairman of the committee, Mr. Masters, is my brother-in-law.*"

Before I could speak, as though afraid I might strike her, she swung round and scuttled off.

I stood quite still . . . long after she had gone.

Now everything was clear, the last thing in the world I had ever dreamed would happen. At one time I had feared that Matron might report me, but never, of all people, never Effie Peek. On her night duty she had seen me leave the pavilion and, after further spying, had informed on me to her worthy relative. It was a sweet revenge. When my first wild fury died, I felt sick and hopeless. How could one fight a thing like this? I had outraged her shrinking sensibilities beyond forgiveness. It wasn't ordinary vindictiveness or spite, but something more. She probably was the victim of a neurotic compulsion, she could not help herself. Yet I had no redress. And after this, I hadn't a spark of hope.

On the last day of the month I received an official communication from the committee of management, signed by Ben Masters, requesting my resignation from my position as medical officer at Dalnair Hospital. I read the letter with a stony face.

The staff were very sympathetic about it. Headed by the matron, they got up a subscription and at a little ceremony, after several agreeable speeches, presented me with a nice umbrella. Then, with an air of melancholy justification, Pim took me to the station in the aged ambulance. I was loose again in the world, faced with the prospect of conducting my experiments in the street. And for a start, as I walked blindly from the platform at Winton Station, I left my new umbrella in the train and lost it.

BOOK THREE

CHAPTER I

AT THE GLOBE Commercial Hotel, in a mean street off the Trongate in the noisy heart of the city, I found a room, uncarpeted, fusty from unopened windows, the wallpaper discoloured, the wooden washstand charred by cigarette ends. I did not like the room, which seemed alien, defiled by the innumerable travellers who had occupied it. But it was cheap.

After a cup of tea in the greasy coffee-room downstairs, I set out for Parkside Crescent, on the far side of Winton. When I reached that quiet residential quarter I found, to my relief, that Professor Challis was at home and would see me.

He came almost at once into the dim, maroon-curtained, book-lined study, moving a little uncertainly, his thin, blue-veined hand shakily outstretched, and a grave welcome in his ash-grey eyes, which, though clear, were deep with age.

"This is an unexpected pleasure, Robert. You called some months ago. I was sorry to miss you."

Wilfred Challis was now over seventy, a frail little bowed figure, dressed in an out-of-fashion frock coat, tight black trousers, and button boots which gave to him an old-world appearance that was both touching and absurd. Because of failing health, he had retired from the University, being superseded by Professor Usher, and, outside of a limited circle of experts in France and Switzerland, where much of his best work had been done, his name was almost unknown. Yet he was a true scientist who, through the purity of his motives and the nobility of his mind, had without any material reward brought light to the darkness of the world. During my student days he had become my ideal, and he had given me in many ways evidence of his regard. His aged face, with its high brow, its look of tranquil distinction, of warm humanity, was mild and serene.

He took an armchair beside me, followed by his old brown spaniel dog, Gulliver, which immediately lay down at his feet; then, giving me his close attention, he listened with deepening sympathy while I told him my story. After a brief pause he asked a few technical questions, then passed his long, sensitive fingers meditatively through his thin white hair.

"Interesting," he said. "Most interesting. Robert, I always felt that you would not disappoint me."

Unexpectedly, I felt my eyes fill up with tears.

"If only I could get a grant, sir," I pressed, earnestly. "Surely I'm entitled to it? I don't want to tie myself up with another job. You see how I've been hampered by lack of money."

"My dear boy . . ." He smiled gently. "A lifelong experience has taught me that the hardest thing about scientific research is to get the money for it."

"But surely, sir, that's what the Research Council is for . . . I'd only need a lab and about a hundred pounds. If you approach them, you have such influence."

He shook his head, with a faint, regretful smile.

"I am a back number now, an old fogey laid away upon the shelf. And what you ask is difficult. But I assure you I will try. Not only to get the grant, but to help you in every way I can." He paused. "One day, Robert, I should really like to find you a Continental appointment. Here, we are still tied down by insular prejudice. In Paris or Stockholm you would have a freer hand."

He would not let me thank him, but led me back with warm interest to the subject of my research. While I talked, the dog, Gulliver, licked his hand, the fire burned
162

clear, from upstairs I could hear the cheerful chatter of his grandchildren. I felt my heart expand towards this kindly old man who, through his hatred of the pompous, still seemed young, and from whom there emanated a sense of gentle humour. Half an hour later, as I took my leave, he made a careful note of my address, and promised he would get in touch with me soon.

Cheered and encouraged, I made my way back across the city. It was a clear afternoon, with high luminous clouds, and the pavements of Manfield Street, the main shopping thoroughfare, were thick with people taking advantage of the mildness of the weather to examine the bargains offered in the spring sales. Near the General Post Office I crossed to the south side of the street.

Then, all at once, I started, my abstraction gone, my body suddenly alive. Directly ahead of me, standing with her mother, holding a number of parcels, and gazing into the window of one of the large department stores, was Jean.

Although I had known she must return for her examination, now only two weeks away, this unexpected sight of her caught me by the throat and left me breathless. My heart began to beat like mad. I started towards her, then held myself in check. Sheltered by the crowd, my pulse still thudding in my ears, I watched her with straining eyes. She looked older, more mature, and although no apparent sadness was discernible in her expression, her interest in her mother's conversation, which related, no doubt, to a dark coat displayed behind the plate glass, was no more than passive and obedient. From time to time, indeed, her attention wandered, and she looked about her with an air of pensive inquiry which sent a fresh pang through me. Why, oh why, was she not alone?

Presently, with a wise shake of her head, Mrs. Law took Jean's arm and the two women moved away from the window. I saw that they had finished their shopping and were proceeding in the direction of Central Station to go home. I followed them, like a thief, my heart burning with desire, longing to approach, yet debarred by a vision of the consternation which my appearance must produce.

Outside a little creamery Mrs. Law paused and looked at her watch. After a moment's consultation, they went inside and sat down at a small marble-topped table. From outside, torn by love and indecision, I watched them order and drink hot milk. When they stepped out I tracked them into the busy station. There, amongst the crowd, under the bookstall, which had so often been our meeting place, I was almost close enough to touch Jean. Why did she not turn and see me? I willed, desperately, with all my force, that she might do so. But no, arm in arm with her mother, she slowly passed the barrier, entered the waiting train, and was lost to view.

Immediately she was gone I blamed myself for my stupidity in bungling this opportunity, and hastening back to my shabby room, after restively pacing its narrow confines, I took a sheet of paper and my pen, sat down on the creaky bed. I wanted to release my long suppressed feelings in a flood of words, but the thought that the letter might be intercepted held me back. Finally, under cover of an envelope addressed to Luke, I sent this message:

"Dear Jean,—I saw you to-day in Winton without having a chance to speak to you. I realize that you will soon be taking your examination again and have no wish to disturb you before or during that event. But when it is over I ask you to meet me without fail. I have missed you terribly and have so very much to say to you. Please reply to this address. Best of luck in the exam.

"Yours,
"Robert."

For the next few days I watched the hotel mail-rack feverishly, waiting for an answer to this letter, my love for her reawakened and renewed. Surely she must reply? My longing to be with her was irresistible.

At the same time, since my funds were running so perilously low that I must soon reach a decision about the future, I was anxious to have word from Professor Challis. I did not wish to commit myself to another job for fear the grant from the Research Council materialized. But as I began to economize on food, to eat a single sausage roll for lunch, and, a little later, to miss my dinner altogether, I began to wish I had more strongly impressed the critical nature of circumstances upon my old Professor. Could it be that he had forgotten, that the main purpose of my visit had slipped from his failing memory? As a precaution I went to the Medical Employment Agency and left my name there, but in the process I had a disagreement with the clerk in charge, an exchange of words which did little to improve my prospects. My failure to hear from Challis, Jean's continued silence, the miserable conditions under which I was living, and, above all, the mounting sense of delay in the progress of my work, began to prey upon me intolerably.

In desperation, I rummaged out a flask from the equipment which encumbered the floor space at the foot of my bed and began to try upon myself a series of skin reactions with heat-killed suspensions of the bacilli, scratching the surface of my arm and inoculating the abrasion with dilutions of attenuated cultures. To my joy, a series of typical ulcers developed, thus enabling me to study the important processes of dermal reaction. I watched these carefully and, since I could do no more, made notes and drawings as the condition spread.

In the intervals, I walked the streets endlessly and took to haunting the approaches to Winton Central, in an effort to catch sight of Jean, coming from the Blairhill train. Several times in the crowds I would glimpse some girl who so resembled her that my heart stopped beating. But as I hastened forward, eager and anxious, it was only to find myself gazing into the eyes of a total stranger.

One wet night while I vainly hung about the station, after a particularly wretched day, I felt a hand upon my shoulder.

"How are you, Robert?"

I swung round, a light of expectation leaping to my face. But it was Spence, buttoned up in a raincoat, the evening paper which he had just purchased tucked beneath his arm. I lowered my head quickly, glad, of course, to see him, yet confused that he should find me here, like this.

There was a pause. Neil never could make conversation, but after an awkward moment he said, in his halting style:

"What are you doing in Winton? Taking a day off?"

I kept my eyes averted, afraid of his pity.

"Yes," I said. "I just got in from Dalnair."

He looked me over, in his sidelong apologetic way.

"Come on home and have dinner with us to-night."

I hesitated. I had nothing to look forward to but another wasted, dismal evening at the Globe, where, if I did not wish to listen to the noisy conversation of commercial travellers in the draughty lounge, I must shut myself in my room. I was damp, cold, and hungry. My head was ringing from a day in the streets, my arm kept throbbing painfully. I had not had a decent meal for a week, in fact for twenty-four hours I had eaten practically nothing. I felt faint and ill. It was a severe temptation.

"That's settled," he said, before I could refuse.

We took the bus which ran to Mount Pleasant, the outlying district where, ever since their marriage, Spence and his wife had rented a small half-timbered house, one of many standing in a row in a modest suburban drive.

During the journey we did not talk. Pretending to read his paper, Spence left me alone, but once or twice I felt his eye upon me and, as we got off and approached his home, he said, as though to put me at my ease:

"Muriel will be so glad you've come."

The house, although not spacious, was brightly lit and warm. When we entered, the change from the outer chill gave me an absurd giddy spell, so that I had to steady myself against the wall. Before he removed his things, Spence took me through the lobby to his study and, having seated me before the fire, insisted on giving me a glass of sherry and a biscuit. There was a look of concern upon his honest face which made me feel most uncomfortable.

"You're sure you're all right?"

I forced a laugh.

"Why shouldn't I be?"

For a moment or two he pottered about, pretending not to watch me, then he left, with the remark:

"Make yourself at home. . . . Muriel will be down presently."

I lay back and closed my eyes, still feeling weak, and fighting an inane desire to break down because of the kindness Spence had shown me. Presently, I relaxed a little; the sherry had revived me, and the comfortable chair almost made me doze off. Ten minutes later I roused myself with a start to find Mrs. Spence standing in the doorway.

"Don't get up." She made a gesture of restraint as she came in.

In spite of Neil's assurance and her own polite smile, she did not seem particularly pleased to see me. She was as attractive as ever, even more so, I thought, wearing a pink, young-looking dress, cut low round the neck, with a tight-fitting bodice covered with sequins. Her hair had been freshly set, and there were reddish lights in it which I had not noticed before. She had on a good deal of make-up, and the heavy lipstick gave her thin lips an artificial warmth.

"I hope I'm not putting you about," I said, awkwardly.

"Oh, no." She shook her head, lighting a cigarette with little affected movements. "Mr. Lomax was coming, anyway. It will be quite like old times for you three to get together."

A silence fell between us which was growing difficult when Spence appeared, washed and changed. He had put on a black tie and a dinner jacket.

"I apologize for these glad rags, Shannon." He smiled placatingly towards his wife. "Muriel insists."

"We don't entertain much," Mrs. Spence said sharply. "At least let us do it like gentlepeople."

Spence flushed slightly, but he busied himself filling up the decanters, and did not say anything. Muriel, with one eye upon the clock, was occupying herself in rearranging, with a slight frown of dissatisfaction, the row of miniature ivory elephants which stood upon the mantelpiece.

"Shall I help you, dear!" said Spence. "These things never stand up."

She shook her head. "I wish we had some decent ornaments."

Somehow it hurt me to see Spence so solicitous, so over-anxious to please his wife—I also observed that he had poured himself a second whisky, and much more of it than usual.

Towards eight o'clock, when dinner had been ready for half an hour, there was the sound of a taxi and Lomax arrived, full of apologies for his lateness. He was charming, easy and composed, delighted, he said, to see me again, his clothes and his manners both quite perfect.

In the dining-room the table was covered by a lace-edged

168

cloth and lit by green wax candles with frilled paper shades. Previously, when I had visited Spence, there was usually a plain and simple meal, but now the dinner was pretentious with lots of courses and nothing much to eat. I did not mind, for although, an hour before, I was ravenously hungry, now my stomach had turned against food and I had no appetite at all. The parlourmaid who waited, drilled by her mistress as to the usages of "the best people," stood at attention by the door, in the intervals of serving, breathing through her mouth and staring at us while we ate. Spence spoke very little, but Muriel chattered all the time, mostly to Lomax, in a gay and vivacious style, knowingly discussing items of society news, picked up, no doubt, from the fashion journals she so eagerly perused, and covering up the delays in the service with an exaggeration of her best social manner which set my teeth on edge.

At last it ended, the rattle of crockery in the kitchen ceased, the waitress disappeared, and Mrs. Spence addressed us prettily.

"You three may go and smoke your pipes in the study. Join me in the drawing-room in half an hour." At the door she detained Lomax with her little laugh. "First you must help me blow out the candles."

Spence and I moved into the study where, silently, he stirred up the fire, poured out some whisky, and passed me a cigarette. He looked on the mantelpiece, then felt in his pockets.

"Have you a match, Robert?"

"I'll get some," I said.

I returned to the hall and there, through the open door of the dining-room, I saw Lomax and Mrs. Spence. Encircled by his arms, she was standing close to him, her hands resting intimately on his shoulders, looking up adoringly into his eyes. It was not her attitude alone but the expression of complete infatuation upon her face which stunned me. I stood for an instant, then, as their lips met, I turned away, found a box of matches in my coat pocket, and went back to the study.

Spence was crouched forward in his chair, staring into the fire. He lit his pipe slowly.

"These evenings cheer Muriel up," he said without looking at me. "I think Lomax does her good."

"Of course," I agreed.

"I sometimes wish I weren't such a dull sort of chap, Robert. I try to be bright, but I can't. I've no small talk at all."

"Thank God for that, Neil."

He threw me a grateful glance.

A moment later Lomax joined us. A brief silence followed his appearance, but it did not disconcert him; nothing seemed ever to leave Adrian Lomax at a loss. Taking a cigarette from his case, he occupied the hearth-rug, began to describe his conversation with the taxi-driver who had brought him out. He was graceful and amusing, and before long Spence, who had at first gazed at him with brooding eyes, was listening with a smile. But I could not smile. I was not squeamish, and I had half suspected Lomax all along, yet even so, I felt within me a sort of burning nausea. If it had been anyone but Spence . . . I kept thinking.

I could not restrain myself. While Lomax went on talking I got up, left the study with a muttered excuse, and crossed the hall to the drawing-room.

Mrs. Spence was standing by the fireplace, one foot upon the brass fender, her elbow upon the mantelpiece, gazing with an absent smile at her reflection in the mirror. She seemed restless, pleased with herself, yet filled with a flickering disquiet. As I came in and closed the door behind me she spun round quickly.

"Oh, it's you. Where are the others?"

"In the study."

She must have guessed from my tone that something was wrong. With a sudden lift of her eyelashes she sped a swift glance at me.

"Mrs. Spence," I said at last in a stony voice, "I saw you and Lomax a few minutes ago."

She paled slightly, then coloured deeply and angrily.

"So you spied on us."

"No. I saw you quite by accident."

Speechless, she struggled for words, her cheeks aflame with vexation. I went on:

"Your husband is my best friend. And the best fellow in the world. I can't compel you in any way. But I beg of you to think of him."

"Think of him!" she exclaimed. "Why doesn't someone think of me for a change?" She choked, overcome by a sudden uprush of passionate resentment. "Have you any idea what I've gone through in these last five years?"

"You were happy enough till Lomax came along."

"That's all you know. I was miserable."

"Why did you marry Neil?"

"Because I was a perfect fool, carried away by sentiment, pity, and popular approval. . . . Such a nice girl, doing a fine thing, so wonderfully noble." Her lip drew back. "I didn't realize what I was letting myself in for. Oh, it was all right at first, during the war. There was lots of excitement then. The bands were playing and the flags flying. They even stood up and applauded him when we went to the theatre. But that's all over and forgotten now. He isn't a hero any more. He's a freak. People stare at him in the street. The boys shout after him. Can you imagine my feelings? Only the other day we were in a restaurant and a group at the next table started laughing at him behind his back, till I could have sunk through the floor."

I gazed at her stiffly, frozen by the cheapness of her mind, but I did not give up.

"People can be horribly unkind. You don't have to go out. You have a nice home."

"A poky little house in the suburbs," she flung back scornfully. "That's not what I was brought up to. I'm bored, yes, bored to death. Sitting here night after night, I could scream. When I was engaged to him we planned he would be a consultant. Can you see him in a fashionable practice now, with that bedside appearance? Once he was called in to a little girl down the street, and when he bent over the cot the child nearly had a fit. He'll never be anything but a laboratory hack."

"That should make you very gentle with him."

"Oh, shut up!" She threw the words at me. "You half-baked idealists are all the same. I've given him enough. I'm tired of making jellies and soups for him. I can't go on wasting the best years of my life."

"He loves you," I said. "That's worth something to both of you. Don't throw it away."

Her eyes met mine, fiercely, like a blow. I expected an outburst. Instead, she turned away and gazed into the fireplace. The slow ticking of the clock sounded in the room like the heartbeats of a mechanical doll. When she faced me again her expression was calm, her gaze open and beguiling.

"Now listen, Robert. You're making a great fuss about nothing. It's only a flirtation really, between Adrian and me. I swear to you there's no harm in it."

She came forward and laid her hand lightly on my sleeve.

"Life is rather dull in this hateful suburb. One does deserve a little cheering-up sometimes. Every woman likes to be flattered and made up to . . . to feel she has some fascination. That's all there is to it. You won't tell Neil?"

172

I shook my head, looking at her fixedly, wondering if she spoke anything like the truth.

"I do make it up to him. I am nice to him really." She smiled, persuasively, still stroking my sleeve. "Promise you won't say a word?"

"No," I said. "I won't tell him. I'm going now. Good night, Mrs. Spence."

In the study, on the pretext that I must take the ten o'clock train for Dalnair, I announced that I must leave, and said good night to Lomax. Spence came with me to the door, rather put out at my abrupt departure. In the porch he slipped an arm round my shoulders.

"I wish you wouldn't rush off, Robert." His dark eyes rested on mine. "In fact . . . I was going to ask you to stay here for a few days . . . if things were difficult for you."

"Difficult?" I echoed.

He glanced away.

"I rang Dalnair last week. They told me you had gone." He groped for words which seemed to come from deep down in his unselfish heart. "You see, I'd love to help . . . I'm so well off here . . . I don't like to think of you knocking around, on the loose."

"Thanks, Spence, thanks. I'm quite all right." My feelings overpowered me, I could not go on. I wrung his hand and ran down the steps into the wet darkness of the night.

I walked all the way back to the city in an effort to pull myself together. My arm felt hot and swollen, but that ache was less than the pain that burned in my breast. A sense of the cruelty of life overwhelmed me.

It was eleven o'clock when I reached the Globe, and as I entered the chilly lobby I saw a letter for me in the rack. I took it hurriedly.

"My dear Shannon,—I am sorry to report that despite my strongest representations, the Research

Council has refused to make a grant towards your work. This I am afraid is final. I shall, however, continue to bear your needs in mind. If in the meantime you should require a room for your equipment I have arranged that you may have this at the old Apothecaries' Hall in St. Andrew's Lane. Do not be discouraged.

"Very sincerely yours,
"WILFRED CHALLIS."

I could not read any more, I simply could not see the words. I had to clench my teeth, to keep the tears from rolling from my eyes.

CHAPTER II

Next morning, like an unskilled boxer who, although knocked down, must struggle to his feet, I went, but without much hope, to the Apothecaries' Hall. This was a rambling old building, situated near the Wellgate, a branch of the Pharmaceutical College, where students for the Licentiate of the Society of Apothecaries took their classes. It was in every sense inferior to the University.

The janitor had been notified of my coming, and when I gave him my name he conducted me to a room on the ground floor, a long, low room, rather dark, with a table, a leather couch, an agate balance in a glass case, a rack of test tubes and two small shelves of simple chemical reagents. It was, in fact, the sort of room I had feared that I might find, a room suited to a student in pharmacy, and as I surveyed its limitations I asked myself if I should ever, under high heaven, secure the proper background for my work. Here, by constant improvising, by straining every nerve, one might push ahead. But alone, without money or adequate assistance, that progress would be slow.

Outside, I gave the janitor a shilling and asked him to call at the Globe with a hand-barrow and bring over my apparatus. At least I should have free storage for my things. This, since I did not know how long I should be able to remain at the hotel, would be some advantage. Whether I should make the effort to carry on here I could not at this moment decide. In my heart, as I came through the ivy-covered archway of the Hall, I was conscious of a slight rankling towards Professor Challis. Yet I could not believe that he would willingly fail me.

On the way back to the hotel, struggling with these thoughts, I went by the Trongate Cross. This was a noisy, congested triangle in the poor section of the city, formed by the intersection of three narrow, busy streets, and hemmed in by cheap shops and tall tenements. All the traffic from the docks flowed through it, a steady stream of drays and lorries, mingling and intermingling with the trams and buses from Old High Street.

I was about to turn the corner into Trongate proper when, suddenly, through my preoccupation, there flashed that strange premonition occasioned by disaster. Amongst the crowd on the opposite pavement a schoolgirl of about fourteen, her satchel under her arm, had been standing with a companion, waiting for an opportunity to cross the street. Now, thinking the intersection clear, with a laughing goodbye to her friend, she stepped off the kerb. At that instant a motor wagon swung out of Old High Street at unexpected speed. The child saw it and ran forward. It seemed that she would escape. But in the same second a heavy lorry lumbered up from the other direction. The space between the two vehicles drew in. She halted dizzily, saw that she was trapped, made an awkward effort to turn back, then slipped full length on the wet asphalt. Her satchel shot across the street, spilling her school-books at my feet. There was a screech of brakes, a shrill scream of terror, and with a grinding noise the wheel of the lorry, weighted with pig-iron from the docks, passed over her body.

A cry of horror arose, there was a general rush forward, and immediately a crowd surrounded the victim. I could not help myself. Although my whole instinct was to shun the public exhibition of my profession, I thrust through the milling throng and knelt beside the injured girl. Beneath the mud which soiled her face she was deathly pale, inert, and moaning feebly. A policeman was supporting her head in the crook of his arm, hampered by well-meaning persons, pressing close and offering advice.

"Get her in somewhere," I said. "I'm a doctor."

His red, resentful face cleared at once. Willing hands passed down a plank from the stationary truck. Amidst more shouting and confusion she was placed on this impromptu stretcher, carried to the back premises of a small surgery, set amongst the shops across the way, and laid upon a couch. A score of curious individuals poured in after us. Immediately the policeman telephoned for an ambulance. But as he joined me at the couch, he said:

"It'll take a good ten minutes in this traffic."

"Please move these people out of here," I told him.

While he cleared the shabby consulting-room I bent down and opened the child's stained and torn blouse. Her rent undervest fell away, exposing her flat little chest. It was the left shoulder, I saw, an impacted compound fracture of the humerus. Her broken left arm hung deformed and limp, but worse than that was the large bluish swelling, growing steadily larger, in the left axilla. With my fingers on her wrist I threw a quick glance of anxiety at her face, completely blanched now, the eyes fixed and slightly upturned.

The police officer was beside me again. We were joined by the surgery dispenser, an elderly man in a short white jacket.

"Whose place is this?" I asked him.

"Dr. Mathers's. It's unlucky he's not here."

"She don't look too well," the officer said in a low voice.

With my gaze upon that pulsing swelling, I was thinking rapidly. The brachial artery was undoubtedly ruptured, too high up to apply a tourniquet, and the bleeding was so profuse it might easily prove fatal before the ambulance arrived.

I could not hesitate. Without a word to the others, I dragged the couch to the window, went to the small enamel instrument cabinet in the corner, took out a scalpel, Spencer forceps, and a glass container of catgut sutures. The ether bottle was on the bottom shelf. I poured some on a pad of gauze, placed this upon the child's nostrils. She whimpered faintly, then lay still.

No time for routine antisepsis. I dashed some iodine over my hands, swabbed the swollen armpit with the same pungent fluid. The other two were watching me with staring eyes. Framed in the doorway was a group of silent spectators. Ignoring them, I took the knife and cut into the puffy arm.

Immediately a great clot of blood welled out. Through it I saw the ragged spurting gap in the torn artery. Instantly I clamped the forceps on it. Then, deliberately, almost at my leisure, I ligatured the vessel. It was very easy, all over in five minutes. Removing the ether mask, I unclipped the forceps, lightly packed the wound, and applied a bandage, reverse spica, to make it extra neat. Already the pulse was stronger, the breathing deeper and more regular. I took the coarse grey blanket from the foot of the couch and wrapped it tight about her skinny form. They might give her a transfusion at the hospital, perhaps an intravenous saline, but the real emergency was over.

"She'll do now," I said briefly.

The policeman gave a gratified sigh, and from the doorway there came a murmur of approval. But, as I turned, I became aware of a short, stocky, vigorous man, with a fiery complexion and a shock of frizzy hair, staring at me with unfriendly eyes.

This jarring personality annoyed me.

"I thought I said to clear the room."

"All right, then," he said brusquely. "Push off."

"You push off," I answered with some heat.

"Why should I? It's my surgery."

I realized that I was in the presence of Dr. Mathers.

At this point the ambulance arrived, a diversion which

caused considerable commotion. When at last the little patient had been made completely comfortable and carefully removed, the police officer closed his note-book, shook my hand solemnly, and took his leave. The dispenser went into the front premises, the remnants of the crowd dissolved, the traffic resumed its roar. Dr. Mathers and I were alone.

"You have a nerve," he resumed. "Walking into my office. Messing it up with blood. And I don't even get a fee for it."

I rolled down my sleeves and put on my jacket.

"When I'm in funds I'll send you a cheque for ten guineas."

He bit his thumbnail for a moment, as though chewing upon my remark. All his nails were bitten close.

"What's your name?"

"Shannon."

"I suppose you're some sort of doctor."

I glanced at his framed diploma, hung on the wall behind him. It was the certificate of the Conjoint Board, the lowest possible qualification with which a man was entitled to practise.

"Yes," I said. "Are you?"

He reddened slightly and, with an air of uncovering a fraud, turned abruptly to his desk and picked up the *Medical Directory*. Slashing through the pages with the energy which characterized all his movements, he quickly found my name.

"Shannon," he said. "Robert Shannon. We'll soon see." But as he read the list of my qualifications and the prizes which I had taken, his face fell. He closed the book, sat down on the Rexine-covered revolving chair, tilted back on his head the bowler hat which he still wore, and fell to studying me in a new manner.

"You've heard of me," he said, at length.

"Never."

"You must have. James Mathers. I've the biggest practice in the city. Three thousand on the panel. The maximum. All the other doctors hate me. I cut the feet from under them. I'm very popular with the people."

Still watching me, he rolled a cigarette, expertly, with his left hand, and stuck it, drooping, in his mouth. His cockiness was amazing. He was dressed in a loud, professional style, with broad striped trousers, short black jacket, winged collar, and a stock with a diamond pin in it. But his chin was blue; he needed a shave.

"So you're out of a job?" he asked, suddenly. "What is it . . . booze or women?"

"Both," I said. "I'm also a morphine addict."

He did not answer—then with a brisk movement sat up.

"How would you like to work for me? Three nights a week. Surgery and late calls. I need time off. The practice is killing me."

Surprised, I reflected for a minute.

"What would you pay?"

"Three guineas a week."

I considered again. It was quite a generous offer which would keep me at the Globe, and save me the humiliation of lining up at the Medical Agency. I'd have time for my research too, if only I could get things going at Apothecaries' Hall.

"All right."

"It's a deal, then. Be here to-night, six o'clock sharp. I warn you I've had assistants before. None of them were any damn good. They went out on their ear."

"Thank you for the hint."

I was on my way to the door when, with a grim smile, he called me back.

"Here. You look as though you needed something in advance."

From his hip pocket he took an overstuffed leather purse and, carefully selecting the money, pushed across to me three shillings and three pound notes.

I had learned a little sense. Without a word, I picked up the money as carefully as he had put it down.

CHAPTER III

THAT SAME EVENING, at six, and thereafter on three nights of the week, I attended at the surgery in Trongate Cross. When I arrived the waiting-room was always packed to the door with patients—women in shawls, ragged children, workmen from the docks—and the hectic session which followed often ran on until eleven o'clock at night, after which there were usually one or two urgent calls which Thompson, the dispenser, gave me as he finally closed up. It was hard work. Dr. Mathers had been guilty of no exaggeration when he spoke of his enormous practice. I soon found that he had an extraordinary reputation amongst the poor people who inhabited this slum district.

His fiery personality alone gave him great prestige, and his methods were abrupt, forceful, and dramatic. He had an instinct for diagnosis and did not hesitate to give his opinion, usually in the broad vernacular. He never spared himself, worked like a galley slave, and bullied his people a good deal. They liked him for it. His prescriptions were drastic. He used the maximum dose of every drug, and a patient who had been severely purged or violently sweated would remark with a knowing shake of his head: "Ay, there's something *in* the wee doctor's medicine."

Mathers was sensitive about his diminutive stature, yet he had all the vanity of the small man, and thoroughly enjoyed his success. He loved to feel that he could triumph where the neighbouring doctors failed, and would chuckle over a case where he had "wiped the eye" of one of his colleagues. But most of all he delighted in the fact that from this drab little surgery, in a poor-class district, with no more than a Conjoint diploma, he was able to reside in style in a large villa in the suburbs, to run a Sunbeam car, educate his only daughter handsomely, present his wife with a fine fur coat—in short, to live, as he put it, like a lord. His money sense was extremely strong. Although he charged only small fees, from a shilling to half a crown, he was insistent upon payment in cash.

"Once they know they can get you for nothing, Doctor," he warned me, "you're done."

In a drawer of his desk he kept a long chamois bag which had once contained midwifery forceps and into which all the fees were poured. Towards the end of the surgery hours it was bulging with cash. Upon my first night, as the surgery concluded, Dr. Mathers walked in unexpectedly, took up the bag and weighed it expertly. He glanced at me, but said nothing. Although he tried not to show it, I could see that he was satisfied.

At the beginning of the second week, when I arrived on Monday evening to begin my consultations, I put my hand in my pocket and brought out a pound note.

"This is yours." As he looked at me sharply, I went on. "The child that was run over is getting on famously. Her father came in last Friday and insisted on paying this fee. He's a decent fellow and very gratoful."

Mathers's expression was extremely queer. He rolled a cigarette and bit away the loose threads, which he spat on the floor.

"Keep it," he said at last.

I refused irritably.

"You pay me a salary. Everything I earn is yours."

There was a pause. He walked to the window and came back, having forgotten to light his cigarette.

"Shall I tell you something, Shannon?" he said slowly. "You're the first straight assistant I've ever had. Let's take the quid and send the kid a bunch of black grapes and some flowers."

That was the strange thing about this little man—he

loved money, but he was not mean, and could spend freely upon himself and others.

After this incident Dr. Mathers's attitude was much more cordial. Indeed, he became quite intimate, proudly showing me snapshots of his wife and of his seventeen-year-old daughter Ada, now finishing her schooling at the exclusive, and expensive, Convent of the Sacred Heart in Grantley. He also exhibited a photograph of his grandiose villa with the big car standing at the door, and threw out hints that he would soon invite me there. From time to time he gave me advice as to how to run a practice, and one day, in an expansive mood, confessed that he was actually making three thousand pounds a year. Intensely curious as to how I spent the rest of my time, he often tried to exact some information from me, but I maintained always a discreet reserve. Although I disliked the work, my spirits were high, for I had an odd premonition that my luck had turned at last. And so, indeed, it seemed.

On Thursday of that week, as I returned late in the afternoon to the Globe, I made out in the gathering dusk, across the street, a man's figure which seemed familiar. As I appeared, he stirred from his attitude of patient waiting, and slowly approached me. Remembering the circumstances under which we had parted, my heart came into my mouth as I recognized Alex Duthie.

A long silence succeeded our meeting and, to my surprise, I perceived that his hesitation and emotion were greater than my own. At last, in a low voice, he said:

"I'd like a word with you, Robert. Can we go inside?"

I took him through the swing doors and up to my room, where, having deposited upon the floor the box which he carried beneath his arm, he sat down on the edge of a chair. Twisting his round stiff cap in his capable hands, he fixed his troubled, candid gaze upon me.

184

"Rob . . . I've come here to beg your pardon."

It cost him an effort to get out these words, but when he had done so he drew an easier breath.

"Last week we were out to Dalnair. We had gathered all of Sim's toys out of the attic, and the wife took the notion to leave them at the hospital for the children. When we were there we had a long talk with the matron. In confidence, she told us everything. I'm sorry I blamed you, Robert. I could cut my tongue out now."

I scarcely knew what to say. Gratitude of any sort embarrassed me beyond belief. At the same time, the break in my friendship with Duthie had worried me, and it was a relief to find myself no longer misunderstood. Without speaking, I held out my hand. He gripped it like a vice, and a slow, grave smile spread over his ruddy face.

"We're all right again then, lad."

"Of course, Alex."

"You'll come fishing with me in the autumn?"

"If you feel like it."

"I'll feel like it," he answered slowly. "One gets over things in time, you know, Rob."

There was a short pause. He rubbed his hands together and with an air of inquiry glanced round the room.

"You're still on with your research?"

"Yes."

"That's good. You remember the milk samples you wanted? I've fetched them along to you to-day."

I sat up, electrified.

"You've had another cattle outbreak?"

He nodded.

"Severe?"

"Quite bad, Rob. Five of our heifers dropped their calves and died in spite of all we could do for them."

"And you saved me milk samples?" I was tense with excitement.

"From all of them. In sterile containers." He inclined his head towards the package he had put down. "In that zinc-lined box."

I gazed at him with overflowing gratitude. So much had gone against me I could scarcely believe this splendid stroke of fortune.

"Alex," I exulted, "you've no idea how much this means to me. Exactly what I wanted . . ."

"It's not so one-sided," he answered, seriously. "I tell you straight, Rob, this business has got us badly worried at the Farms. All the best herds seem to have it. The manager says if you can help us in any way he'll surely appreciate it."

"I'll try, Alex. I promise you I'll try." For a moment I could not continue. "If there was anything needed to make up . . . you couldn't have chosen a better way . . ."

"If you're pleased, then I'm pleased too." He inspected his big silver watch. "Now it's time I was moving."

"Stay a bit longer." I pressed him. "Let me get you a drink."

I would gladly have given him all I possessed.

"No, lad . . . I have to catch that old six-fifteen bus." He gave me his slow, quiet smile. "I waited outside here for over an hour before you showed up."

I went downstairs with him and sent him on his way with my warmest thanks. Having watched his solid figure disappear in the darkness, I came back into the hotel filled with an eager happiness.

I was about to bound upstairs towards the Dreem Farms box when, in the hall rack, I saw a letter for me. The handwriting was unmistakable, it was from Jean. Breathless, clutching the letter, I made my way upstairs, shut the door and, with trembling fingers, tore open the envelope.

"DEAR ROBERT,—Luke has been away at Tynecastle for the past three weeks. Because of this I did not receive your letter until this afternoon, and now I scarcely know how to reply. If I am to be truthful, I cannot deny that it made me happy to hear from you and that I have missed you greatly. Perhaps I am wrong to tell you this. Perhaps I ought not to write this letter at all. But I have some news, and shall make that my excuse.

"For these last few days I have been taking the examination again and, although I made some mistakes, I am so glad to tell you that I did not too badly. Professor Kennerly, for a wonder, was quite nice. And yesterday when I had my final oral he took me aside and informed me that I had passed with distinction, in all subjects. A fluke, of course, but what a relief!

"The graduation won't be till the end of term, July 31; until then I intend taking a course in Tropical Medicine, which starts next week at the Sanderson Institute. The lecture is at 9 o'clock every morning and lasts one hour.
                                                "Yours,
                                                     "JEAN LAW."

Passed . . . passed with distinction . . . and missing me . . . missing me greatly. My eyes glistened towards the words, which after those weary months of sadness and frustration came like a divine balm to my lonely heart. My wretched bedroom was transformed. I wanted to leap, to laugh, to sing. Again and again I read those lines which, because she had written them, seemed invested with a unique and tender beauty. There was a hidden note of longing in the letter which raised me to a kind of ecstasy which gave me, suddenly, an idea, a plan of future action that sent the blood rushing to my head, in a shiver of delight. I took the sheet of note-paper which, so recently, she had touched, and pressed it to my lips.

CHAPTER IV

THE SANDERSON INSTITUTE stood on the far side of the river, in an almost forgotten part of the city, between the Pensioners' Hospice and the ancient St. Enoch's Church. It was a quiet district, and the gardens in St. Enoch's Square gave to it a country look. Rain had fallen the night before, a soft spring rain, and as I made my way along the flagged pavement of Old George Street there was a smell of sap and young grass in the air. A warm breeze came from the river and swung the buds of the tall elm trees where the sparrows were chirping. All at once the cold grip of winter seemed to have relaxed and the moist earth, opening to the sunshine, gave forth a heady sweetness that filled me with longing, with an ineffable yearning, that was like a pain.

Outside the Hospice an old flower woman had her stand. On an impulse I stopped and bought a sixpenny bunch of the snowdrops which hung over the edge of her basket. Too shy to carry them openly, I wrapped the fragile blossoms in my handkerchief and placed them in my pocket. As I hurried into the courtyard of the Institute and took up my position outside the lecture-room, the old clock of St. Enoch's, as though intoxicated by the balmy air, struck ten merry strokes.

A few minutes later the Institute lecture-room began to empty itself. There were not more than half a dozen students. Last of all, emerging with an absent air, alone, came Jean. She was in grey, which always suited her so well, the lines of her slight, thin figure outlined as the fresh wind moulded the stuff of her dress about her. Her lips were slightly parted. Her hands, in their worn gloves, clasped a note-book. Her soft brown eyes were downcast.

Suddenly she looked up, our glances met, and going forward, I took both her hands in mine.

"Jean . . . at last."

"Robert."

She had spoken my name haltingly, as though struggling, with confusion, against a pang of conscience. But now her face was filled with light, a bright warmth flooded her cheeks. I wanted to hold her tightly in my arms. But no, I dared not. Words came huskily.

"It's so wonderful to see you again."

For a moment, gazing into each other's eyes in a kind of rapt intoxication, neither of us could speak. Behind us in the elms the sparrows twittered and, down the river, a dog was barking, far away. At last, still breathless, I exclaimed:

"And you're through . . . with distinction . . . I congratulate you."

"It's nothing." She smiled.

"It's splendid. You'd have done it before, but for my pernicious influence."

She laughed shyly. We both laughed. I was still holding her hands as though I would never let them go.

"You've left Dalnair?" she asked.

"Yes," I answered gaily. "I got kicked out. You see what a rotter I am. Now I'm part-time assistant to a slum doctor in the Trongate."

"But your research?" She spoke quickly.

"Ah," I said. "It's about that I want to talk to you."

I led her across the road to the Square Gardens. We sat down on a green bench which encircled the trunk of a gnarled tree. Pigeons fluttered and strutted before us, giddy as the other birds with the delicious surge of spring. No one was in sight but an old pensioner, hobbling down a path, in his black peaked cap and bright scarlet coat. I took from my pocket the bunch of snowdrops and gave them to her.

"Oh!" she cried, with delight, then paused, afraid that her words or look might say too much.

"Wear them, Jean," I said, in a low voice. "It isn't a crime. Tell me, did they make you promise not to see me?"

There was a sudden pause.

"No," she said slowly. "If I had I couldn't very well be here."

I watched while, with a slightly saddened expression, she deeply inhaled the delicate perfume, then pinned to her bodice, below the soft little necklet of camphory fur around her neck, these white and fragile flowers which so miraculously suited her. Seated close beside her, I felt a glow run through my limbs, my cheeks and forehead were hot. I knew that if I did not quickly broach the subject on my mind, this terrible emotion would conquer me.

"Jean," I said, striving to take a grip upon myself. "Apart from your lecture, your days are free now . . . I mean, after ten o'clock you have nothing much to occupy you?"

"Yes." There was a note of inquiry in her eyes and, as I did not speak, she added: "Why?"

"I need your help," I answered firmly and sincerely, aware that I spoke the truth. Gazing at her steadily, I went on. "I'm halfway through my investigation, ready to begin the next step, and I'm quite wildly excited about it. You know the difficulty I've had, going on by myself . . . Oh, I'm not complaining, but now for this new phase I must have some assistance. There are tests which I can't possibly manage single-handed. Professor Challis has given me a room." I paused. "Would you . . . will you work with me?"

She had flushed slightly and now, for a moment, she looked at me eagerly, then slowly she lowered her eyes. There was a silence.

"Oh, Robert, I wish I could. But I can't. Surely you know how it is with me now? My parents . . . I owe so much to them . . . they've built everything on me . . . I love them . . . Mother especially . . . she's the best in the whole world. And they . . . while they haven't exactly forced me"—she seemed to seek for words to temper the blow—"they don't want me to see you. Even at this moment . . . I'm disobeying them."

I bit my lip. For all her softness there was something irreconcilable about her, a strong fidelity, loyalties that were not mine, a sense of duty which gave her a horror of dissimulation.

"They must hate me pretty thoroughly."

"No, Robert. They simply understand that our ways must be apart."

"It isn't as if this were a personal matter," I burst out. "You're a doctor now and it's for science."

"I'd love to do it. I'm so interested. But it isn't possible."

"It's entirely possible," I insisted. "No one need know. Your people would merely think you were doing some practical work in tropical medicine . . ."

She silenced me with a strained glance.

"It isn't that I'm afraid of, Robert."

"What then?"

"We'd be together."

"Is that so terrible?"

She raised her dark lashes, and gazed at me mournfully.

"I know I'm to blame . . . I didn't realize at first that our feeling for each other was . . . so deep. And if we go on it will get deeper. That will only make it worse for us in the end."

This simple declaration brought back warmth to my heart. I took a quick breath, resolved, at all costs, to persuade her.

"Listen, Jean. If I promise, swear to you that I'll never once make love to you, never even mention the word, will you assist me? I need help so badly. If I don't get it, I'm done."

191

A long, still pause. She gazed at me doubtfully, her colour coming and going, lost in a trance of uncertainty. And quickly I pressed home my advantage.

"It's such a wonderful chance. I'm on the verge of something tremendous. Come and see for yourself."

Carried away, I jumped up and held out my hand. After a moment she got slowly to her feet.

It was not a long walk to Apothecaries' Hall. We were there in ten minutes. I led her directly to my work-room and there, taking from my small incubator one of the culture tubes which I had inoculated with the recent specimens from Duthie, I held it eagerly before her.

"There," I said. "I have it. And it's growing pretty fast. You don't recognize it?"

She shook her head, her interest awakened, a quick look of interrogation in her wide dark pupils.

I returned the tube to the water bath, glanced at the regulator and closed the zinc door. Then, quite simply, I explained what was in my mind.

A flush of enthusiasm crept into her cheeks. Her eyes, bright yet deeply troubled, wandered round the room, back to the culture, then again to me. My heart was beating fast. To hide my emotion, I went to the window and threw it up, letting in a flood of sunlight. Outside, fleecy clouds were racing in the bright blue sky. I turned towards her.

"Robert," she said slowly. "If I work with you . . . because I believe your work to be important . . . will you promise, faithfully, to keep your word?"

"Yes," I said.

I saw her breast heave in a sudden sigh. While I kept my gaze upon her, she put down her book, removed her hat, and began to take off her gloves.

"Very well," she said. "Let's begin."

CHAPTER V

Every morning regularly, shortly after ten o'clock, when her lecture was over, Jean came into the room where I was already at work and, taking her smock from the hook behind the door, slipped it on and began to busy herself, methodically, at the other end of the long table. We did not exchange more than a few words, perhaps only a smile of greeting. Sometimes, when I was occupied with a calculation, I pretended not to notice her arrival—an impersonal attitude which I felt might reassure her. Yet she was there, and later when I guardedly looked up I would see her, measuring and titrating, behind the clamped burettes, entering each reading in the battered black record-book, her expression serious and intent.

As I had foreseen, her neatness and careful accuracy were of the utmost help to me, especially in preparing the hundreds of slides which it was necessary to examine. It was a difficult staining technique, and a dangerous one, for these mass bouillon cultures were highly virulent. But working quietly, with steady fingers, her features deeply absorbed, her eyes unwavering, she never once made a mistake. When she felt my gaze upon her she would give me, interrupting her work, a silent yet speaking glance, binding us more closely in this community of effort to which we were pledged. The light spring airs streamed through the wide open window into our dim little room, bringing faintly the sounds of another world—a hum of traffic, the whistle of a steamboat, a strain of tinkling music from a distant barrel-organ. Her presence, with its control and quietude, stimulated me to a pitch I had never known before.

At one o'clock we stopped for lunch. Although there were one or two good cafés in this neighbourhood, it was easier, more agreeable, and cheaper to take our meal in the laboratory. To this end we clubbed our money, and from the market, which she passed through, on her way from the train, Jean would bring, each day, an assortment of provisions. Having steeped our hands for three minutes in corrosive sublimate solution, a precaution which I insisted upon with inflexible firmness, we sat on the window-sill and, balancing a plate upon our knees, enjoyed an alfresco repast. When the day was grey and chilly we had soup, heated over the Bunsen burner. But usually our fare consisted of fresh scones, slices of cold sausage, and Dunlop cheese, with an apple, or a bag of cherries, for dessert. In the courtyard outside there was a blackbird which came faithfully every day, to share our good things. When he saw that we had cherries, he would perch upon Jean's wrist, whistling his heart out with greedy delight.

Upon the seventh afternoon, as we worked in silence, I heard a step and turned round. Professor Challis stood on the threshold, bent and buttoned-up in his faded frock coat, plucking at his silver moustache, his eyes screwed up towards us.

"I thought I'd look in on you, Robert," he said, "to see how you were getting on."

I rose at once and introduced him to Jean, to whom he bowed with his old-world air. He was surprised, I could see, and although too courteous to show it, both curious and doubtful. But soon it was evident that she pleased him and, reassured, he gave me his twinkling smile.

"Half the battle in research, Robert, is a suitable assistant."

He chuckled at that, as though he had made an excellent joke, then wandered about the room, gently activating the cultures, examining the slides, peering through the pages of our notes, in silence, but with a quiet approval more exciting to us than words.

When the survey was complete he turned and gazed at us.

"I shall get you more samples, more specimens from other areas . . . from the Continent . . . where they still have some regard for me." He broke off and threw out his hands. "Go on, go on. Pay no attention to an old fossil like me. Simply go on."

The words were nothing, but in his eyes I saw a lively gleam which had not been there before.

After that he came regularly to visit us, often at the lunch hour, bringing not only the promised specimens but, more than once, a contribution to our meal. Seated in a chair, his stick between his knees, leaning forward rather shakily on the bone handle, he watched us from beneath his bushy brows, with bright eyes, while we divided a meat pie or a jar of Strasbourg *pâté*. His attachment to Jean had steadily increased, and his manner to her was charming, gently chivalrous, yet with a kind of mischievous benevolence, like a schoolboy. He never ate anything, but when she made coffee he would accept a cup and, having asked her permission with that special gallantry he now displayed towards her, would snip delicately and light one of the small cigars he occasionally permitted himself. While the blue spirals drifted upwards and dispersed, he would recount to us his early experiences as a young research student in Paris, at the Sorbonne, where he worked under the great Duclaux.

"I had no money then." He chuckled, after describing to us a Sunday spent at Barbizon. "And I've none now. But I've always been happy, doing the work that's not like anything else in the world."

When he had gone Jean drew a deep breath. Her eyes were glowing.

"He's sweet, Robert. A great man. And I love him."

"If I'm any judge, the old chap loves you too." I smiled a trifle wryly. "But would your family approve of him?"

She lowered her gaze.

"Let's get back to work."

We had by this time isolated in a pure state, from the numerous milk samples, a Gram-negative organism which I identified as Bang's bacillus, originally discovered by the Danish scientist Bang, and shown by him to be the cause of acute disease in cattle widely prevalent all over the world. This, therefore, was the cause of the trouble in the dairy herds. Indeed, from figures which I worked out, we estimated that probably 35 per cent. of all cattle in the country, to say nothing of sheep, goats, and other farm stock, were harbourers of this germ which we now had cultivated in massive quantity, in a special broth medium.

We also possessed, in a pure state, the Bruce bacillus of Malta fever, which, of course, during my sojourn at Dalnair, I had recovered from human beings stricken during the epidemic of so-called influenza, and which also we had in many instances isolated from the recent human specimens procured by Challis. Thus we were in a position to compare these two organisms—the one from cattle, the other from man—to analyse their varying reactions, and to discover the possible relationship between them.

The tests which we employed were exceedingly complex and at first it was difficult to assess their value. But gradually, as one positive result succeeded another, there emerged a supposition, built in the beginning upon conjecture, but later upon solid proof, which truly staggered us. When it dawned upon us, we gazed at each other incredulously.

"It can't be," I said slowly. "It's impossible."

"It could be," she answered, logically. "And it is just possible."

196

I pressed both hands to my head, irritated for once by her quiet simplicity. Dr. Mathers had kept me late at the surgery the night before; he was increasing his demands upon me, and the strain of this double duty was beginning to tell.

"For God's sake," I said, "don't let's cross bridges before we come to them. We've weeks of work yet before we make the final antigen test."

But still the evidence piled up and, at the end of three months, as we drew nearer to this crucial test, a deep and increasing excitement imposed itself upon us. In the hours when we were obliged to wait for the process of agglutination to take place, we found this nervous strain almost unbearable—and since there was no need to remain in the laboratory we sought relief by escaping for an hour or so to the country immediately surrounding Winton.

Now there was no question of the motor-cycle, for even Luke was unaware that we were together; but the tramway was convenient and took us in twenty minutes to our favourite resort, the Longcrag Hill, a wooded height, not yet built upon, which overlooked the river. Here, on a mossy rock, we would sit and watch the ferry boats and tiny paddle steamers plying up and down the broad stream, with the city, lost in a golden haze, revealed only by a glittering dome or tenuous spire, lying far below at our feet. We spoke mainly of the problems confronting us in our work, and discussed, with agitated hope, the prospects of success. Sometimes, tired out, yet overcome by the magic of the moment, I would lie back, shut my eyes and, with all the longing of my provincial soul, dream aloud, dream of the Sorbonne, pictured so vividly to us by Challis, dream of a life of pure, unhampered research.

Faithful to my promise, although it was not easy, I did not once speak to her of love. Aware of her scruples, of the niceties of conscience she had overcome to help me, I was resolved to prove to her how false was her suspicion that she could not really trust me. Only thus could I justify myself in her eyes and my own.

When the day of decision arrived we set the final batch of agglutinin tubes and went out. It was Thursday, the last day of June, a more than usually lovely afternoon; and, afraid almost of what we might find on our return, we were disinclined to leave the Hill. As we sat there, a little steamer, away beneath us, was setting out upon an evening cruise to the islands of the lower estuary, and upon its after-deck we could see the tiny figures of a German band. They were playing a Strauss waltz. The little ship with flags flying, and paddles churning, swept gaily down the river, and disappeared from sight. But behind there lingered a whisper of the melody, ascending to us faintly yet sweetly, tender as a caress. It was a precious moment. I dared not look at my companion, but in a dazzling flash I felt the exaltation of these days of joint endeavour which, almost without my knowledge, had deepened and strengthened our intimacy. I knew now that, in every way, she had become indispensable to me.

We rose to go. I had no surgery that evening, and Jean, because of the importance of the occasion, had arranged to remain in Winton until eight o'clock.

Five o'clock was striking when we got to our little laboratory. It was now or never. I went to the incubator, and opening the door, made an abrupt gesture to my companion to remove the racked tray of tubes. There were, in that tray, twenty-four tubes, each containing a liquid, perfectly clear some hours ago, but which, if the test were successful, would now show a cloudy deposit. Holding my breath, I watched her nervously take out the tray. Then I gave a short gasp.

Every tube in the rack showed a flocculent white precipitate. I could not speak. Caught by a sudden weakness,

198

I sat down on the leather settee while Jean, still holding the tray of tubes, continued to gaze at me with a transfigured face.

It was true then: these two organisms, regarded for twenty-one years as separate and unrelated species, were the same. Yes, I had proved it. Morphologically, culturally, and by agglutination tests, they were identical. This widespread disease of cattle was intensely communicable to humans, not only by direct contact, but through milk, butter, cheese, and every variety of dairy produce. The Bang's disease of animals was the Malta fever of Bruce and the "influenza" epidemic, all in one, all due to the same bacillus, which we had cultivated here in the lab. I shut my eyes dizzily. We had actually established the existence, and the cause, of a new infection in man, not a minor condition of local interest, but a serious disease capable of producing major epidemics as well as continued ill-health in its milder and more chronic forms, a disease which must number its victims in hundreds of thousands in every country all over the world. As I considered these ramifications I swallowed dryly. Like Cortez, upon his mountain peak, I saw, with startling clarity, the vast extent of our discovery.

At last Jean broke the silence.

"It's wonderful," she said in a low voice. "Oh, Robert, you can publish everything now."

I shook my head. Before me, in a shining glow, I saw a still more splendid vision. Holding down my swelling excitement, trying to behave with modesty and dignity, like a real scientist, I answered:

"We have discovered the disease. And the germ which causes that disease. Now we must produce the vaccine which will cure it. When we have that, we have everything, perfect and complete."

It was a glorious, a dazzling thought. Her eyes kindled.

"We should telephone Professor Challis."

"To-morrow," I said. I felt, jealously, that for the present our triumph must belong to us alone.

She seemed to understand, and as she smiled, a further surge of elation swept over me, toppling my dignity, undermining my pretence of calm.

"My dear Dr. Law," I smiled back at her, "this is an occasion which will go down in history. We really ought to celebrate. Will you have dinner with me to-night?"

She hesitated, her cheeks still warm with ardour, and glanced at her watch.

"They'll be expecting me at home."

"Oh, do come," I said eagerly. "It's early. You'll get your train all right."

As she looked at me with bright eyes in which there lay also a faint entreaty, I jumped to my feet, full of confidence and joy. I laughed as I helped her into her coat.

"We've worked pretty hard. We deserve a little treat."

I took her arm gaily as we went out.

CHAPTER VI

IN OLD GEORGE STREET, not far away, there stood
a small French restaurant, the Continental, which I had
occasionally patronized in company with Spence and
which I now decided was exactly right for our present
entertainment. Kept by a widow, an Alsatian named
Madame Brossard, whose husband had taught languages
at the neighbouring public school, it was a humble establishment, but it was clean, the cuisine was good, and even
in this northern atmosphere it had maintained something
of a native character. The floor was sanded, the coarse
checked napkins were folded like fans and tucked into
tinted wine glasses, each little table bore a red-shaded
rush-light which cast a romantic glow upon the bone-
handled cutlery.

As we entered, Madame bowed to us from her desk
behind the *caisse* and the youthful waiter, clad in a seedy
dress suit too large for him, showed us to a table in the
corner. We were early and, apart from some regular
customers dining at a long table in the centre of the room,
the place was pleasantly empty. In high spirits we discussed the menu, written with violet copying ink in an
angular hand, and ordered *soupe aux oignons, escalope de
veau, soufflé à l'orange*, and coffee.

"It's awfully nice here," Jean said, looking about her
with an animated expression. "We might be in Paris." She
saved herself with a little grimace. "For all I know
about it."

"Let's pretend we are," I answered gaily. "We've come
in from the Sorbonne . . . as described by our friend
Challis. We're immensely famous scientists . . . can't you

see my beard! . . . And we've just made a world-shaking discovery which will cover us with unbounded glory."

"So we have," she exclaimed, practically.

I gave a little shout of laughter. Thrilled by a sense of triumph, escaped from the heavy harness of routine, my usual reticence was gone, a joyous intoxication pervaded me. When the waiter brought our soup and a long thin crusty roll I addressed him in French. As he shook his head, looked apologetic, and answered me in broad Scots, Jean burst out laughing too.

"What were you saying to that poor boy?" she asked when he had gone.

"Something he was too young to understand." I leaned across the table. "I shall tell you later."

We began our soup, which was delicious, filled with thin slices of crisp onion and heaped with grated cheese. In the elation which possessed us we were lifted high above ourselves, buoyant on the crest of our success. The waiter, now our friend, brought, with an air, the carafe of red wine which was included with the *table d'hôte*. Tremulous with excitement, my heart singing with happiness, I poured out two glasses of this simple vintage which was still foaming from the cask.

"Let's drink to our success."

Her gaze wavered slightly, but only for an instant for, as though carried away by a consciousness of the occasion, she took first a sip, then finished the glass.

"Not bad." I nodded approvingly. "When in Paris do as the Parisians. Besides . . . remember that you are now a stout, though still attractive, middle-aged woman who has had a hard day chasing agglutinins at the Sorbonne. As Saint Paul suggested, you need a little wine for your stomach's sake."

She gazed at me reprovingly then, unexpectedly, her composure gave way, she smiled, and a moment later was again dissolved in laughter, a gay and playful laughter which sprang from nothing but the sweet exhilaration of her mood.

"Oh, Robert, you shouldn't . . ." she cried, wiping her eyes. "We're behaving like children."

From behind the cash register Madame Brossard, a stately figure, was regarding us with a benign and sympathetic eye.

When the *escalope* arrived I refilled our glasses and, irresistibly drawn, we began to discuss our adventures during the past three months, smiling now at the difficulties we had encountered, savouring again in every detail the splendour of achievement.

"Do you remember that day you lost your temper, Robert?"

"I deny, emphatically, that I ever lost my temper."

"Oh yes, you did. When I broke the centrifuge. You nearly boxed my ears!"

"Well, now I wish I had."

It was enough to set us off again.

As I bent towards my companion, now so bright and animated, with flushed cheeks and mischievous, laughing eyes, I saw more clearly than ever before the dual nature of her personality. The grave, devoted little Calvinist was gone, and from beneath that imprint of her upbringing, there emerged a warm and vivid creature who, having taken off her hat, leaned her elbows intimately on the table and surrendered unconsciously to her instincts as a woman.

A ground-swell of emotion caught me. As a vision of our relationship flashed before me I felt suddenly that I could not continue to endure the alternate blows of suffering and joy which had composed it. I had kept my word in this strange comradeship; yet, without my knowing it, the deep and painful charm of her presence in the laboratory had worn me down. Freed from the obsession of my work, I could no longer suppress the natural instinct of my heart. I swallowed the last of my coffee to get rid of the sudden choking in my throat.

"Jean," I said. "You've helped me so much in these last three months. Why?"

"Sense of duty." She smiled.

"Then you haven't minded working with me?"

"I've loved it!" she exclaimed, and added absently, "The experience will be so useful to me when I get to the settlement at Kumasi."

The remark, uttered without thinking, sent a knife into my heart.

"Don't," I said. "For God's sake . . . not to-night."

"No, Robert." She gave me a swift and swimming glance.

An immediate silence followed. As though fearful of having betrayed herself, she let her eyes fall.

This evening there was about her a warmth, a quick and vivid pulse of life which made me catch my breath. Overcome with love, I fought to preserve my sanity against this mounting enchantment. It was useless, everything yielded to the wild sweetness of this hour. In my side, fostered by our nearness, there came an actual pain, an inexpressible longing which found a momentary ease when, involuntarily, I took her hand and pressed it tight in mine.

She made no effort to withdraw her imprisoned fingers but, as though she too were striving to be calm, at last she sighed:

"I suppose we ought to go."

During these silent moments which brought us closer than ever before, which seemed formed of the longing that swirled between us, I had quite lost count of time. Now, as I summoned the waiter for the bill while Jean, with a subdued air, slowly put on her hat, I caught sight of the clock above the cash desk. It showed five minutes past eight.

"It's later than I thought," I said, in a low voice. "I'm afraid you've missed your train."

She turned to glance at the clock, then looked back at me. The warmth in her cheeks had deepened, her eyes were bright as stars, so bright that once again, she lowered her lashes in defence.

"I don't suppose it matters."

"When is the next?"

"Not until quarter to ten."

There was a pause. She had begun, almost agitatedly, to crumble a fragment of roll. The nervous movement of her fingers, her downcast gaze, the quick pulse in her throat, made my heart miss a beat.

"Let's go, then."

I paid the bill and we went outside. The street was quiet, the sky overcast, the night air warm and still.

"What shall we do?" I only spoke for the sake of something to say. "Take a stroll in the Gardens?"

"Don't they close the gates at eight?"

"I forgot," I muttered. "I think they do."

We were standing under a street lamp in the deserted thoroughfare. A wave of recklessness passed over me. She was near to me, so near that all my resolutions were swept away in a wild torrent of desire. My heart was beating like mad. I could scarcely speak.

"Let's go back to the laboratory for a bit."

As we started to walk along the pavement I took her arm. We did not say a word. When we reached the Hall I opened the door of our work-room with my key. It was dark, but from the old gas-lamp in the courtyard there stole in a faint glimmer, which cast a lustre that was like a spell, both fatal and predestined, upon her upturned face. Her eyes were closed, the lids translucent, expectant and foredoomed. I felt her sweet breath upon my cheek. As though to still the trembling of her limbs, she clung to me, then we were in each other's arms, upon the little couch.

In the timeless and enchanted twilight, a warm numbness drugged my limbs, a stupor of happiness. The past was forgotten, the future extinguished, this moment now was everything. Her head lay back, exposing the thin arch of her throat, the tender hollow of her neck. Her eyes still were shuttered against the unearthly light, and her pale brow, gathered in a strange deep furrow, was drawn as though by pain. Then, through her quick and troubled breathing, and the rapid pulsing of her heart, which fluttered against her thin, opened blouse, like a frightened bird, I felt the upward rushing of all her being, uniting, soaring into oblivion with mine. Nothing, no tie of heaven or earth, restrained that ecstasy of flight.

CHAPTER VII

On Monday afternoon, four days later, Professor Challis came to see me. He had been away for the weekend at a hydropathic in Bute which he frequented occasionally to have treatment for the arthritis which was slowly crippling him. Finding my message upon his return, he had taken a cab from his house to the laboratory.

When he had shaken hands he laid down his hat and, flicking the raindrops from his umbrella, gazed round the room with an air of mild inquiry.

"Where is our young friend?"

Although I had been prepared for the question, to my annoyance, I coloured slightly.

"She isn't here to-day."

Standing warming his finger tips at the little charcoal stove, he gave me an oddly searching glance, as though surprised to find me here, alone, with a silent air.

"So everything has turned out well."

"Yes."

He shook his head.

"You are suffering from reaction, Robert. You are tired. Sit still and let me look for myself."

A few minutes later he turned to the bench and for the next half-hour occupied himself intently with the report I had prepared, making calculations in pencil upon the margin. Then, with great deliberation, he examined all my cultures. He stooped for a long time over the microscope, and finally slewed round stiffly upon the stool. He looked old, worn, and a little wistful, his cheeks more hollow than before. I saw that he was considerably affected.

"Robert . . ." He said, at last, with his mild eyes fixed on mine: "You must not become proud. Never. Science has no place for vanity or self-seeking. And after all, you are only at the beginning of your career. You have been lucky. Also, you have much to learn—everything, in fact. But what you have done warms my old heart."

After a moment of complete silence he went on:

"Of course, you could announce your discovery immediately. It is without doubt of immense importance. But I agree that it would be better, more perfect and scientific, to take a further three months and finish the work completely by producing a vaccine therapeutically effective in controlling this new disease. Is that what you wish to do?"

"Yes."

"Then you shall do it. But"—his eyes swept the room—"you cannot do it here."

He acknowledged my look of surprise with a slow nod of his head.

"It would be quite impossible to effect the final highly technical stages of your research under these makeshift conditions. I make no apologies, Robert; this was the best I could do for you at the time. But now I must do better. You require, absolutely, a modern, well-equipped laboratory. And there are three possible ways in which you can secure it."

Despite my suffering, I was listening to him with attention.

"In the first place, you can go to one of the large manufacturing drug houses, such as Wilson's or Harlett's. In the face of your present findings, either would be delighted, unquestionably, to offer you all their resources, a highly trained staff, and a large salary to produce your vaccine for sale, commercially, in bulk." He added: "That would be very profitable for everyone concerned."

He waited. Then, as I continued to gaze at him in

silence, without attempting to answer, a faint smile irradiated his lined features.

"So far so good," he said. "The second possibility: To go to Professor Usher."

This time I started involuntarily, but before I could speak he made a gesture of restraint with his thin brown hand.

"The good Professor is beginning to regret that he let you go." He gave a short chuckle, amused, rather than malicious. "From time to time I have caused him some curiosity . . . not to say chagrin . . . by speaking about your work."

"No," I said, in a low tone, and all the secret unrest now within me found expression in that single word.

"Why not? I assure you he would welcome you back to the Department."

"He put me out of the Department," I answered, from between my teeth. "I must go through with this on my own."

"Very well," Challis said. "There remains . . . Easter-shaws."

Forgetting momentarily the turmoil seething in my breast, I stared at him in utter amazement. Was he joking? Or had he suddenly gone out of his wits?

"You know that place?" he inquired.

"Of course."

Again he gave me his faint, grave smile.

"I am quite serious, Robert. They have a vacancy there for a resident medical officer. I have made representations to the superintendent, Dr. Goodall, and he is agreeable that you have the position for the next few months. It is an old institution, you understand, but they have made a recent addition, a complete modern laboratory, in which you would have full and unrestricted opportunity to finish, absolutely, your work."

There was a pause. I looked round the improvised test-room which I had at first despised, but to which I had now, in every way, become attached. Another change, I thought; why can't I for once be left alone?

"I'd rather not leave," I said slowly. "I'm used to it here."

He shook his head.

"It is a necessity, my boy, which was bound to arise. Not even Pasteur could produce a vaccine with this equipage. That is why I have all along been seeking another opening for you." As I still hesitated he asked mildly: "Perhaps you object to living in such a place as Eastershaws?"

"No," I answered, after a moment. "I suppose I could stick it."

"Then think it over, and let me know to-night. Without question, it is a laboratory of which one dreams." He stood up, patted me on the shoulder and pulled on his light-coloured gloves. "Now I must go. Again my congratulations." He took his umbrella, glanced at me over his shoulder. "And do not forget to give my regards to Dr. Law."

I made an indistinct answer as he went out.

I could not bring myself to tell him that I had not seen Jean for the past four days, that in my pocket there burned a letter from her, a pitiful, tear-stained note, filled with self-reproaches, with the deepest, the most desperate anguish of remorse.

Oh, God, what a fool I had been. In the warm delirium of those irretrievable moments I had not paused to consider how deeply the sense of wrong-doing would wound her artless and unaffected soul. I could still see her, as she left me, late that night, her face white and piteous, her lips quivering, and in her eyes the look of a wounded bird, a look so hurt, so mournful and despairing, it almost rent my heart.

Goodness was something one never thought of, at which perhaps one laughed. Yet it was the very substance of her being.

Once, when a child, I had broken a fragile vase of crystal. The same cruel sense of unconsolable bereavement occasioned by those scattered fragments was striking at me now. There were others, I knew, who went through "an affair" with apparent carelessness. Yet we, alas! unlike in every way, had this in common: we could not lay upon our wounds the salve of indifference. A phrase from her letter kept grinding through my brain.

The mistake we made was in thinking we could be together. We must never make that mistake again. I cannot, must not see you again.

A deep sigh broke from me. I felt, desolately, as though I had cast away, and lost for ever, a pearl of great price. Weary and unsettled, filled with a sort of burning sickness, I blamed myself bitterly. Yet we had crossed this invisible brink less because we were together than because of those forces which would have drawn us apart. And now? The end of enchantment . . . death of the heart? No. I longed for her more than ever, desired her with all my soul.

Abruptly, I stood up. Although since I had received her letter I had thought of nothing else, I made a great effort now to shake off my despondency and to fix my mind on this offer which had come from Challis. My mood was not attuned to the idea, yet I had to admit the justice of his arguments. And after, in restless brooding fashion, I had paced the floor for perhaps an hour, I decided to accept. As it was nearly half-past five, I locked up and set out for the surgery in the Trongate.

The waiting-room, as usual, was hot and overcrowded, filled with a prevailing odour, with hushed murmurs, coughs, heavy breathing and the shuffling of feet on the bare floor. Condensed moisture was running down the chocolate-coloured walls. As I took my place at the desk, Dr. Mathers came bustling in with a slip of paper in his hand.

"Full house to-night, Shannon. Business is good. I wonder if you'd mind doing these calls for me when you get through."

There were five visits written on the slip he handed me. Gradually, in an off-hand, genial manner, he had been increasing my work until now I was doing far more than that originally agreed between us.

"All right," I said, in a flat voice. "But I'd like to talk to you."

"Go ahead."

"I'm afraid I'm leaving."

According to his custom, he had begun to transfer handfuls of cash, the fees taken during his afternoon round, from his trouser pockets into the chamois bag, but now he stopped abruptly and looked at me sharply. After a moment he began to laugh.

"I wondered how long it would be before you tried to hold me up for a rise. How much do you want?"

"Nothing."

"Come off it, Shannon. You're not a bad chap. I'll give you another guinea a week."

"No," I said, with averted eyes.

"Two guineas, then, damn it."

When I shook my head his expression altered and became serious. With his foot he closed the door in the face of the waiting patients, sat down on the edge of the desk and considered me.

"This is a fine thing to land on a man when he's going off for the evening. I'm taking the missus and Ada to Hengler's Circus. You've no idea how much they liked you when they met you the other day. Now tell me. How much do you really want?"

I had to hold myself in check. In my present state of mind, it revolted me, the manner in which he reduced everything to the common denominator of cash.

"Money has nothing to do with it."

He did not believe me—impossible that I should not care for the precious stuff. He bit his thumbnail, eyeing me calculatingly, all the time.

"Look here, Shannon." It came with a rush. "I've taken to you. We've all taken to you. I don't say you're much of a doctor yet, but I could teach you. The thing is, you're dependable. You're honest. You don't let the half-crowns stick to your fingers. I've been meaning to put this proposition up to you for a long time. Now listen. Come in with me here, as a full-time assistant, at two-fifty, no, say even three hundred a year. If you do well, in twelve months, I'll take you into partnership, and let you pay out of receipts. Can you beat that? This practice is a regular gold-mine. We'll work it together. Why, if Ada and you was to hit it off, we might make it a family business, and in the fullness of time you would succeed me."

"Oh, go to hell." My nerves suddenly gave way. "I don't want to succeed you. I don't want your money. Or anything else."

"Oh, come now," he muttered, quite taken aback. "I gave you a job, didn't I, when you were down and out?"

"Yes," I almost shouted. "And I'm grateful for it. That's why I've let you sweat me to death these past three months. But now I've had enough. I'm sick of picking half-crowns out of one-room tenements to shove in your shammy bag. Keep your gold-mine to yourself. I want no part of it."

"It's not possible," he said, staring at me. "I make you

a gilt-edged offer. And you throw it in my teeth. You're crazy."

"All right," I said. "We'll leave it that way. Now let me get on with the work."

I banged the admission bell on the desk and straight away the first patient, an old man, came shambling in. As I began to examine him Dr. Mathers continued to stare at me with his hat pushed back on his head, in complete bewilderment. Finally, he took up the bag of money, locked it securely in the safe and, without another word, went out. I regretted my outburst immediately he had gone. He was not a bad-hearted fellow, and he gave good service to the district, but his relentless quest of a full money-bag was more than I could bear.

It was past eleven o'clock when I finished the last call. I made my way towards the Globe, tired out, yet knowing that I would not sleep. Now that I was no longer occupied, the pain returned and, like a sharp-toothed animal, started gnawing at my breast. Yet, as I tramped through the damp streets, I sneered at my suffering. What a model I would make for the gay, successful Lothario! Young Romeo . . . Casanova . . . these were the names I threw at myself with bitter self-derision.

When I reached my hotel room I tore off my clothing and flung myself into bed. I lay there in the darkness, stiffly, with tight-shut eyes. But as I tried to get to sleep these words branded themselves upon my brain: *I must never see you again . . . never . . . never.*

BOOK FOUR

CHAPTER I

A WEEK LATER, towards nine o'clock in the evening,
I was carrying my bag along a deserted road, straining my
eyes in the misty darkness for the first sight of Eastershaws
Place, still quite invisible in the illusory emptiness of the
night. I had missed my train at Winton and, arriving an
hour late at Shaws Junction, which lies in the lonely,
wooded pastures of Lothian, some forty miles from the
city, I found no conveyance awaiting me. At the village
station they had given me directions, yet in that deserted
countryside I would almost certainly have lost my way but
for striking a high and solid wall, topped by a row of iron
spikes. I had followed this for the past ten minutes and
now, with a sudden sweep, it brought me to the entrance
gates, sentinelled by a turreted stone lodge with a lantern
in the window.

Setting down my bag, I knocked upon the heavy, nail-
studded door which gave access to the lodge. After a short
interval someone plucked the lantern from the window
and came out of the lodge, an unseen figure peering from
behind the gate.

"Who is it?"

I gave him my name, adding:

"You're expecting me, I think."

"I know nothing about you. Where's your pass?"

"I haven't a pass. But surely they told you I was
coming?"

"They did not."

The gateman appeared on the point of returning to the
lodge and of leaving me in the outer darkness. But at that
moment, another lantern swung into being, and a

feminine voice, high, rather pretentiously cultured, and with an Irish accent, came from behind the porter.

"Is that Dr. Shannon? All right, Gunn, open up and let him in."

Not without some grumbling from the lodge-keeper, the wrought-iron gates swung open. I picked up my bag and stepped forward.

"You've got your gear with you. Good. Come along."

My conductress, so far as could be made out by the sickly lantern light, was a woman of about forty, bareheaded, wearing blue glasses and a loose ulster of rough tweed. As the gates clanged shut, while we set off up a long, dark drive, she introduced herself.

"I'm Dr. Maitland, in charge of the Women's Side." I brushed against a clump of shrubs, and almost missed my footing. "Dr. Palfrey would have met you . . . he looks after Men's East and West, but it's his half-day and he has gone to Winton." After a due pause, she added: "That's our main building straight ahead."

I raised my eyes. Some distance in front, upon a slight eminence, a castellated shape was dimly visible, a honeycomb of lights which swam hazily in the moist blackness. The mist subdued these lights, gave to them a quality luminous and elusive. As I watched, striding on, some lights went out and others came to being, which made the constellation dance and flutter.

The end of the avenue brought us at last under the high façade, and Maitland advanced to a stone portico illuminated by an overhead lamp in a metal grille. Pausing, key in hand, at the top of the wide and shallow granite steps, she explained:

"This is Gentlemen's South. Your quarters are here."

Within, the hall was large and lofty, tessellated in black and white marble, with an alabaster statue at the end and three dark enormous landscapes, in oils and heavy gilt, upon the walls. Two buhl cabinets flanked by green-and-gold state chairs completed a picture which stupefied the senses by its rococo splendour.

"I hope you approve." Maitland seemed to be hiding a smile. "Entrance to Valhalla, eh?"

Without waiting for an answer, she continued up the broad carpeted staircase, to the third floor. Here, using, with remarkable dexterity, the same key, which I now saw to be attached to her waist by a thin steel cable, she threw open the door of a self-contained suite.

"Here we are. And you know the worst. Bedroom, sitting-room and bath. Complete Victorian-Gothic."

Despite her cool amusement, the rooms, although somewhat archaic in their style of furnishing, were unusually comfortable. In the sitting-room, where the chenille curtains were already drawn, a coal fire threw a warm glow upon the brass fender and red pile carpet. There were two easy chairs and a sofa, a reading lamp beside a secretaire which held shelves of leather-bound books. The bedroom beyond showed a snug mahogany bed, the tub in the bathroom was of thick rounded porcelain. I was tempted, with a stab of bitterness, to tell my superior companion that, by contrast with the inadequacies I had experienced at the Globe, this was luxury.

"Want to unpack?" she asked, standing discreetly near the doorway. "Or perhaps you'd like some supper sent up?"

"Yes, I would. If it isn't too much trouble."

I dropped my bag behind the sofa, and while she rang the bell beside the mantelpiece and ordered something for me, I had a better look at her. She was extremely plain, with a mottled, shiny pink complexion and drab-coloured hair untidily gathered into a knot at the back of her head. Her eyes were obviously weak, for even behind her violet lenses, the lids were visibly red and everted. As though deliberately to accentuate her lack of beauty, she was dowdily dressed, beneath her ulster, in a pink-striped flannel blouse and a baggy tweed skirt.

In five minutes a maidservant wearing a bulgy black uniform and starched white apron came in silently with the tray. She was short and stocky, almost a dwarf, with muscular black-stockinged calves and a grey, expressionless face.

"Thank you, Sarah," Maitland said pleasantly. "That seems nice. By the by, this is Dr. Shannon. I know you'll look after him well."

The maid kept her eyes upon the carpet, with no relaxation of her drawn blankness. But suddenly she bobbed, an automatic little curtsy. Without speaking, she went out.

I followed her with my eyes, then turned to my companion in meaning interrogation.

"Yes." Maitland nodded carelessly. She watched me with her challenging, half-mocking smile as I poured a cup of coffee and began to eat a sandwich.

"They do one rather well here. Miss Indre, who looks after the housekeeping, is most efficient. Incidentally, I'm not going to drag you round the staff for introductions. Palfrey is the man you'll see most of; you breakfast with him at Men's East every morning. Then there's Dr. Goodall . . . our Chief . . . that was his house, with the red blinds, on the left of your entrance."

"Oughtn't I to report to him to-night?" I looked up.

"I'll let him know you're here," Maitland answered.

"What are my duties?"

"Morning and evening rounds. Deputize for Palfrey on his day off and for me on mine. Official duty in the refectory. Occasional dispensary. Otherwise make yourself generally useful and agreeable to the good people of our little world. It's quite simple. I understand you're doing some research. You'll have ample chance for that between times. Here's your pass key."

From her coat pocket she produced a key, similar to her own, with a length of fine steel chain attached.

"You'll soon get the knack of it. I warn you that you'll get nowhere without it in Eastershaws. Don't lose it."

There was no mockery in Maitland's manner as she handed over the large, old-fashioned key, incredibly smooth and polished like silver from constant use.

"Well, I fancy that's about everything. I'm off now to see the Duchess. She's been quite obstreperous and needs a good lecture and a spot of heroin."

When she had gone I finished my supper, which was very different from the usual hospital food, and altogether in keeping with this sumptuous establishment. I wondered if I should make a short tour of inspection with my new, indispensable key. As I came up the staircase with Maitland I had observed, on each landing, a mahogany door with faded lettering above, and thick glass panels through which there was a vista of a long gallery, faintly illumined, reaching out mysteriously to another door, a further gallery.

Despite Professor Challis's recommendation, already borne out, that this place was one of the best of its kind, a vague disquiet troubled me. In the profession one always tends to look askance at asylum work as being just a little off the normal track. There are some splendid people in that service, of course, but on the other hand some who are distinctly queer—and who get queerer, as time goes on. It is an easy life and much medical flotsam drifts into it. Besides, once you're in, somehow it is less easy to get out. Not to put too fine a point on it, some of these peculiar mental states are as "catching" as the infectious fevers.

However, I would have to take these chances. I got up abruptly. My bed had been neatly turned down, disclosing linen whiter and finer than any I had known. Retrieving my bag from behind the sofa, I unpacked, distributing my text-books, papers, and few poor belongings to the best advantage. The previous incumbent, name unknown, had not troubled to remove all his possessions, leaving a half-tin of cigarettes, an old red-striped bath robe, several novels, and a score of knick-knacks scattered in careless profusion.

I had only one small photograph, cheaply framed in passe-partout, a snapshot taken, one sunny day, on the moors behind Gowrie: a simple, open little face, in sepia, with wind-blown curls and a pointed, courageous chin . . . with dark eyes smiling . . . could one believe it . . . actually, smiling with a strange awakened happiness. Were they smiling now? At least, as I placed it on the mantel-piece, beside the clock, I had no answering smile. Instead, I went over to the calendar on the secretaire and, with a queer, fixed expression, I put a mark opposite the date JULY 31.

At that moment, a quick knock upon the door caused me instinctively to start and, as I saw the tall and craggy figure upon the threshold, I realized that my visitor was the Superintendent.

"Good evening, Dr. Shannon." His voice was mild and halting. "Welcome to Eastershaws."

Long and loosely built, Dr. Goodall had a gaunt and sagging air, with iron-grey hair that needed cutting hanging untidily over his collar. His face was long and saturnine, with a biggish nose, undershot chin, and heavy-lidded, jaundiced eyes which, although aloof, were deeply human, warm with understanding, and holding strange hypnotic depths.

"I have heard much of you from Professor Challis." He smiled meditatively. "It struck me you must be anxious to see our laboratory."

With a gesture, he indicated that I should accompany him. We went downstairs and, by a tiled subway, lit by

222

electric frosted domes, he led me a considerable distance under the main building, then up an incline to a small central courtyard, open to the stars, but surrounded by high walls. Silently unlocking another door, he switched on the light.

"Here we are then, Dr. Shannon. I trust you will find it satisfactory."

I was speechless. I could only gaze in dumb wonder, completely overcome. Naturally I had hoped for a reasonably good work-room, although in the light of my past experience I had not dared to build upon it. But this exceeded even my wildest expectation. It was the finest small unit I had ever seen, better even than the Department laboratory, with rack upon rack of stoppered reagents, an Exton scopometer, conditioned hoods, electric grinder, and sterilizing vault—all fitted up, from the tiled walls to the last pipette, regardless of expense.

"I'm afraid," Goodall commented with mild apology, "it hasn't been used much. Some of the apparatus may need adjusting."

"But it's perfect." My voice failed me.

He smiled faintly.

"It is a recent addition. And we had the best technical advice when we installed it. I am happy to think that it is to see some service."

In that remote yet sympathetic manner he concluded:

"We shall expect great things of you. I am a lonely bachelor, Dr. Shannon. Eastershaws is my child. If you can bring credit to it, you will make me happy."

We retraced our steps. In the hallway, beneath the staircase which led to my rooms, he paused, that heavy-lidded gaze once again barely touching mine.

"I trust you are satisfied with what Eastershaws can do for you. Your quarters are quite comfortable?"

"More than comfortable."

Another pause.

"Good night then, Dr. Shannon."

"Good night."

When he had gone, I entered my room, my head whirling from the impact of his strange, compelling personality.

I undressed slowly, took a hot bath, and got into bed. As I settled myself to sleep I heard, through the overhanging silence, a sudden, wailing cry. It came like the wild and desolate hooting of an owl. I knew that it was not an owl, yet I did not care. I had no place now for dismay.

The cry was repeated, fading slowly into the outer darkness.

CHAPTER II

NEXT MORNING, from the small iron balcony which spanned the coping of my window, I was able to view the impressive prospect of Eastershaws.

The mansion, built of grey granite, shimmering in the morning air, was in the baronial style, with castellated gables, and four massive turrets. In front lay a broad, balustrated terrace with a central fountain surrounded by ornamental designs in boxwood. A lawn, edged by rose beds, stretched beyond, merging to a stretch of playing sward, served by a little Tyrolean chalet. Avenues cut across the green acres, and the high stone wall which circled the wide estate gave to it an air of privacy, as though it were some privileged domain.

I shaved and dressed; then, as it struck eight o'clock, I set out to breakfast with Dr. Palfrey. In the sitting-room above Men's East I discovered a short, plump, pink, baldish man of fifty seated at table eating vigorously behind the morning paper. Our eyes met.

"My dear fellow, come along in." Still eating, he raised his hand in welcome, then completed the gesture by filling his mouth with buttered toast. "You're Shannon, of course. I'm Palfrey—Edinburgh man, took my degree in '99. Kedgeree, bacon and eggs over there . . . and here . . . the coffee. A lovely morning . . . blue sky and clear air . . . what we call a 'real Eastershaws day.' "

Palfrey had a warm, inoffensive, and slightly foolish air, his cheeks were smooth and chubby—with every movement they wobbled like jellies. He looked thoroughly washed and manicured, his cuffs were starched, gold pince-nez hung primly round his neck by an invisible cord. Across his pink scalp a few strands of pale hair, faintly speckled with ginger, were carefully arranged from the fringe behind his ears. He kept dabbing his rosy lips and white moustache with his napkin.

"I should have made your acquaintance last night. But I was out. Out in the outland, as we say. At the opera. *Carmen*. Ah! Wonderful, unhappy Bizet. To think that he died, broken-hearted, after the failure of the opening production at the Opéra Comique, without an inkling of the glorious success it would afterwards attain. I have been to that opera precisely thirty-seven times. I have heard Bressler-Gianoli, Lehmann, Mary Garden, Destinn . . . de Reszke as Don José, Amato as Escamillo. We are most fortunate to have a Carl Rosa season in Winton." He hummed a few bars from the "Toreador Song," strumming with his fingers on the *Herald* before him. "In the critique here it says Scotti was in good voice. I should think so! Ah, that moment when Micaela, emblem of sweetness, enters the wild and rocky defile of the smugglers' camp! '*I try not to own that I tremble.*' Exquisite . . . melodious . . . superb! Are you interested in music?"

I gave an inarticulate murmur.

"Ah! You must come down to the piano in the auditorium with me. I go there most evenings, to run through a few things. I might as well confess, music is my delight. I count the three great moments in my life . . . when I heard Patti sing 'Sicilian Vespers,' Galli-Curci 'Pretty Bird' from *The Pearl of Brazil*, and Melba Massenet's 'Sevillana.' '

He ran on like this until I had finished breakfast; then, with a ladylike gesture, examined his wrist watch.

"The Chief has asked me to take you round. Come along."

He led off fussily, his short, plump legs twinkling with

unexpected speed along the subway—then, taking a concrete incline to the left, as by an astral materialization, he brought us unexpectedly to daylight in the corridor beneath my own quarters.

Here an obese, stupid-looking man of fifty in an untidy, grease-stained grey uniform and rubber-soled shoes was padding up and down officiously. At Palfrey's appearance he threw out his stomach and saluted with a mixture of obsequiousness and pomp.

"Morning, Scammon. Dr. Shannon—this is Samuel Scammon—our Head Attendant . . . and also, may I add, our valued conductor of the Eastershaws Brass Band."

Joined by Scammon's assistant, Attendant Brogan, a young, good-looking fellow with a bold blue eye, we advanced towards the first gallery, over which I now saw, in faded gold, the name BALACLAVA. Like a conjurer, Scammon manipulated his key. We were inside.

The gallery was long, lofty and restful, well lit by a row of high windows upon one side and with a score of doors, leading to the individual bedrooms, upon the other. The furniture, like that in the entrance below, was of buhl, the carpets and hangings, though faded, were rich. There were easy chairs in plenty, racks of books and periodicals, in one corner a revolving globe of the world. The atmosphere was that of a comfortable but old-fashioned club, smelling of age, soap, leather and furniture polish, just faintly tinged with the scent of the commode.

About twenty gentlemen sat quietly enjoying the gallery's amenities. In the foreground two were occupied by a game of chess. Another, in the corner, with a meditative finger, was revolving the geographic sphere. Several had their morning newspaper. Others had nothing, but kept still, very erect, on chairs.

Palfrey, having scanned the report which Scammon handed to him, swept forward blithely.

"Morning, gentlemen. Having a good game?" Beaming, he placed a companionable hand on the shoulder of each chess player. "It's the most glorious day outside. You'll enjoy your little walk, I promise you. I shan't be a moment running through . . . then you may be off."

He moved down the gallery, pausing at intervals, full of good humour and affable advice. His flow of small talk, though somewhat to a pattern, never failed. He heard complaints with an indulgent and soothing ear. He hummed between times. Yet he wasted not a minute in his expeditious passage.

ALMA was the next gallery, then came INKERMAN; altogether there were six and when, at last, we emerged to the ground-floor vestibule, having completed the entire circuit, it was almost one o'clock. Palfrey, without delay, escorted me into the fresh air and along the terrace towards the West Wing for luncheon.

"By the by, Shannon, perhaps I ought to warn you . . . Maitland and our housekeeper, Miss Indre, are a very close little mutual admiration society. They're not particularly enamoured of me." He passed this off airily. "I don't mind a bit. But it's all the more reason for us to support each other."

In a small parlour off the vestibule of Ladies' West, tastefully arranged as a dining-room, the square table set with fine linen and shining silver for four, Miss Indre and Maitland were already waiting. The housekeeper greeted me with a small, quiet inclination of her head, a slender, faded, aristocratic woman of over fifty, immaculate and fragile in a blue voile uniform with narrow soft white wrist-bands and collar.

As we sat down veiled glances of understanding and quiet, intimate remarks passed between the two women. It was a strained and uncomfortable meal. After the soup a joint of meat was brought in and placed before

Palfrey, who carved in an embarrassed manner, humming strenuously as he sliced the undercut on to the various plates. Occasionally, with masculine directness, Maitland addressed a breezy remark in my direction—she asked me if I would make up the stock solutions after lunch for her sister-in-charge. Once or twice when Palfrey spoke she shot an amused glance at Miss Indre.

Oppressed by my morning experiences, and by the unexpected difficulty of adjusting myself to this strange environment, I kept silent. When Palfrey rose, after the dessert, with a muttered excuse, I followed him towards the terrace.

"These women!" he exclaimed. "Didn't I tell you? I can't stand these two, Shannon. In fact, I detest all women. I thank Heaven I have never had anything to do with one of them in my life."

He flounced off to take duty in the refectory, leaving me to proceed, with mixed emotions, towards the dispensary.

Here, Sister Shadd and a nurse were awaiting me, with an official air. Shadd was a coarse, middle-aged, strongly bosomed woman with a good-natured eye. She was examining her watch, pinned on the front of her uniform, as I came in.

"Good afternoon, Doctor. This is Nurse Stanway. May we have our supplies?"

As Shadd placed her empty basket on the counter, the nurse glanced at me, sideways, and across her pale, composed, flattened face there passed a faint smile. She was about twenty-five years of age, dark-haired, carrying herself with an air of indifference, and wearing a wedding ring on her right hand.

"Let me show you where things are," Shadd said. "A friend in need is a friend indeed."

I was to discover that Sister Shadd had a collection of proverbs such as, "Six and half a dozen," "It never rains

229

but it pours," "A stitch in time saves nine," which she constantly produced with an air of wisdom. Now, very cheerfully, she aided me to fill her basket with the standard drugs, mostly hypnotics; then, with another glance at her pinned-on watch, she took her departure, remarking over her shoulder, as she went through the door, in that friendly, well-disposed tone she adopted towards Stanway:

"Get the East dressings from Dr. Shannon, Nurse. Then come back and help me in the linen-room."

There was a pause when Nurse Stanway and I were left alone, an alteration of the atmosphere, an imperceptible drop from the official plane. As she slid forward her basket she gave me a casual glance.

"You don't mind if I sit down?"

I made no objection. I guessed she wanted to get into talk with me, but although I had a rule of never looking twice at any nurse, this place, frankly, was getting on my nerves, and I felt that a little human conversation might help.

Perching herself upon the counter, she gazed at me, expressionless, yet with slightly mocking air. She was not exactly good-looking, she was too pale, with pale, full lips, flat high cheek-bones, and a pushed-in nose. Yet she had an attractive quality. Under her eyes there were faint blue shadows, and the skin there was stretched tight. Her black hair, cut square across her forehead, had a bluish sheen.

"Well," she said, coolly. "What brought you to Eastershaws?"

In the same manner, I answered:

"I just came in for a rest."

"You'll get it. This place is practically a morgue."

"Some of it seems pretty old-fashioned."

"It was built over a century ago. I shouldn't think it's changed much since then."

"Don't they use any modern methods?"

"Oh, yes. Not Palfrey, poor dear. He only eats, sleeps, and hums. But Maitland sweats away at hydrotherapy, shock-treatment, and psycho-analysis. She's very earnest, means well, quite decent, in fact. Goodall's idea is the best. He lets well alone. But he sees that the patients are taken care of, and he sort of helps them along by pretending that they're normal."

"I like Goodall. I met him last night."

"He's all right. Only he's a little cracked himself." She glanced at me satirically. "We're all slightly off the beam."

I filled the East list for her, gauze, lint, and g.p. tissue, solutions of valerian, bromide, and chloral hydrate. I had never met paraldehyde before, and as I took the stopper from the bottle the ether smell of it almost knocked me over.

"That's powerful stuff."

"Yes. It has a kick in it. Not bad for a hangover."

She laughed briefly at my surprised expression, and crooked her arm in the handle of the basket. As she moved to the door, she gave me, from her oblique eyes, that peculiar, direct half-smile.

"It's not so bad here, when you know your way around. Some of us manage to have a fairly decent time. Drop into our sitting-room when you're bored."

As she went out I found myself frowning slightly. Not that I was puzzled. Although she was quite young, her air of experience, the stretched blue skin beneath her eyes, that pushed-in, expressionless face which gave nothing away, suggested an eventful history.

When I had finished in the dispensary it was only three o'clock, and now I was free to begin my own work. With a sigh of relief, I went outside. But there I drew up suddenly, arrested by the scene before me.

On the lawn beneath the terrace a group of gentlemen had been marshalled by Chief Attendant Scammon for a game of bowls which, from their frequent exclamations, was proving highly exciting. The tennis courts on the other side of the Tyrolean pavilion were in full blast, with Palfrey umpiring one match. From the pavilion itself came the strains of brass music: pleasant little broken snatches, runs and rallentandos from one of Sousa's marches: indicating that the Eastershaws band was engaged in practice. Colour was added by a party of ladies, headed by Sister Shadd, trailing in elegant fashion—some were even sporting parasols—round the orchard. Nor was the picture entirely given over to diversion. In the kitchen gardens a large body of men from the East Wing were working industriously, spaced at regular intervals, hoeing the newly planted furrows with well-directed strokes.

I looked at the scene for a long time, then gradually a strange and startled feeling came upon me, a recurrence, an intensification of the sensation which had troubled me ever since I set foot in the Place. This was pleasant, this was pretty, but, my God, it was almost more than I could stand. My nerves were not in a good state, perhaps, but I'd had about enough of Eastershaws for the present, with these Crimean galleries, and the gentlemen inside them, and Palfrey, and the pass key with chain attached, the doors with no handles, the smell of Sanitas, and all the rest of it. In fact, I was getting a queer, confused dizziness at the back of my head. I spun round sharply, went straight to the laboratory and locked the door. As I shut my window against the distant cries of the bowlers, a terrible weight of desolation, of loneliness, struck at me and crushed me down. Suddenly, despairingly, with all my heart, I longed for Jean. What was I doing in this accursed spot? I should be with her. We should be together, I couldn't stand it here . . . alone.

But at last I conquered myself and, at the bench, set myself to begin the last phase of my research.

CHAPTER III

On the thirty-first of July, that date I had so
determinedly anticipated, I obtained Dr. Goodall's con-
sent and started, early, for the graduation ceremony at the
University. Although Palfrey had occasionally tried to
enveigle me to one of his favourite operas and Maitland
several times had suggested that I ought to "go out"—
because of my activities in the laboratory, since my arrival
I had not once been beyond the confines of the Place.
I was beginning to settle down. In fact, it felt unreal to be
in a tram again, and to see cars and people moving at will
about the streets.

When, towards eleven o'clock, I reached the summit of
Fenner Hill, the Moray Hall was already crowded with
students and their relatives, buzzing with the usual antici-
pation, its musty dignity rent, from time to time, by the
demonstrations of the younger and more exuberant undergraduates, who were singing student songs, chasing up the
aisles, whooping and catcalling, unrolling paper streamers.
It all looked childish and stupid to me. I did not go in,
but hung about in the crowd standing by the door, hoping
to meet with Spence or Lomax and, in the meantime,
searching the auditorium and balconies with a strained
and nervous gaze.

Jean was not visible. But suddenly, amongst that sea of
faces, I caught sight of her family, her father, mother, and
Luke, seated in the second row of the left side balcony,
with Malcolm Hodden beside them. All were in their best
clothes, bending forward eagerly, with such animation, so
pleased, proud and expectant, I had to repress an instinctive reaction of hostility. I took cover behind the nearest
pillar.

At that moment, by the dexterous use of his umbrella, a corpulent spectator poked and manœuvred into position beside me—then, with a gasp of triumph, accosted me.

"Hello, my dear Dr. Robert Shannon."

I found myself confronted by that fount of gossip and good nature, the ever-beaming Babu Chatterjee.

"How extremely agreeable to meet you, sir. We miss you continually at Rothesay, but, of course, follow your career with interest. Is it not a splendid assembly here to-day?"

"Splendid," I agreed, without enthusiasm.

"Oh, come, sir! Tee hee! No disparagement to our dear Alma Mater." His remarks were punctuated by little grunts as, periodically, from the thrusting crowd, he received an elbow in his abdomen. "Although I am not myself graduating, hoping to do so shortly, the splendid ceremonial pleases me greatly. I have not once missed it the past ten years. Come, sir. Shall we press forward and secure two front adjacent seats?"

"I think I'll wait here. I'm looking out for Spence and Lomax."

At that instant the great organ above us pealed out, drowning all other sounds; and, realizing that the proceedings had begun, a fresh wave of people pressed into the hall, swirling us apart, sweeping the Babu up the central aisle.

I held my ground for a few minutes, while the Principal made a short speech and, aided by Professor Usher, who stood beside him with the parchments, started the usual business of "capping" the long procession of graduates. But the crowd was too dense for me to view the spectacle; in any case I had no wish to see all of it, and, since my frustrated gaze kept stealing upwards to the balcony, the sight of Hodden and the Law family, smiling and applauding, became more than I could endure. In the face of protests and opposition, I fought my way out of the hall.

A public telephone booth stood in a corner of the cloisters, and, on an impulse, I entered and rang up the Pathology Department. But Spence was not there. Nor could I find him at his house. The phone simply rang; no one answered.

Defeated, I came out of the cabinet and went slowly up the worn, shallow stone stairway, along the corridor, to the robing-room. It was here that, for a fee of half a guinea or so, the students hired their gowns and hoods, and I knew that after the ceremony Jean would come back, to return her borrowed robes. This was the only place where I could be sure of finding her alone, and I sat down in a corner by the long wooden counter, to wait.

Under the depressing sound of forced applause, which rattled out every thirty seconds beneath me, my mood sank to depths of bitter sadness. A rush of returning graduates caused me to raise my head abruptly and presently, amongst the others, I saw Jean, hurrying along the corridor, wearing her gown over a new brown costume, new brown stockings and shoes. She was flushed, talking to the girl beside her, with an air of excitement, of momentary animation which, after these weeks of separation, cut me to the heart. Because I loved her I wished to find her bathed in tears.

She had not noticed me. Slowly and carefully, I got up and stood by the counter, close beside her. I was at her elbow, but she did not dream that I was there, and I did not say a word.

For several seconds nothing happened; then, all at once, she paused, arrested in the act of handing in her gown. She could not have seen me, yet the warm blood ebbed, slowly, from her face and neck, leaving her very white. For a long, long moment she remained inanimate—then, as by the exercise of an immense, an almost superhuman, effort she forced herself to turn her head.

I looked straight into her eyes. She seemed turned to stone.

"I wasn't invited, but all the same, I came."

A long pause. Her pale lips may have shaped an answer. But she could not speak it. I went on.

"I don't suppose you have a few minutes to waste? I'd like to speak to you alone."

"I am alone now."

"Yes, but we're sure to be interrupted here. Can't we go off somewhere for a bit? I seem to recollect that we've done it before."

"My people are waiting for me downstairs. I have to go back to them at once."

Although all my bones were melting towards her, I answered bitterly.

"I've kept out of your way for four weeks, I haven't contaminated you with my presence. I think I'm due a short conversation with you."

She moistened those pale dry lips.

"What good would it do?"

I looked at her cruelly. I had longed to see her and now that we were, at last, together, my one desire was to wound her as deeply as I could. I searched for the hardest and most cutting words.

"At least it would give us a chance to say goodbye. Now you've got your degree I've no doubt you'll be only too glad to be rid of me. You probably know I'm at Eastershaws. Yes. The asylum. I've come down even more in the world."

As I went on like this, causing the dark look of pain to deepen in her eyes, I suddenly saw a solid form advancing towards us. Quickly, I bent forward and, in a different tone, said:

"Jean. Come out and see me at Eastershaws . . . some afternoon . . . just once . . . for old time's sake."

I could see the struggle going on behind her pale, tormented brow then, even as I realized what it must mean to her, she barely whispered:

"Next Thursday, then . . . I may come."

No sooner had she spoken than Malcolm Hodden was upon us, breathing a little rapidly from having bounded upstairs, curving his arm around Jean's shoulders, as though to protect her from the jostling crowd, and at the same time giving me, with his steady blue eyes, a glance of quiet recognition.

"Come, Jean, dear," he reasoned, but without reproach. "We've all been wondering what was delaying you."

"Am I late?" she asked nervously.

"Oh, no." He smiled with reassuring calm, escorting her towards the steps. "I engaged the table for one o'clock— we have plenty of time. But Professor Kennerly is with your father and asking for you."

At the foot of the staircase, while Jean slipped away, without even a glance, to join her parents, who stood in a group near the quadrangle, Malcolm turned upon me his serious yet unhostile gaze.

"Don't look at me like that, Shannon. We are not enemies. Since we have a few minutes together, let us talk things over sensibly."

He led the way through the stone archway to the front terrace, where, at the University flagstaff, there stood, in an open space upon the summit of the hill, a circular iron bench. Seating himself, he made a sign for me to do likewise. His calm was admirable. He was, in fact, all that I was not. Strong, practical, dependable, with a clear eye and a fine physique, conscious of his own inner equilibrium, he showed no sensitive flinchings. There were no secret doubts or dark places in his soul. I envied him with all my imperfect, anguished heart.

"At least we have one thing in common," he began, as

237

though reading my mind. "We both want Jean to be happy."

"Yes," I said, my lips compressed.

"Then think, Shannon," he argued, logically. "Don't you see it is impossible? You and she are unsuited in every way."

"I love her," I said doggedly.

"But love isn't marriage," he answered quickly. "That is a serious undertaking. One simply cannot rush into it. You would be wretched, married."

"How can you tell? We would take our chance. Marriage is something inevitable . . . a calamity, perhaps, from which there is no escape . . . but not a blueprint for a new mission hall."

"No, no, Shannon." He countered my jibe with greater earnestness. "Marriage should confirm, and not disrupt two lives. Before you met Jean everything was arranged . . . her work . . . her life. She was settled, contented in her mind. And now you are asking her to give up all this, to estrange her family, cut herself off from the very sources of her being."

"None of these things need happen."

"Ah, that's what you think. Let me ask you a simple question. Would you like to attend service at Jean's chapel?"

"No."

"Exactly. Then how can you expect her to go to yours?"

"That's just the point. I don't. I have no wish to force her into anything. We should each have complete freedom of thought and action."

He shook his head, unconvinced.

"It's a pretty theory, Shannon. In practice it won't work. There are scores of opportunities for friction. And what about the children? Ask your own priest. He will tell you that I'm right. Your Church has always frowned on mixed marriages."

"Some have succeeded," I maintained, with heavy stubbornness. "We would be happy together."

"For a little while, perhaps," he said, almost with pity. "But in five years' time, just consider . . . a hymn tune overheard, a revival meeting in the street, some recollection of her childhood, the realization of what she has given up . . . she will look at you and hate you."

The words fell upon my ears like a knell. In the silence which followed I could hear the heavy drumming of the flag, transmitted through the pole, as though the vibrant wood were striving to be alive.

"Believe me, Shannon, I am trying to think only of Jean. To-day she had almost regained happiness when you reappeared. Do you wish to hurt her always? Ah, I know you better than that! As man to man, Shannon, I am sure your better nature will prevail."

He brought out his watch, encased in a horn guard, studied it, and, in a lighter key, declared:

"We are giving a little celebration for Jean. Lunch at the Windsor Hotel." He paused. "If circumstances were different, I would wish you to be with us. Is there anything more that I can say?"

"No," I said.

He stood up and, after a firm, forbearing pressure upon my arm, moved steadily away. And there I sat, hearing the drumming and singing of the flag, isolated by my own acts, trying not to hate Malcolm, feeling myself more and more an outlaw. A party of well-dressed visitors glanced at me curiously, in passing, then turned away polite eyes.

CHAPTER IV

BREAKING THE LONG SPELL of fine weather, Thursday dawned damp and misty. I watched anxiously for it to clear, but even at noon the sun was blanketed and, although it was not raining heavily, the lawns were drenched, and in the avenues a steady dripping came from the trees.

Immediately after lunch I walked to the Lodge, keyed, nervously, with longing. I was in good time, yet she had already arrived, and was sitting, neglected and distraught, in the waiting-room, which, since this was visiting-day, was noisy and steamy, crowded with the relatives of East Wing patients.

Concerned, I went forward and would have taken her hand had she not risen to her feet.

"Why didn't you ask the porter to telephone me?"

"It's my own fault." She gave me a distant, wavering smile. "I took an earlier train. It was a little difficult at home . . . and as I had nothing else to do, I just came out here."

"If I'd only known."

"It's nothing. I didn't want to disturb you. But they might have let me walk about the gardens."

"Well," I explained, "they have to take a few precautions here. It's like crossing from one country to another. We're an exclusive lot. But if you'd told Gunn you were a doctor, he'd have let you in right away."

Although I was trying to win her from her depression, she remained silent and withdrawn, looking small and forlorn in her raincoat and a soft hat with a grey wing all beaded with raindrops. My longing for her hurt me, yet I tried to force my stiff features to a semblance of composure.

"Well, never mind," I said, making a fresh start. "You're here . . . and we are together."

"Yes," she answered in a subdued voice. "It's a shame it's turned so damp."

In silence we walked up South Avenue, past the wet-roofed chalet, under the dripping trees, which stood silent, bent over the wet path as though cowed by the rain.

The misery of the weather hung over us, blurring all outlines in this lost and silent city. Would she never speak?

Suddenly as we approached the main building she raised her gaze slowly—then, at something visible behind me, gave a startled cry.

A body of men from the East Wing had loomed out of the mist, led by Scammon and his assistant Brogan, approaching in mass formation at the double. They were only exercising, but as the dark figures swung down on us, closely packed, their feet thudding rhythmically on the soft gravel, Jean closed her eyes, holding herself rigid until they had passed and the sound of their pounding footsteps was lost in the grey fog.

"I'm sorry," she said, at last, miserably. "I know it's absurd of me: I'm all on edge."

Everything was going wrong. Under my breath I cursed myself. The rain came on, quite heavy.

"Let's go in," I said. "I want to show you the laboratory."

After the raw outer air, it was comfortable in the laboratory, but although she removed her gloves she did not unbutton the collar of her raincoat. We stood side by side at the bench and, when her eyes had swept the place, she took up all the cultures, one by one, in a reminiscent way, as of something past, clouded by memory, never to be renewed.

"Careful," I murmured, as she touched the stopper of the strongest culture.

She turned towards me, and her dark dilated pupils softened slightly. Yet she said nothing. No one was there, we were together, but we were not alone.

"I've made a vaccine," I told her in a low voice. "But now I have a better idea. To extract and concentrate the nucleoprotein. Challis agrees it should be far more efficacious."

"Have you seen him lately?"

"No. I'm sorry to say he's laid up again, at Bute."

There was a pause. Her apparent calmness, this pretence of normality, made everything unreal. We stood and looked at each other as though hypnotized. It was suddenly chilly.

"You're cold," I said.

We went to my sitting-room, where Sarah had already lit a good fire. I rang the bell, and almost at once she brought up the well-laden tray I had asked her to prepare.

Sunk in a wide chair and warming her hands at the blaze, Jean drank a cup of tea gratefully, and ate one of the *petits fours* which I had brought in specially from Grant's. Her mood seemed flagging, as though the prospect of life were a load from which she shrank. I simply could not break this cold constraint which lay upon us. Yet, watching the colour flow back slowly to her pinched cheeks, I hoped that she was thawing out. She looked pathetically small and slight. As her fresh and tender bloom returned, a white heat burned in my breast. But my pride would not let me show it. In a stiff voice I said:

"I hope you feel better."

"Yes, thank you."

"This Place takes some getting used to."

"I'm sorry I was so silly outside. But here . . . It's as though someone never stops watching you."

Again there fell a silence in which the slow tick of the clock sounded like fate. The room was beginning to darken. Except for a flicker from the hearth, there was barely enough light for me to see her face, so still, as if asleep. A quiver went over my nerves.

"You have barely spoken all afternoon. You cannot forgive me . . . for what happened . . ."

She did not raise her head.

"I am ashamed," I said. "But I could not have been different."

"It is terrible to fall in love against one's will," she said at last. "When I am with you I no longer belong to myself."

This admission gave to me a feeling of hope, that grew, gradually, into a strange sense of power. I gazed at her across the shadows.

"I want to ask you something."

"Do you?" she said. Her face had a tense look, the look of someone expecting a blow.

"Let us get married. At once. At the registrar's office."

She seemed to feel, rather than to hear me, sitting silent and stricken, her head averted, as though trying to turn away.

Seeing her so helpless, a sudden exultation flamed over me.

"Why shouldn't we?" I insisted softly, rapidly. "Say you'll marry me. This afternoon."

Breathless, I waited for her to answer. Her eyelids were lowered, her face half dazed, as though the world rocked about her and she were lost.

"Say yes."

"Oh, I can't," she murmured, inarticulately, tormented, in the tone of one about to die.

"You can."

"No," she cried, facing round to me hysterically. "It is impossible."

A long, a heavy pause. That sudden cry had made of me an enemy, her enemy, the enemy of her people. I tried to collect myself.

"For God's sake, don't be so unloving, Jean."

"I must be. We have suffered enough. And others too. My mother goes about the house, looking at me, simply saying nothing. And she is ill. I have to tell you, Robert. I am going away for good."

The finality in her voice stunned me.

"It's all arranged. There's a party of us going out to West Africa on the maiden voyage of the new Clan liner, the *Algoa*. We sail in three months' time."

"Three months." I echoed her words—at least it was not to-morrow. But sadly, with enforced calmness, she shook her head.

"No, Robert . . . I shall be busy all that time . . . doing temporary work."

"Where?"

She flushed slightly, but her gaze did not waver.

"At Dalnair."

"The cottage hospital?" Surprise broke through my despair.

"Yes."

I sat dumb and overcome. She went on:

"There is a vacancy there again. They want to try a woman doctor for a change . . . a short, experimental appointment. The matron recommended me to the Committee."

Crushed by the news of her departure, I nevertheless kept trying, in a stupid sort of way, to picture her against the familiar background of the hospital, traversing the wards and corridors, occupying the very quarters that I had used. At last, I muttered brokenly:

"You did get on with Matron. You get on with everyone but me."

Her breast heaved. She gave me a strange, unnatural smile.

"If we had never met . . . it would have been better. With us, there is a penalty for everything."

I guessed her meaning. But although my eyes were smarting and my heart almost bursting, I struck back with a last, despairing bitterness.

"I won't give you up."

She was still calm, but tears were flowing down her cheeks.

"Robert . . . I'm going to marry Malcolm Hodden."

I stared at her, frozen. I barely whispered:

"Oh, no . . . no . . . you don't care for him."

"Yes, I do." Pale and tremulous, she defended herself with quivering distress. "He is a worthy, honourable man. We grew up together, went to school, yes, to Sunday school together. We worship in the same chapel. We have the same aims and objectives, he will be good for me in every way. In fact, when we are married we shall go out together on the *Algoa*, I as a doctor, Malcolm as head teacher in the settlement school."

I swallowed the enormous lump which had risen in my throat.

"It can't be true," I muttered, inaudibly. "It's all a dream."

"You and I are the dream, Robert. We must go back to reality."

I clenched my fists against my forehead and while, helplessly, I did so, she began in real earnest to cry.

It was more than I could stand. I got to my feet. At the same instant she rose, blindly, as though driven by the instinct to escape. We met. Then, for a moment, she was in my arms, weeping as though her heart would break, while my own heart was choked by a wild intoxication and delight. But as I held her more closely, she seemed suddenly to summon all her strength. Abruptly and passionately, she broke away.

"No . . . Robert . . . no."

The anguish in her face, in every line of her fragile, flinching form, held me rooted to the spot.

"Jean."

"No, no . . . never again . . . never."

She could not stop the sobs which choked her, sobs which wrung my heart, and made me long to soothe her upon my breast. But that look in her glistening eyes, broken and tortured, yet fiercely unwavering, welling up from the depths of her soul, drained me slowly of all hope. The burning words of love I meant to speak died upon my lips. The arms I had raised towards her fell to my side. There was a dull and heavy beating in my head.

At last, stiffly, she brushed away her tears with the back of her hand, then wiped her lips. With a face hard as iron, I helped her to put on her raincoat.

"I'll come with you to the gate."

We walked to the entrance lodge without a single word. The rivulets which channelled the avenue had a sound almost living, but our steps were dead upon the sodden ground. We drew up at the gateway. I took her fingers, wet with rain and tears, but quickly she disengaged them.

"Goodbye, Robert."

I looked at her as for the last time. A car rushed past in the road outside.

"Goodbye."

She faltered at that, but recovered herself with a shiver and hurried off, her eyes wrinkled up against fresh tears, not looking back. The next minute the heavy gate clanged shut; she was gone.

I came up the drive, sullen and wretched. Twilight was

falling and the rain at last had ceased. Above the western horizon the sky was livid, as though the sunset had committed bloody murder amongst the clouds. Suddenly, over the still Place, the evening bugle sounded and from the tall flagpole on the hill the flag descended, slowly, slowly, while outlined upon the ridge there stood, rigidly, in the tense attitude of salute, the erect and solitary figure of the inmate deputed to this task.

Long live Eastershaws, I thought bitterly.

Back in my room I found the fire almost dead. I gazed at the dull grey ashes.

CHAPTER V

I<small>T WAS</small> S<small>UNDAY</small>, and the bells of the ivy-clad church broke upon the Eastershaws air. As though to aggravate the darkness of my mind, the morning once again shone bright and warm. Fruit hung heavily on the orchard trees, and in the formal beds of the balustraded terrace geraniums and begonias traced out vivid arabesques.

From my window, as I finished dressing, heavy, and only half awake, I could see the inmates of the Place converging upon the holy building, a goodly sized Gothic structure of mellow brick, appropriately shaded by a cluster of tall elms.

The men of the East Wing came first, flanked by Brogan and three of Scammon's staff, a large and solid body, dressed in workmanlike grey, with strong boots and serviceable caps, most of whom worked in the fields or craft shops. Some were cheerful and smiling, others silent, a few gloomy—for there were "bad" morons amongst the "good" who were often at odds with the authorities. One group had a superior, though less hardy air, with darker suits and white starched collars—these were men who had risen and were entrusted with special tasks, such as checking cartloads of coal or wood at the weighbridge, or marking off the laundry, on paper sheets, with pen and ink. Palfrey, already in the porch, shepherded them in with a benign smile and pink nods of welcome.

The women of the North Wing approached a minute later, wearing their Sunday black, some of them recognizable as the waitresses and chambermaids of the Place. They fell into the same category as the men.

Next upon the scene were the gentlemen of the Place, accompanied by Scammon who, in the full finery of his best uniform, set the tone of sartorial perfection. At least a dozen of the party sported morning coats and top hats. Here, if you like, was the "upper crust" of Eastershaws.

A moment's pause when the gentlemen had crossed the sacred acre. . . . Inside the church an organ voluntary had begun; then, as though aware that they brought the final touch, the ladies of West Wing made their appearance, not in a solid troop like those of lesser consequence, but singly and in pairs, chaperoned by Sister Shadd. They came leisurely, in all their finery, careful that their skirts did not touch the dust. In the very centre of the group, surrounded by her own adulatory coterie, a lady advanced with great dignity towards the porch. Small, grey-haired and slight, with a drawn little beak and bright darting eyes in a parchment face, she was attired in lavender silk, with lace at her bosom and a large hat with an ostrich plume upon her head.

They were all in now, the bells ceased and, stepping briskly up the path, in a plain everyday suit, came Goodall, to conduct the service. When he had vanished into the church I turned from the window with a bitter frown, clipped on my key and went downstairs.

This was the third Sunday of the month, I was on official duty all day, at least until six; but I went first to the laboratory, which I had left only six hours before, to check upon the collodion sac I was using as a dialysing membrane. Yes, it was functioning perfectly. That was the way of it now. In my work everything went well. I took the rack of twenty sterile paraffined tubes, and ran into each 1 c.c. of the dialysed fluid, corked the test tubes carefully, numbered them, and put them in the incubator.

I stood a moment, heavy and brooding, feeling at the back of my head that hard pain which comes from overwork. I wanted my coffee, but could scarcely gather myself to go for it. Yes, this time there was no mistake. I was not far from isolating the nucleo-protein which should prove far more effective than the primary vaccine. Then I should have finished. Everything. My nerves bunched together at the thought. But I felt no real excitement. Only a kind of sullen, bitter satisfaction.

In the breakfast-room at Men's North I ate a slice of toast and drank three cups of black coffee. It was good to be alone—not that I minded Palfrey much, he was an amiable, inoffensive creature. The rhyme Nurse Stanway had made suited him:

> *"I like little Palfrey, his coat is so warm,*
> *And if you don't hurt him, he'll do you no harm."*

I lit a cigarette and inhaled deeply, as though to dull down that perpetual ache in my side. It was over, yet there came always an unguarded moment when Jean was close to me, when, with a wincing spasm, I must thrust her savagely away. At first, in sadness, I had pitied myself. Now a slow, burning resentment had mingled with the pain, and tempered it like steel. There raged in me a deep, corroding anger against life.

I rose and went down to the dispensary, where I began to make up the stock bromide and chloral solutions for the galleries. The dispensary was quiet and dim, panelled in dark mahogany, with an aromatic smell of drugs, old wood, and sealing wax which vaguely soothed my warring senses. Lately, the place had grown upon me. My earlier uneasiness was gone. I accepted, without a second thought, the key, the warm rococo galleries, the social structure of this cut-off little world.

Footsteps sounded in the passage and, an instant later, the hatch went up, framing Nurse Stanway's head and shoulders.

"Ready?" she asked.

I answered briefly.

"In a minute."

She stood watching while I filled the last of the West Side list.

"You didn't go to church?"

"No," I said. "Did you?"

"It's much too nice a day. Besides, it isn't in my line."

I looked at her. She met my gaze without any discernible change in her expressionless face. Her bang of glossy hair had a bluish glint and showed square on her white forehead under her uniform cap. I knew now that during the war she had married a flying officer who had later divorced her. She did not appear to care. One never knew what she was feeling, it seemed that nothing could break her casual air, her complete indifference, as though life were something worthless, to be spent carelessly, or simply thrown away.

"You haven't come to our sitting-room yet." She spoke deliberately, almost with the slowness of mockery. "Sister Shadd's very cut up about it."

"I haven't had time."

I made the excuse abruptly.

"Why don't you look in to-night? You might find it amusing. One never knows."

There was a faintly malicious challenge in her tone which sent a stark impulse along my worn nerves. I gazed at her with moody attention. Her rather full eyes still were mocking, yet they held a glint of meaning.

"All right," I said, suddenly. "I'll come."

She smiled slightly and, still looking at me, gathered up the medicines I had placed on the ledge of the hatch. Then, without a word, she turned away. Her slow movements had a physical casualness, a sensual grace.

For the rest of the day I was unsettled, ill at ease. After lunch I wrote up the case-book for Men's East, and at three o'clock went to deliver it at Dr. Goodall's house, set in the façade of the main building.

An elderly maidservant answered the bell and, having gone within to inquire, returned a moment later to say that the Superintendent was resting, but would see me. I followed her to the study, a large, untidy room, panelled in nondescript brown wood and sparsely lit by a yellowish leaded Gothic window with a stained-glass coat of arms inset. Stretched upon a sofa by the wide fireplace, covered by a plaid rug, was Goodall.

"You must excuse me, Dr. Shannon. The fact is, after church I did not feel well, and took a stiff dose of morphine." He proclaimed the fact simply, his eyes heavy in the griped and sallow face. "Wasn't it Montaigne who compared biliary colic to the tortures of the damned? I am a sufferer too."

He laid down the book I handed him and fixed his lined and heavy-lidded gaze upon me.

"You seem to be settling down very nicely. I am glad. I don't like changes in my staff. We have a great opportunity here, Dr. Shannon . . . in this little planet of ours." He paused, with a musing, strangely distant air. "Has it never struck you that we are a race apart, with our own laws and customs, virtues and vices, our social and intellectual strata, our reactions to the stress of living? People of the other world do not understand us, laugh at us, perhaps fear us. But we are citizens of the universe, nevertheless, a symbol of Man's indestructibility under the forces of Nature and of Fate."

My heart missed a beat as, leaning towards me, he went on with that remote gleam in his dark, pin-point irises.

"My task, Dr. Shannon, my life's endeavour is to create a new society, out of an order that is diseased and decadent. Difficult . . . ah, yes, but not impossible. And what a chance, Doctor! . . . When you have finished your present research I can open up for you a scientific field of unimaginable scope. We are only upon the threshold of understanding those maladies which affect our people. The brain, Dr. Shannon, the human brain, in all its mystery and majesty, pink and translucent, shining like a lovely fruit within its delicate membranes, its cranial sheath . . . What a subject for investigation . . . what a fascinating enigma to be solved!"

There was exaltation in his voice. For a moment I thought he was about to soar to dizzier heights but, as with an effort, he recollected himself. He threw me a quick glance and, after a moment of silence, dismissed me with his dark yet winning smile.

"Don't work too hard, Doctor. One must occasionally pay tribute to the senses."

I came away from his house in an even greater tumult of my feelings, attracted, yet excited and confused. He always had that effect upon me. But this evening it was worse than ever.

I simply could not rest. A surging ferment overcharged my veins, ready to burst forth. One must occasionally pay tribute to the senses, he had said.

Although, several times, I had told myself I would not go, towards eight o'clock I knocked on the door of the sisters' sitting-room and opened it. I must find a way of escape from these fevered and tormenting thoughts.

Seated at the end of the long table, which gave evidence that most of the staff had already supped and left the room, were Shadd, in uniform, Miss Paton, the dietician, and Nurse Stanway, dressed for "off duty" in a blue skirt and white silk blouse. The three were talking in intimate voices and it was Shadd, perking up like a pouter pigeon, who saw me first.

"Why, Mahomet has come to the mountain." She

brought out the "saying" in a pleased voice. "We're highly honoured, I'm sure."

As I entered, Miss Paton, a middle-aged woman with a ruddy face, gave me a nod of greeting. Nurse Stanway's expression was calm and indifferent. It was the first time I had seen her out of uniform. Her bang of glossy hair fell more conspicuously over her forehead, and the soft, shiny stuff of her blouse was loose over her flat chest and breasts.

"Haven't you finished?" I asked.

"As a matter of fact, we haven't begun." Shadd met my inquiring gaze with a robust laugh. "We may as well tell you . . . since you're one of us now. Sometimes we get tired of our menu. It wouldn't be good discipline, for the others, to complain. So we just wait and go down for supper, we three, to the kitchens."

"Ah, I see!"

At my tone, a faint blush penetrated Shadd's dermal toughness. She rose.

"If you breathe a word of it, I'll never speak to you again."

The kitchens, reached by the subway, were entirely underground, but lofty, cool and softly lit by clusters of frosted ceiling globes. Against one white tiled wall stood an array of old-fashioned ranges, on another hung a copper *batterie de cuisine*, while along a third ran a series of insulated white doors leading to the cold-rooms. Three mixing troughs, a bread-cutter and a ham-slicing machine with a heavy steel wheel stood at the far end beside a scrubbed deal table on which a great pan of oatmeal was already soaking for the next morning's porridge. A gentle whirring from the ventilation system filled the air of the immaculate vault.

Miss Paton had acquired a new briskness in her own domain. She advanced to the refrigerator marked Ladies' West, and with a turn of her wrist on the nickel handle threw open the heavy door, disclosing an assortment of cold meats, tongue, ham, sardines in a glass container, blanc mange, jellies, and preserved fruits.

Sister Shadd smacked her lips.

"I'm hungry," she said.

When plates and forks had been passed round, we began to eat in picnic fashion. Out of the corner of my eye, I saw Stanway perch herself on the wooden table with a detachment and assurance which swelled the dark forces of exasperation within me. Her legs were crossed, so that one swung loose, stressing the silken slimness of the limb. Her posture, slightly inclined backwards, emphasized the line of her thigh, waist, and breasts.

A harsh tightness rose in my throat. The desire to subdue her, to break through the barriers which restrained me, to destroy and desecrate, dominated me like a fever. I took no notice of her, remaining beside Sister Shadd, replenishing her plate from time to time, bearing with her stupid conversation. Yet while I pretended to listen, I could still see Stanway, balancing a plate of salad, her eyes charged with a sly and secret irony.

At last, having finished her dessert, Shadd heaved a regretful sigh.

"Well! All good things come to an end. I must go now and check my wretched linen-room. Be a sport, Paton, and come with me. It'll only take me half an hour if you help me."

On our way back through the underground the two older women took the West incline. I continued with Nurse Stanway towards the North Wing vestibule. We stood there.

"What next?"

"I think I'll take a walk," Stanway said, carelessly.

"I'll come with you."

She indicated her indifference with a slight shrug, an

255

instinct of cruelty, yet flattered, in a feline way, by my attention.

Outside, the night was dark, a few stars showing, but moonless. Once she was free of the buildings Stanway halted to light a cigarette. The cupped flame haloed for an instant her pale unconcerned face, with its high cheekbones and flattened nose. Why, I asked myself, am I doing this? I knew practically nothing about her and cared less. An accommodating stranger who would help me to roll in the gutter, to escape. A greater hardness took hold of me. In a controlled voice I said:

"Which way?"

"Down to the farm . . ." She seemed to smile. "And back."

"Just as you like."

Setting off along the West drive, suiting my step to hers, I kept a distance between us, looking straight in front. But, in the darkness, her own sense of space was less exact, and from time to time she brushed against me. The soft collision of her hip-bone as it made contact with mine increased the tortured hardness of my thoughts.

"Why don't you talk?" she asked with a light laugh. She was like a cat, in that the night seemed to excite and strengthen her.

"What about?"

"Anything. I don't care. What star is that ahead of us?"

"The Pole star. Look for it when you get lost in the woods."

Again she laughed, less scornfully than usual.

"Are we likely to get lost? You don't see Venus, by any chance?"

"Not just yet."

"Well . . ." She was still laughing. "There's still hope."

I did not say anything. I felt myself harder and more uncaring now, despising myself and her. That laugh,

256

keyed too high, shorn of assurance, had given her away, revealed her pretence of indifference as a sham, a secret invitation, from the beginning.

At the turn of the road under the farm elms there was a five-barred gate, held by two high turf walls. I stopped.

"This is as far as you want to go?"

She stubbed out her cigarette against the gate. I took her by the shoulders. I said:

"I'd like to break your neck."

"Why don't you try?"

Pressed back against the turf wall her face was dead-white, the stretched skin under her eyes bluer than ever. Her nostrils were slightly dilated. Her smile was fixed, almost a grimace. A wave of repugnance went over me, but the desire for oblivion had gone too far to be dispelled.

Her lips were dry and slightly bitter from the cigarette. They opened in an experienced manner. I could feel a shred of tobacco on her tongue. Her breath came quicker than mine.

There was an instant while Jean's face floated up before me, then the moon went behind a cloud and it was dark beneath the elms, where nothing remained but disillusion and despair.

CHAPTER VI

Aᴜɢᴜsᴛ ᴘᴀssᴇᴅ ɪɴ ᴀ wave of stifling heat. Although the watering cart went round each morning, clouds of dust rose from the driveways of the Place, and the leaves hung limply on the trees. The sun, streaming through the window-panes, upon which a fly buzzed quietly, gave to the dim galleries a mellow and nostalgic charm.

On the last evening of that torrid month it was so close I left the door of the laboratory half open. As I bent over the Duboscq colorimeter, with my shirt-sleeves rolled up and sweat rolling down under my unloosened collar, I heard a step behind me.

"Good evening, Shannon." To my surprise, it was Maitland's voice. "No; don't let me disturb you."

She had never visited me here before. Judging by the wool-stuffed workbag upon her arm, she was returning from one of her long, close sessions with Miss Indre, wherein the two women, knitting together, confidentially reviewed the current problems of the Place. Now, pulling forward a stool, she seated herself near me.

"How is it going?"

I laid down my pen, and rubbed my strained and slightly bloodshot eyes. I could feel the twitching of my left supra-orbital nerve. I said shortly:

"In a few hours I'll have finished."

"I'm so glad. I guessed you were near the end."

She had taken no offence at my abruptness. I did not dislike Maitland, but it was annoying to have her in the way at this particular moment. I could see her better now, her mottled face had a serious expression, as she gazed at me steadily through her violet lenses, studying me, and at the same time nerving herself to speak.

"I'm not an interfering person, Shannon . . . under my shell of bravado, I am rather a weak and pitiful creature. And I am wondering if I dare offer you some advice."

I stared at her in complete surprise. With a formal gravity which increased my irritation, she resumed:

"It's terribly important to find one's proper place in life, Shannon. Take my own case, for instance—dull though it is. I'm Irish, as you know, but actually my family is English, settled in Wexford on a demesne granted them by Cromwell. For over three hundred years we Maitlands have lived there, isolated, alien, separated from the people by blood and tears, burned out twice in five generations, suffering an insidious decay, a blight, soft and relentless as a sea fog, which rots the soul."

There was a pause. I looked at her coldly.

"You seem to have escaped that unhappy fate."

"Yes, Shannon. I escaped. But only by running away."

Her gaze was charged with such significance I moved impatiently.

"Frankly, I don't know what you mean."

"Don't you recall Freud's definition of a psychosis? A flight away from life into the realm of disease."

"What's that got to do with me?"

"Can't you guess?"

"No, I can't." My temper unexpectedly got out of hand; my voice was disturbingly shrill. "What are you driving at?"

She took off her glasses and slowly polished them. Then, forgetfully, she let them fall into her lap, gazed at me with those weak and browless eyes.

"Shannon . . . you should leave Eastershaws."

I was absolutely staggered.

"What! Leave?"

"Yes," she repeated. "Whenever you complete your research."

I felt myself flush, deeply. I stared at her with angry, incredulous eyes.

"That's an excellent joke. I thought for a moment you were serious."

"I am entirely serious . . . and so is my advice."

"Then wait until I ask for it. I happen to like this Place as well as you. And I have friends here too."

"Nurse Stanway?" Her lip curled faintly. "She's had a few followers in her time. Attendant Brogan, for instance . . . and your predecessor . . ."

"That's none of your business. I've been treated pretty badly outside. I'm not going to throw up a good job and a first-class laboratory because you get some wild idea in your head."

That, I could see, had silenced her.

She sat still for a few moments, then stood up.

"All right, Shannon. Let's forget about it. Good night."

She smiled and quickly went out.

I turned angrily to my bench. At the back of my mind I was dully aware of how I had spent myself in this final effort. I had lost weight and there were hollows in my cheeks; when I caught a glimpse of myself in the mirror I seemed to be confronted by a stranger. In the past, I had been able to do with three or four hours' sleep. But now I couldn't sleep at all. Complete insomnia. To calm my nerves during these night long seances I smoked so constantly my tongue and throat were raw. And there were these strange tricks and fancies—fetishes, in fact—which I had developed under this growing strain. Every time I left my bench, I had to go back, three times, to reassure myself that I had actually turned off the tap of my burette. I had developed the habit of shutting my left eye when I made my readings, and of writing my figures backwards. Each day, before I began work, I counted all the tiles in the section of wall above the incubator. There was a word, too, which somehow had got into my head, "abracadabra," and I found myself muttering it to myself, as a kind of invocation, as a spur to goad myself on, and as a low exclamation of triumph, whenever I completed another step in my experiments. And still I went on, like an automaton, testing and titrating, bearing forward, forward . . . I had to go on. I'd gone too far to draw back, it was all or nothing now . . . yes, all or nothing.

At eight o'clock I set the vaccine extract to filter, and as this process would take about an hour, I rose, switched off the lights, and left the laboratory, bent upon a short respite in my room.

Outside, I could hear preliminary tunings from the auditorium where, at the end of each month, an entertainment was held, half-dance, half-concert, sponsored by Palfrey, ostensibly for the benefit of the patients, but mainly to permit the little *maestro* to sing, with his hand upon his heart, Gounod's "Even bravest heart may swell . . ."

I rarely went to these junketings, and to-night I assuredly would not go.

Anxious to stretch out on my sofa, I entered my room, but as I did so I found that I was not alone. Seated by the open window, with a droop to his shoulders, and a peculiar fixity in his gaze, was Neil Spence.

"Why, Spence!" I exclaimed. "It's good to see you again."

He acknowledged my welcome with a faint smile in his wide, immobile eyes, and after we had shaken hands, sank back in his chair, his face shadowed by the curtain.

"I can't stay long, Robert. But I took a notion to look you up. You don't mind?"

"Of course not." I had often pressed him to visit me—yet, strangely, I wondered why he had come. "You'll have a drink?"

He looked at me broodingly, that shadowy smile still flickering in his dark pupils.

"Please."

I saw then that he had already had several, but that made no difference, besides, I wanted one myself. It was easy to come by good spirits from the stimulant cupboard, and lately I had drawn pretty heavily upon that store. I scarcely ate anything now, but kept myself going on black coffee, whisky, and cigarettes. I poured out two stiff drinks.

"Here's luck, then, Robert."

"Good health."

He nursed his tumbler between his hands, his eyes wandering about the room. There was in his calmness something which made me uneasy.

"How is Muriel?" I asked.

"Quite well, I believe."

"You should have brought her along."

He sat stock-still; his immobility was strangely terrifying.

"Muriel left me last week. She's with Lomax—in London."

He made the statement in a tone so matter-of-fact it took my breath away. There was a pause. I had not guessed it was as bad as this.

"What a rotten trick!" I muttered at last.

"Oh, I don't know." He answered logically, with that same inhuman self-control. "Lomax is a good-looking fellow, and Muriel is still a most attractive girl. And after all, I'm not much fun to live with."

I looked at him quickly. He went on, musingly, in that same flat tone:

"I suppose she went on as long as she could, before she fell for Lomax."

I had to say something.

"What a swine he must be!"

Spence shook his head. In spite of the whisky, he was completely sober.

"He's probably not any worse than the rest of us." A long, low breath escaped him. "I ought never to have married her in the first place. But I was so damned fond of her. And God knows I did my best. Took her out every Friday night." He repeated this, as though it comforted him. "Every Friday night in life."

"She'll come back to you," I said. "You can make a fresh start."

He looked full at me, and the smile in his dark eyes was tragic.

"Don't be a fool, Robert. It's all over." He paused, reflectively. "She has asked for a divorce. Wants to be free. Well, I'll attend to that for her. Isn't it extraordinary . . . I see now that she is shallow and worthless . . . but I can't hate her."

I poured him another drink, and one for myself. I scarcely knew what to say. In a vain effort to divert his mind, I asked:

"Have you been going to the Department?"

"Yes. You see, no one knows about this yet. Lomax is on vacation . . . Muriel supposed to be visiting her sister. But what's the use, I've lost interest. I'm not like you, Robert, I never was cut out for research." He added, in a flat voice: "It wouldn't have been so bad, except that when I saw how things were going and spoke to her, she said, 'Leave me alone. I hate the sight of you.' "

There was a prolonged silence. Then, softly, the sound of a two-step came through the open window, stealing across the night air into the room. Spence looked at me, his impassive features showing a vague inquiry.

"It's a dance they have once a month," I told him. "The staff and some of the patients."

He considered for a moment.

"Muriel would have enjoyed that . . . we occasionally used to dance on Friday nights. I dare say Lomax will take her out."

He listened till the two-step was over, then put down his empty glass.

"I have to go now, Robert."

"Oh, nonsense. It's quite early."

"I must. I have an appointment. There's a good train at nine."

"Have another spot, then?"

"No thanks. I want to be right for my appointment."

I guessed he had to see his lawyer about the divorce. I wasn't happy about him, but there seemed nothing I could say. It was twenty minutes to nine.

I went down to the lodge with him and opened the gate —Gunn had gone up to the dance.

"I'll walk to the station with you."

He shook his head.

"If I know anything, you want to be back in that laboratory."

There was a slight flush on his thin cheeks, and the expression in his fine sombre eyes startled me.

"Are you all right, Spence?"

"Perfectly." His voice held a hint of ghostly laughter. A pause.

We shook hands. As I gazed at him doubtfully, he did actually smile, his old distorted smile.

"Good luck, Robert. . . . Bless you."

I made my way back up the drive slowly. What he said was quite true. I had to finish, absolutely, or it would finish me. In the darkness, as I went towards the laboratory, I could still hear the soft beat of the music. That night fog we so often got was coming down.

As I entered, the white cool room was silent, save for the low and muffled throbbing of the music. I freed my mind of everything, except my work. Despite the barred double windows of frosted glass, the stealthy fog had penetrated, and floated in a soft swathe, like a disembodied spirit, under the domed roof. Beneath, in the centre of the tiled floor, upon my bench, stood the filtration apparatus. I saw that the flask was nearly filled by a clear, translucent fluid. It took me but a moment to remove my jacket, roll up my shirt-sleeves, and pull on my soiled smock. Advancing to the bench, I took up the flask, gazed at it with a strange and thrilling emotion. Then, intently, I set to work.

It was only a short process to standardize and encapsulate the final product. At quarter to ten I had done it. At last, in spite of everything, I had reached the summit of the endless hill and looked down upon the kingdoms spread before me.

I felt so dizzy I had to hang on to the edge of the bench. The buzzing elation in my ears transformed the distant music. Faintly, then more clearly, I conceived the strains as a celestial symphony, with high angelic voices, clarion-sweet, mingling with bells and a sonorous counterpoint of drums. As these ecstatic harmonies swelled I kept muttering to myself tensely.

"I've done it . . . oh, God Almighty . . . I've finished it at last."

With an effort I broke off, put away the ampules carefully in the ice box, locked up the laboratory, and went out.

I directed my exhausted footsteps towards my room. As I reached the vestibule I heard someone call my name, and turning, I saw Brogan, the attendant, running after me.

I stopped and waited till he came up. He was white and breathing fast.

"Dr. Shannon, I've been looking for you all over." He caught his breath. "There's been a little accident, sir."

I stood quite still, staring at him.

"Look, sir." Despite his experience, the man shuddered. "It's your friend . . . we just had word from the station."

Spence! I suddenly felt sick. A cold sweat broke on my brow. I swallowed with an effort.

"He slipped and fell, sir. Just as the nine o'clock train came in. It was instantaneous."

CHAPTER VII

THE NEXT FEW DAYS were raw and foggy, a chill and early breath of autumn, melancholy presage of the coming winter and, as I went about my duties, I felt an equal foreboding bearing coldly down upon me. Spence's funeral had been held in his native town of Ullapool in the distant county of Ross, and I had been unable to attend it. But in a letter to his parents I had tried to temper the blow by attributing the occurrence solely to tragic chance. I had heard nothing of Lomax and Muriel.

The laboratory was locked, the key in my pocket, and it seemed strange that I should not be going there. Professor Challis would return to Winton at the end of the week, I would leave all arrangements concerning the announcement in his hands. Inevitably, news of my achievement pervaded Eastershaws, and I was obliged to endure the embarrassment of congratulations—restrained from Maitland and Miss Indre, effusive from Palfrey, warm and dignified from Dr. Goodall. There came also an extraordinary trunk call from Wilson's, the great pharmaceutical house in London, which, until Challis should advise me, I refused to answer.

But on Thursday I received a visitor whom I had expected least of all. After supper, as I paced up and down my room, smoking endless cigarettes, trying to concentrate my scattered thoughts and to control my still unruly nerves, Professor Usher was shown in.

I gazed blankly at his tall, distinguished figure as he came forward and shook my hand with a cordial smile.

"My dear Shannon, how are you? I hope I haven't come at an inconvenient moment?"

"No . . ." I said stiffly. "Not at all."

"May I sit down?" He took a chair and crossed one leg over the other. "I dare say I should have let you know I was coming, but I enjoy acting upon impulse. And I did wish to be amongst the first to felicitate you."

"Thank you."

"I was in my office when Professor Challis telephoned me from Bute, working out a little idea." He smiled and caressed his neat imperial. "Despite my heavy administrative burdens, I try to get down occasionally to some real research. Well, I did not hesitate a moment."

I could not think of a suitable response, so I said nothing at all.

"Of course, I knew this was coming. I flatter myself I keep my ear pretty close to the ground. After all, the main purpose of my Department is to foster all that is worth while in modern scientific advancement and, despite our little disagreement, I realized that one day you would justify my belief in you."

I bit my lip at this airy insincerity.

"It would have saved me considerable trouble if you had acted upon that assumption."

"Yes," he agreed in his most winning manner. "I'm prepared to admit frankly that I was hasty. And now I've said it, I hope you'll meet me halfway and forget what's past."

My head was aching more than ever. I could not fathom his purpose. His tone grew more confidential.

"Now, listen, Shannon. I'll be perfectly open with you. Lately, we've had a run of shocking bad luck at the Department. We have not been getting satisfactory results. To cut a long story short, I want you back."

I made an instinctive gesture of refusal, but he held me with an impressive eye.

"Don't misunderstand me. I mean something considerably more important than merely handing you back your

268

old position. Significant changes have been shaping up at the University. At last I have been won over to the idea of incorporating a biochemical laboratory in the Pathology building, and the Board of Trustees has decided to found a chair for experimental research in that particular field. The salary has been fixed at seven hundred pounds per annum, and the duties of the new director, subject, of course, to my most cordial co-operation, will be to organize and promote the work of the laboratory. He will have the status of a junior professor, with the privilege of delivering a course of lectures each session. Now, Shannon——" He drew a long, important breath. "I want you to consider the results a young and brilliant man might achieve in this position, aided by trained technicians and eager young students." He leaned forward and tapped me on the knee. "What would you say if the chance were given to you?"

I tried to keep steady in my chair. The offer took my breath away, an opportunity the like of which I had never dared, even, to contemplate. I saw that Usher's motives were completely selfish, he wanted me for the sake of the Department, and for his own sake too. The scientific and popular interest created by the publication of my discovery, the newspaper acclaim, the new health legislation which would be introduced in Parliament, all this was too infinitely valuable for him to miss. Even so, was he less human on that account? In my perplexity and distress I pressed my hand across my forehead, not knowing how to answer him.

"There, there," Usher said, easily. "I've a fair idea of how hard you've been at it. I won't bother you any more at present. What I suggest is this. You'll come to dinner at my house, Monday night. The Chancellor will be there, together with a few of my colleagues, members of the Senate who are keenly interested, to meet and congratulate

269

you. There may also be present, though whisper it not in Gath"—his incisive expression became arch—"an editor or two, distinguished representatives of the Press. I think I can promise you a stimulating evening."

I tried to express my thanks, but he stopped me with a smile.

"Not a word, my dear fellow. You must accept this as my *amende honorable*. Eight o'clock sharp then, at my house on Monday. Splendid. Again my congratulations, coupled with the hope that in the future we may further the noble cause of science together."

He stood up, clasped my hand, flashed upon me his histrionic smile and left the room.

I sank back in my chair. This brilliant turn of events was too much for my tired brain, I still could scarcely grasp it. The first start of excitement was over, I felt no elation, only a strange inner tensity. This was the copy-book reward of industry, perseverance, and high endeavour. I was the prize student now, at the head of the list. They all professed their friendship, were eager to shake my hand; even the Dalnair committee would want to claim acquaintance with me now. But they had been against me, every one of them, when I was really struggling, bogged in the morass of adversity.

Yet I knew I would not be so heroic as to disown success. I had suffered too long the cruel pangs, the back-breaking effort of independent effort. Usher wouldn't interfere too much. And the money . . . seven hundred pounds a year . . . I had never once thought of that, but now, despite myself, I would be rich, I might even dress like a well-off practitioner, quite the gentleman . . . it was all going to end up well, after all.

It was not good for me, this bitterness, but I could not check it, my future had never seemed brighter, yet a shroud seemed cast over my joy. Only one person would truly care, honestly rejoice in my success. I could see her face at this moment. For weeks I had buried that picture in the secret recesses of my mind, now I could not free myself of it. And suddenly, through the hardness which pervaded me, there came a soft and tender yearning. She had broken with me. Her prolonged silence indicated that. And I had betrayed her. But I wanted to speak with her, only for a moment, to tell her that my research was over; only for a moment, to hear her voice.

And so, against common sense, against my pride, against everything, I got up, went slowly to the telephone and, after a final moment of hesitation, called up the cottage hospital at Dalnair.

It was a toll call and I had to wait some time, but at last I succeeded in getting through. My voice sounded harsh and forced.

"I'd like to speak to Dr. Law, please."

"Oh, I'm sorry, sir, you can't."

The abrupt refusal surprised and disconcerted me.

"Isn't she in?" I asked.

"Oh, yes, sir, she's in."

"You mean she's on duty?"

"Oh, no, sir, not on duty."

"Then what do you mean? Please go to her room and tell her I'm here."

"She's not in her room, sir. She's in the wards."

Who was at the other end? I tried to recognize the voice, but could not. In addition, the country exchange was acting in its usual fashion and the wire began to sing and crackle loudly. Restraining my impatience, I changed the receiver to my other ear.

"Hello, hello . . . Who is that talking?"

"It's the maid, sir."

"Katie?"

"No, sir, the under-maid. I'm new, sir."

My nerves were now so taut I had to shut my eyes.

"Please fetch the matron. Tell her Dr. Shannon wishes to speak to her."

"Very good, sir. Will you hold on, please?"

I hung on, with increasing vexation and anxiety, for what seemed an interminable period. But finally, with relief, I heard a sharp step, followed by Miss Trudgeon's unmistakable tones.

"Yes, Dr. Shannon?"

"Matron," I exclaimed. "I'm sorry to trouble you, but I did want to have a word with Dr. Law. Could you reach her for me?"

"I'm afraid you can't speak with her, Doctor. You haven't heard our news?"

"No."

There was an appreciable pause. Then:

"Dr. Law has been ill, quite ill, for the past three weeks".

As my heart turned over in my breast, there came a crackle in the instrument which cut off further speech. But I had already heard enough to turn my swift suspicion into certainty. I hung up the receiver. It was always my failing to leap impetuously to a premature conclusion, and that, precisely, was what I did just now.

CHAPTER VIII

Next morning I went early to the laboratory, then across to Dr. Goodall's house. He had not risen, but when I sent in word that I was obliged to take the day off, he gave me his permission.

The sky was still grey as I walked down the drive and through the big gates. After my long and unbroken sojourn within the high walls it was painful to make this journey to Dalnair. I reached Winton at ten o'clock. The city lay damp and warm beneath a low smoke pall. The noise and bustle of the streets, the crowds pushing with luggage towards the barrier at the Central Station, were strangely jarring after the order and tranquillity of Eastershaws. But I had to see Jean—yes, at whatever cost, I must see her.

Yet, as I sat brooding in the swaying train, while the sooty fields and sidings drifted past, my feeling was less pity than a slow and smouldering anger. More and more I was obsessed by the vision of her fingers—touching the cultures . . . crumbling the biscuit to her lips.

At Dalnair Station I couldn't get a cab, so, under the grey and humid sky, I walked to the hospital by the steep path which I used to race up at top speed. But now I climbed slowly, wishing I had stopped at the Railway Tavern for a drink. I was out of breath as I reached the crest of the hill, entered the drive, and rang the front door bell.

There was no delay. It was Katie who answered my ring. I had not told them I was coming, and she gave me a queer look. But she had always liked me and, with a restrained air of welcome, she admitted me to the reception-room. A moment later Miss Trudgeon appeared.

"Well," she exclaimed, bustling in with her brisk and energetic smile. "This is a surprise. I'm very glad to see you again."

Gazing at her heavily, I saw that she had spoken quite sincerely; yet, while I felt grateful for her friendly reception, I was not deceived by the specious brightness of her manner, which I recognized at once as a mere professional disguise, a cloak that I had often seen her adopt when interviewing anxious relatives.

"But I must say," she went on with a sideways glance, "you don't flatter your new job. You're thin as a rake. What have they been doing to you? You look as though they'd put you through a mangle."

"Oh, I'm all right."

"Don't they feed you out there?"

"Yes . . . the food's excellent."

She shook her head slightly, as though doubting the truth of my words.

"You need a course of my good nourishing curries."

There was an awkward pause during which, as she hadn't asked me to sit down, we both remained standing. The cheerful, rather encouraging smile, which from long practice her tough facial muscles seemed capable of sustaining endlessly, had lost a little of its glitter.

I moistened my lips.

"How is she?"

"As well as can be expected. She's been ill three weeks now." The matron hesitated; then, observing that I was waiting for further information, she proceeded on that same note of optimism, choosing her words so as not to commit herself. "At first she seemed to be holding her own. But these last few days there's been a slight loss of ground."

I felt my heart contract. I knew that phrase so well.

"Who's looking after her?"

"Dr. Fraser, the Medical Officer of Health."

I had a vision of this middle-aged man, with thinning sandy hair, thick fair eyebrows, and a plain, square, lined face made coarsely ruddy by a reticulation of red veins upon the cheeks.

"He's a good man."

"Excellent."

"Tell me the truth. What does he say?"

The matron was silent. She shrugged her shoulders slightly.

"She's quite ill. If only she'd gone down with it at once, she'd have had a better chance. She went on for a week with persistent headache and temperature, before she collapsed. But that often happens with scarlet fever."

"Scarlet fever!" I exclaimed, in an indescribable tone.

"Yes, of course," Matron said, surprised. "I told you on the phone last night."

A rending silence. I drew a quick sharp breath, which seemed to burn to my finger-tips. So rooted was my idea I could not bring myself to surrender it.

"I'd like to see her," I said.

Miss Trudgeon's gaze slid over my head.

"She's not altogether conscious."

"All the same, I would like to."

"What good can it possibly do?"

"All the same . . ." I said.

The matron now looked thoroughly embarrassed. She spoke directly.

"Her parents and her brother are here . . . in the sitting-room. And her fiancé. Unless they were willing, Doctor, I couldn't take the responsibility."

I felt a sinking of dismay. This was something unthought of, a difficulty to be overcome, a penance to be endured.

Yet for nothing, nothing must I abandon the purpose which had brought me here. I sighed.

"I'll go in and see them."

Once again she shrugged.

"Very well. You know your own business best. If you want me, I'll be in the ward."

Without further comment Miss Trudgeon briefly nodded, spun round and moved off, leaving me to make my way, as best I could, along the corridor to my old sitting-room. Outside the door I stood for a full minute, hearing the sound of a deep voice within, then summoning all my courage I turned the handle and went in.

Daniel Law was at the table, reading aloud from a Bible, with Luke, in the next chair, close beside him. Seated in the window embrasure and facing in my direction were Mrs. Law and Malcolm Hodden. I stood there in hangdog fashion, holding my breath until the recital finished.

There was a momentous silence. Daniel removed his glasses and, with his handkerchief, dried them openly, then half-turned in his chair. Although his attitude was fixed, his grave, anxious countenance gave no sign of anger or accusation. He simply gazed at me with silent dignity.

Malcolm, however, had risen. He came towards me. His undertone was audible in the silent room.

"How can you intrude at a time like this?" His full eyes, near to me, were veined. "Can't you respect our privacy . . . forcing yourself . . ."

"No, Malcolm," Jean's mother interposed in a low tone.

I kept my gaze on the floor, all that I had meant to say congealed upon my lips.

"He has no right to be here!" Hodden cried, suddenly, in a racked voice.

"Oh, be quiet," Luke muttered.

"Hush, son," whispered Mrs. Law. With a steady glance

towards me, she stood up. "I am going to see our daughter now. Will you come with me to the ward?"

Speechless, not having spoken a word, I accompanied her from the room, across the driveway, to the side room of the little pavilion. Waves of light rippled across the clean gravel yard, a young nurse crossed before us, under a veranda a group of children, convalescent, in red coats, were throwing a rubber ball.

My heart was hammering unbearably in my side as Matron opened the door and we joined her in the white-painted room. Only one of the three beds was occupied, half-surrounded by a screen, with a white enamel chair at one side. Upon this chair, leaning forward in an attitude of watching, was Sister Peek. As I followed Matron slowly round the edge of the screen and stood at the foot of the bed, I dared not raise my eyes. Only by the greatest exercise of will did I succeed in lifting my head, inch by inch, until my gaze, travelling along the white counterpane, came to rest on Jean.

She lay upon her back, her eyes wide open, constantly muttering, with tremulous movements of her dry lips and tongue, her thin hands all the while plucking at the bed-clothes. Against the low white pillow, beneath her tied-back hair, her facial bones were sharp and fine. Her cheeks showed, not the usual bright patches of fever, but a dull and heavy flush, while a crop of reddish points, some of which had already faded, leaving brownish stains, disfigured her drawn brow . . . the typical rash of toxic scarlatina.

Already, amidst the rushing in my ears, I felt myself slipping down the slope.

Above the bed, beyond reach of those plucking fingers and twitching wrists, there hung the chart upon which was traced the sharp ridges, the depths and hilly contours, of the fever. My eyes went straining towards it. Yes, I thought, after a long moment, there is no doubt at all. What a fool I had been, what a fool I always was. . . . It was, with certainty, scarlet fever.

In muted voices Mrs. Law and Matron began to talk together. I was not there. Useless as a piece of unwanted furniture, I was ignored. I did not exist. My eyes fell, in anguished confusion, wandering amongst the paraphernalia of sickness which neatly covered the bedside table, medicine bottles, feeding cup, a hypodermic, ether, and camphor in oil. If it had reached that stage it was bad enough.

The scene hung, suspended, from a remorseless thread of time which swung slightly from side to side, and slowly attenuated, became more fragile as seconds were stripped away and cast one by one into an unknown void. You could not bear this indefinitely. I went out, crossed the narrow passage to the opposite side room, which was quite empty, and there sat down upon the edge of a bed, staring at the blank yellow distempered wall with direct and haggard eyes. I had hoped to do so much, and now I could do nothing . . . no dramatic and impassioned act to prove myself, to establish a reason for existing . . . nothing. Filled, more and more, with self-contempt, denying myself all value, I took from my pocket the large ampule I had wrapped in cotton wool that morning and, under the unconscious pressure of my fingers, the brittle snap of the glass was magnified to a high resonance, ringing in my ears like bells. Shreds of damp wool stuck to my fingers. Impossible to describe the white heat burning in my mind, my sense of distressed ineptitude, the burden, without feeling, which bore upon me, the string of mocking echoes in the silence which encircled me.

Still, time kept swinging, the seconds falling, feather-soft. How had this come upon her? Ah, if one were tired, or wrapped, despite oneself, in some melancholy dream, might it not then be easy to forget those simple precautions which make the difference between health and sickness? Voices fell upon my ear through the frozen emptiness of thought. I heard Mrs. Law and Matron come out of the sick-room and move along the passage. Miss Trudgeon was trying to soothe the troubled mother.

"Rest assured, everything is being done. We should know in twenty-four hours. Dr. Fraser is giving every attention. As for Sister Peek, nothing could surpass her devotion to this case. She's been specialling on it for over three weeks, and has often taken double duty. I've never known such self-sacrifice."

So I had been wrong there also. It was like me to think the worst of everyone. I'd misjudged the matron, too, fought with her, distrusted her. That was my special quality, getting on the wrong side of people, acting against convention and the grain of decency, standing against the universe, belonging to no place, and to no one, but myself.

A gong vibrated in the far main building, sounding for the nurses' luncheon, a sign of normal life which deepened the hollow present. The two women had passed through the outer door now, their voices, faint and sad, dwindled away to nothing. I stood up, automatically, and, like a figure moved by strings, went out of the pavilion. No one was in sight. As though wearing shackles, I started down the hill towards the station. Huddled in an empty compartment of the returning train I was still in the ward, up there, on the darkening hill.

CHAPTER IX

WHEN I GOT BACK TO Eastershaws I found a note saying that Professor Usher had telephoned me twice, leaving word that I should call him when I came in. I hesitated, then told myself I would put it off till later. I had a splitting headache; I wanted to be let alone, to cut myself off, to nurse my sadness, and my fears, in secret.

At five o'clock I drank a cup of tea. I was glad of it. All my faculties seemed numbed. On the tray was another slip.

"Mr. Smith of the Pathology Department telephoned you at 3 p.m. Urgent."

Vaguely, through the weight that was myself, I felt annoyed by this persistence, and puzzled, until I remembered that Usher had hinted at sending a reporter from the *Herald*. Smith must have been deputed to arrange that interview. I could not bear that just now. Time enough at the dinner on Monday. I rolled up the slip and dropped it in the fire.

Goodall had given me the whole day off. There was no need for me to leave my room. I sat, in a heavy daze, counting the hours, until nine o'clock; then, rousing myself, I telephoned the hospital at Dalnair. There was no change in Jean's condition. They could tell me nothing more.

Dead tired, throbbing with anxiety, I supposed I had better turn in, but my neuralgia was so bad I knew I would not sleep. The aspirin bottle in my bathroom cabinet was empty. I went downstairs and, as I was in the dispensary, took some pyramidon. Then, on my way back, in the central subway, I saw one of the nurses approaching. It was Stanway.

She was alone, walking slowly towards the hostel. When she noticed me, she stopped, leaned back casually against the wall of the passage until I came near.

"Where have you been?"

"Nowhere in particular."

"You're quite a stranger."

Although she spoke with an assumption of indifference, she was studying me closely. She added:

"I hope you don't think I missed you."

"No," I said.

"There are lots of others I can go out with."

"Yes."

There was a pause. I looked at her, and looked away, overcome by a revulsion of feeling which turned me sick and cold. There is a penalty for everything, I thought, bitterly regretting those many dreary nights when, skirting the walls like a thief, I had gone to her room. Promiscuous and cheap . . . all without meaning . . . or a single tender thought. The frosted lights crackled overhead, artificial and unreal. She cared nothing for me and I, oh God, how tired I was of her.

"What's the matter?" She spoke sharply, still watching the changes in my face.

Still I didn't answer. And, mistaking my hesitation, a slow provocative smile touched her lips.

"I'm going off duty now." She glanced at me indolently. "If you want to come along."

"No," I said heavily, gazing straight ahead.

Quite taken aback, she stiffened, from wounded vanity, and, for once, her pale skin reddened, an angry and unexpected stain. There was a pause.

"All right." She shrugged. "Don't think I care. But

don't come round, disturbing me, when you happen to change your mind."

She stared at me, with open contempt, her small head silhouetted like a skull against the light, then she spun round and went off, along the subway, her heels clicking on the concrete, clicking away to silence.

Well, that was the end, thank God. I turned and went back to my room and flung myself upon my bed. After a while the pyramidon took effect. I slept heavily.

But next morning, when I awoke, I felt worse than ever. My sleep had merely prepared me for the day to come.

During the forenoon, I got through my work somehow, and without meeting Maitland or Palfrey—lately, I had become adept at avoiding the other members of the staff.

After one o'clock, with a deep foreboding, having forced delay upon myself until I could no longer bear it, I telephoned Dalnair again. Sister Cameron spoke to me. Her voice sounded cheerful, but she was always cheerful. And the answer which she gave me was the same. No change. Holding her own. No change at all.

In a burst of good intention she tried to help me.

"At any rate, the worst hasn't happened yet. While there's life there's hope."

Outside it was raining, a heavy shower which darkened the sky and cast a stormy shadow over all the grounds. I mounted the staircase slowly to my room. Then, as I entered, I perceived in the indistinct light that someone was seated on the sofa, at the far side of the fire. I switched on the shaded lamp above the bookcase and, with dull surprise, I saw that my visitor was Adrian Lomax.

Without altering his position, he met my long, heavy stare in a manner which at least simulated his habitual and superior calm, but which, at the same time, betrayed, underneath, uncertainty as to how I might receive him.

"Lomax," I said, finally, as from a distance. "You're the last person I expected here."

"You don't seem very glad to see me."

I made no answer. There was a pause. He had not changed much, indeed, scarcely at all. I had imagined that, after what he had come through, he must be broken up by a sense of responsibility and guilt. On the contrary, he was still as well turned out as ever, paler perhaps, with a more listless droop to his lips, but perfectly composed, and prepared to defend himself.

"You didn't know I was back?"

"No."

Although actually there had been little scandal, I saw that his pride had driven him to return. He lit a cigarette, with an attempt at his former ease. Yes, he was embarrassed and was trying, with this air of bravura, to hide it.

"I suppose you have your knife in me. But I wasn't altogether to blame."

"Weren't you?"

"Far from it. From the very beginning it was Muriel who ran after me. Wouldn't leave me alone. Oh, I dare say it was foolish of me, but I just couldn't disentangle myself."

"Where is she now?"

"I offered to marry her. I wanted to do the right thing. But we had a filthy row. She's gone back to her people. I'm not sorry. She would have been a damned nuisance."

"You've got out of it very well. Better than Spence."

"You know it was an accident. It was a foggy night. He missed his footing on the platform. It all came out at the inquest."

"For God's sake don't excuse yourself. You sound as though you felt you'd pushed him over."

283

The colour went out of his face.

"Don't you think that was a little uncalled-for? At any rate, I mean to show that I'm not the rotter they say I am. I'm going to work, really work at the Department, do something this time that'll make them all sit up."

He gave the impression that he had been the victim of uncontrollable circumstances, and that the future would completely justify him. I knew that he would never achieve anything, that he was, under his air of brilliant superiority, weak, vapid, and self-indulgent. It made me uneasy to have him in the room. I stood up and poked the fire, hoping that he would take the hint and go.

But he did not go. He kept looking at me in a curious manner.

"You've been doing good work lately."

Standing away from him, I made a gesture of dissent.

"They were very excited about it at the Department."

I raised my eyes slowly. Through the mists which encircled me his use of the past tense struck me as strange. A moment's silence followed.

He sat up and leaned towards me, that odd, thin smile of condolence more apparent upon his lips.

"Usher has asked me to come and see you, Shannon . . . to break the news. You've been forestalled. Someone had published your work before you."

I stared at him, wondering, dully, what he was driving at; then suddenly I started.

"What do you mean?" I could scarcely bring out the words. "I checked all the literature before I began. There was nothing."

"No, Shannon, there wasn't. But now there is. A research worker in America, a woman doctor named Evans, has just come out in this month's *Medical Review* with a full report of her experiments. Two years' work. Her conclusions are practically the same as yours. She has isolated the bacillus, shown the world-wide incidence of the disease—the figures are amazingly large—identified the infection in dairy herds, in fact, everything."

A long silence. The room was spinning round me.

Lomax was speaking again, with too obvious tact.

"It was Smith who told us first. He's been following Dr. Evans's work for months. He actually had an advance proof of the report in his possession. He brought it into the Department yesterday."

"I see."

My lips were stiff and cold, I felt as though I had been turned to stone. Eighteen months of unsparing effort, of feverish application by day and night, in the face of every difficulty, all wasted, and of no avail. If the results were already before the scientific world, proved and published, I should get no credit now for what I had done, the problems I had solved at such cost to myself. It had happened before, of course; as though by some strange telepathy, a current passed between two workers, continents apart, starting them off, unknown to each other, upon the same quest. And doubtless it would happen again. Yet this did not ease the frightful pang of finding another at the goal before me, nor dull the deathly bitterness of defeat.

"It's a damned shame." Lomax spoke without looking at me. "I needn't say how sorry I am."

His pretence of pity was more crushing than indifference. He got up from his chair.

"By the by, in case you wanted to read it, I brought along the article." He took some printed sheets from his coat pocket and laid them upon the table. "Now I'll push off. Good night, Shannon."

"Good night."

When he had gone I sat staring at nothing, in a hollow, hopeless calm. Then, with a deep sigh, which seemed to spring from the bottom of my heart, I rose, went over to the table, and taking up the report, steeled myself to read it.

As Lomax had said, it was a masterly investigation of the disease, later to be named brucellosis, and one that came to be regarded as a monumental work. When I had twice gone over it carefully I had to acknowledge, with a swift surge of jealousy, that Dr. Evans was a brilliant and resourceful scientist, whose work was perhaps better than mine.

I folded the sheets with intense calm, and stood up. This new calm, false though it might be, was like a sudden intoxication filling my head with a sense of power and light. It was now three o'clock and time for me to ring Dalnair again. Without a tremor, I went towards the telephone. But before I could take up the instrument there came a knock upon the door, the maid entered and handed me a telegram. I opened it with steady fingers.

"ACCEPT MY SINCERE SYMPATHY PUBLICATION IN REVIEW WHICH IN NO WAY DETRACTS INTRINSIC MERIT YOUR EFFORT. AM STILL UNABLE TO TRAVEL BUT HOPE SEE YOU SOON TO ARRANGE FUTURE WORK. REGARDS. WILFRED CHALLIS."

If reaction had been delayed, now it fell upon me with an added force. I had leaned on Challis, forgetful of his years and gathering enfeeblement. This message of condolence struck away the last support, and as I gazed at the blurred words I felt, suddenly, a queer snap behind my brow, as though an elastic band, stretched too tight, had finally yielded to the strain. At the same instant my nerves escaped me, the world spun round, and the splendid humour of the whole thing came before me in a flash. I smiled, at first vaguely, yet after a moment with growing

286

conviction, until, presently, I began to laugh . . . at my-self, my present situation—then, like a quick-change artist, upon whom is forced the necessity of another part, I suddenly became sedate, serious and resourceful.

With an air of purpose, I looked at my watch, forgetful that I had done so a few minutes before. It was only a quarter after three, which reassured me, for I suddenly was filled by a pressing desire to be busy. All sense of disappointment was gone and, through the general insensibility which affected me, I was conscious of a vague pervading comfort, a recognition that what occurred outside, at the Department or Dalnair, was of slight importance in the general movement of my life. Was I not safe here, well-housed and fed, insulated from the shocks and sadness of the outer world, in this splendid, this sheltered, retreat? For that matter, if it pleased me, I need never leave it.

Reinforced by this thought, I set out briskly to the West Wing, there, on Maitland's day off, it was my duty to make the afternoon round. Lately I had been remiss in this obligation, perhaps I had not been pulling my full weight in the Place. That would not do at all, it was not fair to Dr. Goodall, not up to Eastershaws standards. Reproachfully, I told myself I must make fitting reparation. There were many things I could attend to before the day was over.

In the West vestibule I joined Sister Shadd and made a thorough round of the six galleries. I did not rush or scamp the work, but was painstaking and solicitous. The quiet of the galleries was strangely soothing, and I talked at length with several of the inmates, even drank a cup of tea with the Duchess in her own room, a lofty apartment with faded green curtains, a bearskin hearthrug and an ormolu chandelier. She wore a mauve velvet dress with a great deal of ornate jewellery and several necklaces of freshly strung melon seeds. At first she kept her beady eyes appraisingly upon me, but as I exerted myself to please she gradually unbent and, when I rose to go, extended to me, coquettishly, her parchment-yellow hand.

Mildly amused by my success, I turned to Shadd as we stood together at the outer door.

"Remarkable, Sister, isn't it . . . how the Duchess, despite her extravagances, epitomizes certain phenomena observable amongst your ladies here."

"Most remarkable." All through my visit she had been constrained and silent. Now, she gave me a peculiar, sharply disapproving look.

"I mean," I smiled, "they're all interested in dress. Even the oldest of them keeps trying to come out with something new, adding a ribbon here, altering a flounce there, in an effort to outvie the rest. Often their creations are grotesque, yet if they're sufficiently different they immediately become the vogue. Of course, the Duchess's large wardrobe enables her to reign supreme."

Sister Shadd, still staring at me, opened her lips, then compressed them tightly in acute displeasure.

"Their attitude towards the opposite sex is interesting also . . ." I went on. "Take, for example, the passive virgins who blench at the very sight of man . . . and those others, of a mild romantic strain, who give coy glances while walking in the grounds, towards the male of their fancy . . . And those desperate creatures who alternately beseech and complain of ravishment by lightning, thunderbolt, electric waves, solar and lunar rays, or even through the supernatural visitation of Goodall himself!"

"Excuse me, Doctor," Shadd cut in abruptly. "Miss Indre wants me. I have to go now." As she went off, her brow like thunder, she added, "Really, you surprise me. Why don't you go and lie down for a bit?"

So she thought I had been drinking, confound her.

Philosophy was wasted on her, anyhow. I resented her departure, yet refused, positively, to permit it to upset me. I turned with renewed briskness, and made my way to the dispensary.

The stock solutions had got very low. It took a full hour's work to replenish them. As I measured the crystals of chloral hydrate and shook them into the blue glass bottles I found myself humming—Palfrey's favourite phrase from *Carmen* . . . by poor, unhappy Bizet. Very pleasant and agreeable. If my head had not felt so numb, as though beaten by hammers, I should have been thoroughly at ease.

Suddenly the house phone rang. The sharp, shrill note gave me an agonizing start. Yet I was calm as I picked up the receiver.

"Dr. Shannon?" It was the porter at the lodge.

"Yes."

"I've been trying to find you all over the building. There's a young fellow here who wants to speak with you."

"With me?" I stared blankly at the wall in front of me. "What's his name?"

"Law . . . he says, Luke Law."

Oh, of course, I remembered Luke, my young friend with the motor-cycle. What did he want at this time of day?

I'd barely time to begin humming again when Luke's voice came through, eager and excited, the words tumbling over one another.

"Is that you, Robert . . . come down at once . . . I want to see you."

"What's the matter?"

"Nothing . . . everything . . . it's good news . . . Jean's much better."

"I beg your pardon?"

"She's out of danger. At two o'clock this afternoon she

289

had her crisis. She's conscious now. She's talked to us. Isn't it wonderful?"

"Quite so. I'm delighted."

"I just had to get on the bike and come flying over to tell you. Come down to the lodge. I want to see you."

"Sorry, dear boy." My tone conveyed the polite regret of one preoccupied by many affairs. "I couldn't possibly manage it at the moment."

"What!" A pause. "After me coming all that way . . .? Robert . . . Hello . . . hello . . .`."

Although, remotely, it hurt me to do so, I cut him off, hooking up the receiver with a quiet smile. Much as I liked Luke, I had no time to waste on futile errands! Naturally, it was quite a relief that Miss Law should be better, no doubt very gratifying to her relatives. A quiet sort of girl, she was, with brown eyes and hair. I recollected the song . . . *Jeannie with the light brown hair* . . . Charming melody, I must mention it to Palfrey. I remembered her, vaguely, as a student in my class, clever, but something of a nuisance. Of course, I bore her no ill-feeling, not the slightest ill-will in the world.

Bizet, again . . . poor, unhappy Bizet . . . *I try not to own that I tremble* . . . I finished my stock solutions, tidied up the dispensary, and again, briskly, with unclear gaze, deciphered the time on my watch.

Seven o'clock. I had always disliked duty in the refectory, but now, despite the pain in my head, it seemed a pleasing, a logical necessity.

Supper had begun when I entered the dining-hall, and the waitresses were bringing tray after tray of food to the long tables, where, amidst a great clatter of dishes, scraping of chairs, and chatter of voices, everyone had begun to eat.

I stood for a moment; then, not mounting the dais, strolled up and down, watching with benign, possessive interest. The rising clouds of steam and the spicy smell of food made me feel my lack of sleep, and as my thoughts drifted, the scene grew rich and warm, feudal, almost, in its trenchered assembly of hind and gentle, its constant flow of servitors, like a canvas by Breughel in its life and colour, its bizarre diversity of human physiognomy, its abundance, movement, and high hubbub. . . .

Ah, I was back in the subway again, returning, with measured paces to my room. Outside the pantry of Balaclava the night attendant had come on duty and was mixing the evening cocoa.

"I brought up the mail, Doctor. There's a letter for you."

"Thank you, my good fellow."

In passing, I took the stiff envelope, stamped with the University crest. My smile was fixed now, as though printed upon my face, a mask for all the whirling chaos that went on behind. The heavy sledges struck harder on my skull, a sudden sweat broke over me, and in a transient, haggard gleam I knew that I was ill. But swiftly, the light went out, and eager to go on, aware of work waiting to be done, smiling more fixedly, I entered the vestibule and opened the letter.

Department of Pathology, University of Winton. From Usher, Professor Usher, head of that most excellent foundation. A nice letter, yes, indeed, a charming letter. The good Professor regretted, in fact, he deeply regretted that, under the circumstances, it was impossible to hold out any hope of the new appointment. If only the results had been published sooner. The delay was tragic, the disappointment intense, and his feelings quite understandable. There was a postscript over the page. Ah, yes, the dinner party was off too. Most unfortunate, when the invitation for Monday was extended, a previous engagement had been over-looked. Profuse excuses. Some other time. Why, yes, of course, it was all perfectly agreeable and correct. Come back to your bench in the laboratory. Work under me in a less intractable spirit with proper co-operation and supervision. A generous offer. But thank you, no.

Under the high light in the vestibule, beside the statue of Demeter and the tall buhl cabinets, I tore the letter carefully into four pieces. I wanted suddenly to shout out loud. But my lips were too stiff, as though glued together, and the pain in my head had risen, swelled in a crescendo of sound and shivering vibrations, as though someone were smashing wood with blunt axes on the back of my neck. In spite of this, I saw at last, with my wavering and dream-like gaze, what I wanted to do. Essential and important. On, on . . . don't stop . . . not an instant to be lost.

I went outside and hastened towards the laboratory. It was quite dark now and a wind had risen, swaying the trees and bushes, sending strange whisperings across the night. A leaf, brushing my cheek like ghostly fingers, made me spur my flagging footsteps to a stumbling run.

Now I was in the laboratory. Surveying the scene of my labours with an expressionless yet tortured eye, I advanced, independent of my own volition, and opened up the storage cabinet. The round, cotton-wool-stoppered flasks stood there in a row, opalescent and glittering, like luminous suns. Dazzled, I faltered and hung back. But that weakness was momentary. Collecting myself, I took up the precious flasks and smashed them quietly and carefully in the porcelain sink. I turned on both taps. When the last drop of fluid had run through the drain I bunched together the sheaf of papers on the bench, those pages filled with my calculations and conclusions, the toil of many midnight hours. Again, quietly, carefully, I struck a match to set a light to them, to hold them, burning, over the sink until the last charred fragment should be destroyed. But before I could do so the sound of quick footsteps made me turn round, slowly, balancing the insufferable burden of my head. Maitland stood in the doorway.

"Don't, Shannon," she cried, and hurried forward.

The match scorched my fingers and went out. The hammer strokes rang harder in my brain. I put both hands to my brow. Then everything gave way.

CHAPTER X

THE OCTOBER AFTERNOON was still and golden, filled with tranquil space. In my old room at Lomond View the slanting daylight made a bright patch upon the wallpaper, brought to life from beneath the yellow varnish its faded roses, glinted, also, upon the brass end knobs of my bed, dented years ago, when I had tried to straighten a crooked skate. Through the window I could see the early tinge of autumn upon the crimson curled leaves of the beech across the road, and in the distance, above the violet haze, the blue humped shoulders of Ben Lomond. As a boy, in this same room, I had often gazed with ardour upon that far-off prospect of the mountain. I gazed upon it now.

Lying comfortably on my side, I felt relaxed, conscious that my indolence was sanctioned, since Dr. Galbraith, supported by Grandma Leckie, was always insisting that I must rest. Yet the splendour of the afternoon was irresistible—I decided I must be up. Was I not practically well again and able to be about, after lunch, for a few hours each day? I threw off the bedclothes and began to dress, carefully however, for I was still unsteady on my feet and had proved how slowly one may gather strength after a complete breakdown. Well, I had deserved it. All my own misguided fault.

I went downstairs, demonstrating my progress towards recovery by not even holding to the banister. I had not yet got used to the queer sensation of living again in this house which, during my childhood in Levenford, had been my home. Now the property of my grandmother, it was quite unchanged, and although peopled only by the shades of most of its former inhabitants, still maintained its familiar air of pinched but aspiring respectability. They had brought me here after my smash-up, and with a grim devotion which made me heartily ashamed of all the hard things I had said of her, the old woman had nursed me back to health.

In the parlour the paper fan had been removed, a good fire burned in the black-leaded grate. Grandma had lit it for me before departing upon one of those shopping pilgrimages to the town, from which she returned, slowly, encumbered by packages of good things for me to eat. She had nourished me nobly, and according to her own peculiar precepts, on such proved restoratives as were sanctioned by her country traditions. Ten minutes ago, before leaving, she had whispered in my ear, with an air of significant promise:

"A nice boiled fowl for to-night, Robert." She was a staunch believer in a boiled fowl, served with the broth, which she named "the goodness" of the dish.

Alone in the house, this silent house filled with memories of the past, I had always to struggle against reverie, and the intolerable nostalgia which it evoked in me. Here was the couch on which Dandie Gow had bade me rest when I came in from my schoolboy combat with Gavin Blair. There, on the mantelpiece, lay the old wooden pen he had used for his legal copying. On that window-seat I had studied hard and fruitlessly to win the Marshall Bursary. At this very table they had told me I could not go to the University to study medicine. But I had gone. Ah, yes, I had always followed stubbornly my own solitary path, that tortuously winding path which had brought me back to where I had begun.

Quickly, I took myself in hand and, with a glance at the weather, decided on a short walk. In the hall, conscious of my cropped head, I pulled my cap well down, slid the key under the doormat in case the old woman should return before me, and set out.

Although the air was crisp and cool, my paces were not lively, and once or twice I had to pause as I strolled up the road to the hamlet of Drumbuck. It was the same quiet little village, set beneath a slow rise of moors, traversed by a brook which ran beneath two stone bridges. Some children were bowling their hoops towards the smithy, and their thin, high cries broke cheerfully upon the scene. On the village green I rested upon the seat under the great Scots fir which had stood there for a hundred years. From fissures in the blue-grey trunk little streams of sap had run and hardened. I scraped one with my finger nail and, rubbing the grey dust between my palms, inhaled the clean resinous tang. It made me feel that strength was coming back to me, that my life, after all, was not without a future.

Yet by the time I had made the round of Barloan Toll, I had more than had enough. I was glad to get back to the armchair, to put on my slippers and warm my feet at the fire. The morning paper lay folded on the table beside me, the *Herald*, which I always enjoyed, the main diversion in my convalescent day. I lifted it and laid it upon my knees, at the same time hearing the front door open and shut. There were steps in the hall, sounds of bustling movements in the back of the house. Presently the old woman came into the parlour. We looked at each other. I smiled.

"Did you get your fowl?"

"I got two," she answered. "I've asked McKellar for supper."

"That sounds like a party."

"Aye." She nodded calmly. "Dr. Galbraith will be here as well."

"I see."

Before I could engage her in controversy, she changed the subject.

"It's time you had your hot milk. Don't scorch your shoes like that. They'll go through in the soles."

She turned and went out, leaving me thoughtful and subdued.

I had sensed for some time what was coming, and now I knew that it was here. Dr. Galbraith was getting on in years. His large practice, which extended widely from Levenford town into the Winton countryside, had become too much for him. He wanted a partner and, to my sorrow, the suggestion had been made that he might want me.

Yes, the trap had been long and patiently prepared, the hands that had set the trap were kind and friendly hands. Yet, alas, despite the promise I had given, I shrank away from it. It touched me that the hard-headed McKellar should be willing to advance the purchase price—a thousand pounds was a deal of money to a Scots lawyer. I liked the old doctor well enough, with his weather-beaten face, his grey goatee beard, and that dry twist to his lips, his manner, once abrupt and choleric, now mellowed by age. As I drowsed by the fire I tried to see myself driving a Ford along the country roads, bumping over dry ruts in summer, ploughing through winter snow, calling at outlying farms, bearing my black bag into snug steadings and white-washed cottages standing lonely on the moor. But my heart was not in it. I understood myself too well to feel anything but unwillingness towards such a prospect. I was not suited to general practice, and from my past experience I knew that I should grind along, without interest, blunting the edges of my ambition, mediocre, indifferent, and defeated.

Suppressing a sigh, I took up the paper and in an effort to distract my mind began to scan the sheets. I read here and there, all the pieces that looked interesting. There was not much news. I was turning to the editorial columns when, on the back page, an item caught my eye. It was a small item, a bare three lines, but it caused me to start painfully; then, for a long time, held me motionless.

Under the heading, *Departure of Ships*, was the simple announcement:

> "The Clan Liner, S.S. *Algoa*, sailed to-day from Winton for Lagos and the Gold Coast. She carries a group of workers bound for the settlement at Kumasi."

I read the notice several times, like a child learning a lesson, as though uncertain of its meaning, and as I did so, the warm room chilled, and that faint quickening, sanguine and instinctive, which I had felt in the afternoon beneath the pine tree, diminished within me. So that was over, too . . . finished for ever. Since I had known that Jean would sail upon this ship I had dreaded the moment of its departure. Now it had gone. And, in that act, that separation of the vessel from these shores, that slow recession towards the horizon, there was a sense of final, irrevocable cleavage . . . a lonely lighthouse searching the empty sea, the flickering beam extinguished. And she had not come, had not even written her goodbye. That failure was the real martyrdom of love, it hurt me most of all.

For a long time, perhaps an hour, yet how long I did not know, I remained staring into the fire. Distantly, through my sad and painful thoughts, I heard the sound of an arrival, of footsteps and voices in the hall. I did not stir. Whether it was McKellar or the doctor, I could not bring myself to face the hearty handclasp, the tactful sympathy, which either would surely offer me.

Then, as I sat mute and motionless, the door opened

almost without sound, behind me. Awaiting the impact of a robust voice, I did not trouble to move, but gradually the consciousness of someone standing there, standing with perfect stillness, at my back, caused me to turn my head. And then, slowly, I raised my apathetic eyes.

At first I thought I was ill again. This must be some fresh hallucination, another of these fevered visions which had not so long ago afflicted me. Then, in a flash of understanding, I saw that it was she, saw also the explanation of her presence.

I had forgotten that out-going vessels often lay overnight at the tail of the Bank to pick up passengers, and await a favourable tide. She had come, after all, to say goodbye.

The heavy thudding of my poor heart sounded in my ears, and a mist rose up before me, through which I gazed at her in utter silence. In equal silence she gazed at me. Although she still was thin, with a slight pallor persisting in her cheeks, little trace of her recent illness could be seen in those brown eyes, that clear complexion and lustrous hair. I could not but contrast my own condition with this serenity. Here I crouched, spent and broken, while she set out, steady and intent, almost fully restored to health. Her dress, too, of dark grey material edged with a lighter braid of silk, was quite new, bought, no doubt, in preparation for her journey. I saw, with a further stab of pain, that around her neck were clasped the green beads I had given her.

Slowly, I straightened in my chair. I could see her lips shaping to speak to me. I wanted to be ready to meet the blow.

"How are you, Robert?"

"Never better. Won't you sit down?"

"Thank you." Her voice was low, yet controlled.

She seated herself, opposite me, very erect, her gloved

hands clasped together, her eyes still bent upon me. Like a little plaster saint, I told myself, embittered by a composure that I could not match. I gritted my teeth to keep back the weak exhibition of my emotion.

"You have quite recovered," I said.

"I was very lucky."

"The sea voyage should set you up."

She took no notice of this thrust. Her silence caused me a fresh paroxysm of heartache. I tapped the news sheet on my knee.

"I just happened to read that you were sailing. Nice of you to look me up. How is Malcolm? Has he gone on board?"

"Yes, Robert; he has gone on board."

The barb, turned back, gently, without rancour, sank deep in my breast. I tried not to flinch. Because of her glove, I could not see the ring, but if Malcolm were going with her they must certainly be married.

"Well——" I tried, casually, to smile, but my pale lips were drawn back in an anguished spasm. "I ought to congratulate you. He's a good fellow. I hope you have a nice trip."

She did not immediately answer; then, seriously, she said:

"And what about you, Robert?"

"I'm quite all right. I have a chance to get into a good practice here in Levenford."

"No."

The single word, uttered with a burst of feeling, drew me up short.

"What do you mean? It's virtually settled."

"No," she repeated. "You must not do it."

A short, strained pause. She was less calm now, and her eyes had taken on a sudden depth.

"Robert," she said, earnestly. "You cannot, you must

not throw yourself away in a country practice. Oh, I'm not decrying country doctors. But they are not you. You've had a bitter disappointment, a terrible reverse, but that isn't the end. You'll try again, you'll do finer, greater work. You can't bury your talents. You must, you must go on."

"Where?" I asked, bitterly. "In another back room . . . another asylum?"

With greater earnestness she leaned a little forward.

"You feel badly towards Professor Challis, don't you? It was a mistake to send you to Eastershaws. But he's an old man, and he never really had an opportunity to put you in the right place." Her throat swelled. "Well, now he has. Robert, how would you like to lecture in Bacteriology at the University of Lausanne?"

I gazed at her, immobile, in fact scarcely breathing, as she went on, more rapidly.

"They wrote to Professor Challis, asking him to recommend the best man he knew, a young man who could organize the laboratory. He sent them a full report of your research. Yesterday he showed me their reply. If you wish it, the appointment is yours."

I brushed my hand across my eyes as though shading them from too bright a light. A fresh start, away from the restrictions of this narrow land, in Lausanne, that lovely Swiss city on the sparkling waters of Lake Leman. But no, no . . . my confidence was gone . . . I dared not undertake it.

"I couldn't," I muttered. "I'm not fit."

Her lips came together. Under her cloak of stiff formality I saw a sudden trembling of resolution. She took a quick grave breath.

"You must, Robert. All your future is at stake. You cannot admit that you are beaten."

I was silent, my eyes, unseeing, fixed upon the floor.

"I am beaten," I said, in a leaden voice. "I've given them my word. They are coming here to-night. It's easy to fight one's enemies. But against friends . . . and kindness . . . and my own promise . . . I can't argue . . . I can't fight any more."

"I will help you."

In slow surprise, I raised my gaze.

"You? . . . You'll be away."

She was very pale, and for a moment her lips quivered so convulsively that she was unable to answer. She sat looking at her clasped hands.

"I am not going."

"But Malcolm?" I cried.

"The *Algoa* sailed at six this morning. Malcolm was on board."

There was a mortal silence. Bewildered, incapable of believing, I felt myself grow rigid. Before I could speak, she went on again in a voice that seemed strangled by the immensity of her effort.

"When I was ill, Robert . . . and afterwards, I seemed to see things which were not apparent to me before." She almost broke down, but forced herself to go on. "I had always recognized my obligations to my parents, to the people with whom I meant to work. I didn't realize my obligation to you . . . and because I love you most in all the world, it is a greater obligation than to any of the others. If you had succeeded, if you hadn't had your breakdown, I might never have understood this . . . but now . . . I do."

She paused, striving for breath, gazing at me with strained intensity, as though burdened by the burning necessity of conveying to me difficult and unformed thoughts which recently had come to her. In the stress of her emotion tears began to roll down her cheeks. Her words came quickly.

"All the time, as I was lying there, in a kind of dream, I kept wondering why I had refused to marry you . . . I loved you . . . really I had got ill through loving you, and not caring what I did in the wards . . . but behind that love there was pride and fear and prejudice against your religion, of which I really knew nothing. God had caused you to be born a Catholic and me a member of the Brethren. Did that mean He hated one of us and loved the other . . . wished that one should live in the darkness of lies, and the other in the light of truth? If so, Christianity was meaningless. Oh, Robert, you were kinder towards my belief than I was to yours. And I felt so terribly ashamed I told myself, if I got better, I would come and beg you to forgive me."

Now she was weeping uncontrollably and, while I sat white and rigid, unable to move my stiff lips, she whispered:

"Robert, dear Robert, you must think me the most difficult . . . the most inconsistent person in the world. But there is a pressure in events we cannot withstand. Oh, my dear, I've left Blairhill, left my parents, left everything, for good. And if you still want me, I will marry you, when and where you wish. . . . We will go to Lausanne . . . work together . . . be kind and considerate of each other. . . ."

The next instant she was in my arms, her heart against mine, her voice stifled by sobs. My lips moved without making a sound. My breast, dilated with an immense joy, seemed about to burst.

As from a distant world I heard the front door open again, heard the stamping arrival of McKellar and Dr. Galbraith, the cautious undertones of the old woman as she met them in the hall.

It did not matter now. I was no longer alone, darkness had turned to the light of day, life was for ever remade.

We should make our way into the unknown together. Yes, in the mystical warmth of that moment everything became possible, there was no thought of failure, and happiness seemed eternal.

THE END